Nicholas Montemarano is the author of a story collection, *If the Sky Falls* (a *New York Times Book Review* Editor's Choice), and a debut novel, *A Fine Place*. His fiction has been published in *Esquire*, *Zoetrope*, *Tin House*, and *The Pushcart Prize* (2003), and cited as distinguished stories of the year in *The Best American Short Stories* four times. He is Associate Professor of English at Franklin & Marshall College in Lancaster, Pennsylvania.

By Nicholas Montemarano

IF THE SKY FALLS
A FINE PLACE
THE BOOK OF WHY

NICHOLAS MONTEMARANO

The Book of Why

headline
review

First published in Great Britain in 2013
by HEADLINE REVIEW
An imprint of HEADLINE PUBLISHING GROUP

First published in paperback in Great Britain in 2013
by HEADLINE REVIEW

1

Cataloguing in Publication Data is available from the British Library

ISBN 978 0 7553 9414 2

Typeset in Bembo by Palimpsest Book Production Ltd, Falkirk, Stirlingshire

Printed and bound in Great Britain by Clays Ltd, St Ives plc

Headline's policy is to use papers that are natural, renewable and recyclable products
and made from wood grown in sustainable forests. The logging and manufacturing
processes are expected to conform to the environmental regulations of
the country of origin.

HEADLINE PUBLISHING GROUP
An Hachette UK Company
338 Euston Road
London NW1 3BH

www.headline.co.uk
www.hachette.co.uk

For Nicole Michels

Contents

THIS *IS* A self-help book.

Didn't think it was, but it is.

It's also a revision, a question, a confession, an apology, a love letter.

This book is for you, of course, and now for Gloria Foster, who might read this when she's older, might chance upon this book online or in a used book store in Philadelphia or New York or San Francisco, open to a random page, and see her own name. She might be struck by that and sit where she had been standing in an aisle and begin reading. She might put the book back on the shelf, though I doubt it – human curiosity is much too strong. The desire to know. The sense that there's too much we don't know. She might tell her parents, if her parents are still alive; her boyfriend, if she has a boyfriend; her husband, if she's married.

She might tell no one. She might be frightened, and for that, in case it happens, I apologize. Add it to my list of apologies. She might think, But I don't remember the man and woman who stayed with us. The man's dog. The big storm. Maybe, after she reads what I've written, it might begin to return to her. She could let it go, put it out of her mind: what happened when she was five no longer matters, what happened before she was born – if the book is true – matters even less. But, the desire to know. She might try to find me, search my name on the Internet – by then, twenty years from the time of this writing, you'll probably be able to find someone just by thinking his name. Maybe that's just science fiction. But she'll find me, if she wants. I'll still live, if I'm still alive, on Martha's Vineyard, at the end of a dirt road that turns to bog in rain or snow. She'll find me if she's supposed to.

And what happens then? Does she believe me? Does she ask why I didn't tell her sooner – why *this* way, in a book? Does she ask for more details about you – your likes and dislikes, your joys and struggles? Does she need to? Does she ask for a cup of tea? Does she sit on the couch and stare at me as if she's sorting through memories she's not even sure are her own? Does she become an intimate, a daughter figure, or perhaps even—

No. She'll be twenty-seven by then, a woman. But now she's a girl, and so I'll close that path in my mind.

Celebrate Life Conference, Phoenix Convention Center, 1996

HELLO AND WELCOME. Thank you all for coming.

You are here for a reason.

Close your eyes, take a deep breath, and ask yourself why.

What would you like to accomplish today? What would you like to change about your life?

Maybe you're drowning in debt. Maybe you're stuck in a stressful, unrewarding job. Maybe you've chosen a career you know isn't your true calling. Maybe your marriage is falling apart. Maybe you're estranged from your children or your parents. Maybe you're battling an addiction or a serious illness. Maybe you're happy but want to be happier.

If any of these are true, you've come to the right place. No need to move for the next two hours; the only shift will take place inside you.

You have creative control over your own experience. You have the power to change your life, to revise the story you've been telling yourself — consciously or subconsciously — for years, or to write a new story entirely. This transformation begins now with your next thought. In this room today there's no such thing as the past. By focusing on the present, by recognizing your conditioned way of thinking and reprogramming your default settings, you will create a future without limits.

Write this down and underline it: Happiness is an inside job.

Let me say that again: Happiness is an inside job. Happiness doesn't depend on what anyone else is doing. It doesn't depend on circumstances. If only this would happen, I'd be happy. If only that would happen, I'd be happy.

No more excuses. Happiness is an inside job. Your mind is the ultimate gift-giver. You need to understand: we live in an abundant universe. The universe is listening to your every thought. You are always broadcasting a signal to the universe, and this signal — this wave of energy — will always return to you. Every request is granted.

There are no accidents in this universe, only laws, and ignorance of the law is no excuse.

A current of energy runs through all things, including you and me; it doesn't know the word no. *The law of attraction is no less absolute than the laws of physics and mathematics. Two plus two always equals four; this is true everywhere in the universe. It's something you can be certain about, a fact you can count on. No different with the law of attraction: you'll be able to create your future. No need to worry anymore — you are in charge, you are the scriptwriter, the director, the editor; you have final say. There's no need ever to feel like a victim; there are no circumstances beyond your control. It's as simple as simple math: if you focus your attention on something you desire, then by law it must come to you.*

Ask, believe, receive – these are the three steps we'll be practicing today. Three steps to changing your life.

Number one: ask. Changing your mind's default settings. Redirecting your thoughts. Focusing on what you desire.

Number two: believe. Living as if you already have what you want. Keeping faith no matter what. Expecting miracles.

Number three: receive. Allowing abundance into your life. Getting out of your own way. Removing obstacles in your path, especially negative thoughts.

Because, believe me, negative thoughts can hurt you. Doesn't matter if they're conscious or subconscious. Our brains are computers; we're programming them all the time whether we're aware of it or not. You must be careful. Thoughts repeated become dominant thoughts. Dominant thoughts become default settings. Default settings become beliefs. Beliefs sustained manifest. Dangerous enough when thoughts and beliefs are conscious; much more dangerous when they're subconscious. Sometimes we become aware of subconscious beliefs only when they manifest in our lives. You can say you deserve a better job, you can say you deserve the break you've been waiting for, you can say you deserve health and peace and happiness, you can believe that you believe, but watch out for the subconscious. The conscious mind may say yes while the subconscious mind says no. So if you don't get that job, if you don't get that break, if you do receive a serious medical diagnosis, then in the deepest, darkest parts of the computer inside your skull, you must not have believed that you deserved that job or that big break or that clean bill of health.

Let me be clear: the mind is always creating whether we want it to or not. We really do get what we're thinking about. When we desire, we create; when we worry, we create. Nothing can enter our lives *without our invitation. Some people are uncomfortable with such responsibility, but we couldn't forfeit it even if we wanted to. No more cruel twists of fate to blame, no more acts of God, it's all up to us now. Which is why we need to reprogram our brains with positive thoughts; we need to clean out our files, scan our hard drives for viruses.*

Ask, believe, receive.

If you spend a lot of time thinking about how terrible life is, then the universe says, 'Your wish is my command,' and sends back to you people and events and circumstances that reflect your thinking. If you focus your thoughts on the joy and abundance in life, then the universe will say, 'Here you go, more joy and abundance.' I assure you, I didn't make this stuff up. I'm just the messenger. I believe it, I try to live it, and I want everyone to know about it. I want you to have everything you want.

This isn't about greed. This isn't about being selfish. This isn't about people thinking about wealth and receiving a check for a million dollars in the mail. If you want more money, fine. Money's not a bad thing. Your poverty won't make a single poor person rich. Your sickness won't make a single sick person healthy. Imagine that line of thinking: Well, there are so many poor people in the world, I'm going to be poor, too. There are so many sick people, I should be sick, too. There's so much suffering, I'd like to help by suffering, too. Listen, the more you have, the more you can give. The universe has deep pockets. Abundance is meant to be recycled. There is always enough. You are a reflection of the universe, and the universe is generous; the universe never says no.

Part One

Accidents

WINTER ON MARTHA's Vineyard, five years after.
The tree in the yard, its limbs heavy with ice, leans toward the house. Branches crack under their own weight, shatter on the walkway. Wind swings the ice-coated hammock low to the ground. The front door is frozen shut.

It's been a few months since I've heard her sing, so I put on my favorite song. Her voice will never grow old, but this is the smallest consolation.

What changes is the listener, forty-two now, long-bearded, going gray, heavier than he used to be but still what most would describe as thin.

Her music isn't all that I have. I have photographs and a box of keepsakes – letters and doodles, a few sweaters, a pair of socks, her favorite books, notes in the margins, ditties that ended up in her songs.

I have the dog, too – a long-haired German shepherd. She used to be hers, then ours, now mine, but I think of the dog, still, as ours. Twelve years old a month ago, on Valentine's Day.

Hello is the beginning and goodbye the end of every story, the refrain tells me. First and last words – hers to me and mine to her. Unless you count the many times every day that I speak to her – sometimes in my head, but more often aloud. I can do that. Now that I live in Chilmark year round, I don't see other people very often. Every few months a ferry, then a long drive to see my mother in Queens. Otherwise, my life is solitary. There's Ralph, of course, and she counts as company. She wakes me with her nose each morning and waits for me to say hello, which is the word I greet her with, and then I allow her up on the bed, only her front paws, and scratch her ears until she moans, and then the day – this happens every day, and there's some comfort in this – begins. She follows me from room to room, but spends most of the day sleeping, twitching her way through dreams, unless I take her with me to town or to the beach to play fetch. When I drive or walk to the market, I wear a baseball hat; I don't want people to recognize me, though I suppose by now they might not.

It could be you here, singing, if it weren't for the fact that I know this recording so well by now, every note and pause and breath. I listen closely, but it never changes. I roll a tennis ball across the floor and Ralph brings it back to me. She holds it in her mouth, tail wagging. When I reach, she moves her head. A game we've played since she was a puppy. I point to my lap, she comes closer. I point to my lap again, she drops the ball. When I try to roll it past her again, she plays goalie and stops it with her front paws, crushes the ball between her jaws.

Enough with the ball; I want her close. She lies on my lap, and I close my eyes and pet her face, rub her belly, put my hand by her mouth to feel her panting, and you might be in the next room singing.

The song suddenly ends. I'm never prepared for this silence. Except I hear a voice, a woman saying hello, a knock at my door. I'm not sure how anyone could have gotten here. More than a few times, even in weather not as inclement as today's, I've had to abandon my car on the steep dirt road leading to the house. This happened on our honeymoon. Our shoes stuck in mud three inches deep, we walked the rest of the way up barefoot. I had to carry Ralph, who was still a puppy but getting heavy, maybe thirty-five pounds. It wasn't yet our home, just a house we rented. We talked, after our honeymoon, about how much we'd love to own the house, and by the following year we did. I might have said then that I'd intended it: I tacked photos of the house on the corkboard above my desk; I ordered address labels; on the first of each month I mailed myself a letter here.

Before I look out the window, I wonder what I'll do if no one's there, if I'm hearing things. I used to be afraid of ghosts when I was a boy, but for the past five years I've wanted to see one. Any ghost would do, would provide a kind of answer, but one in particular would be most welcome, no offense to the others out there, including my father. That is, if there are such things. I'm not sure if I believe in literal ghosts. Spirits, phantasms, apparitions. I certainly do believe in ghosts if you mean things that haunt you – memories, feelings, regrets.

I'm disappointed to see that there really is a woman at my door. She appears solid, flesh and blood. Literally, I see blood – running from her nose and staining the tissue she's holding. She's pressing her other arm against her stomach as if she's wearing a sling, though she's not. I fear a scam of some sort – a robbery, a man with her, perhaps hiding behind my ice-covered car – but I quickly change my thoughts lest they become reality. Some old habits never die. I have to shoulder the storm door three times before the ice gives, then I gesture for her to step back so that the door, which opens with my next push, doesn't further injure her.

She's tall, almost as tall as I am, and has long red hair. A face young and old – dimples and crow's feet. Constellations of freckles on her forehead and nose. Blue eyes. Late thirties, I'm guessing, but probably gets proofed when she buys wine. She looks familiar, but then again, everyone looks familiar to me. She's smiling but sniffling. I can't tell if she's laughing or crying.

'I'm sorry to bother you,' she says. 'My car is stuck down the road. I can't move my wrist. And my nose – maybe it's broken, I don't know.'

'Come in,' I say, and I can see now that she *is* crying but trying to laugh.

I pull out a kitchen chair and she sits, though not comfortably. She seems concerned about the blood dripping on the floor. 'Don't worry about that,' I tell her.

'I'm lost,' she says.

Ralph walks over to her, sniffs her jeans, her boots, rests

her head on the woman's lap. 'Sorry, sweetie,' she says. 'I don't have a hand to pet you with.'

I give her a towel and try to take the bloody tissue, but she won't let me; she balls it and lays it on her lap, where Ralph sniffs it.

'I'm not sure you should put your head back,' I tell her. 'I think it's one of those things we're taught that's really not true.'

'God, it won't stop,' she says.

'It doesn't look broken,' I say.

'The bump's mine,' she says. 'My father gave it to me.'

I tear off a piece of clean tissue and give her the wad. 'Try putting this in your nostril.'

She pushes the tissue in, and her eyes water.

'Now pinch the bridge – somewhere in the middle – and hold it.'

As she does, she winces. 'Not too hard,' I tell her.

The tissue in her nostril is soaked with blood. Gently, I pull the tissue from her nose, then quickly wad the clean half and push it into her nostril.

'I'm Sam,' she says. 'Sam Leslie.' She reaches out her left hand and I shake it. 'Weird,' she says. 'Doing that with my *left* hand.'

'Harry,' I say.

'I'm really sorry about this,' she says.

'Was there an accident?'

'I don't believe in accidents.'

'But something happened with your car.'

'Lost control coming up the hill and hit a tree. But the nose happened after – I pretty much fell on my face.'

'Do you need another tissue?'

'I don't think so. Hey,' she says, 'do you think I can let go now?'

'Probably been long enough.'

She releases her nose, then reaches into her back pocket and pulls out a piece of paper. 'I was trying to find someone,' she says. 'The address is 95 Old Farm Road.'

'You must be freezing.'

'Some guy at the market told me left after the chocolate shop. It was all ice.'

'Can I make you some tea?'

'Yes, thank you. And if you have some ice, for my wrist.'

The ice tray is empty. I go outside with a knife and chip some from inside an empty flower pot. Telephone wires sag close to the ground. Trees, some almost ready to bud, sparkle in the last light of day. I bring Sam a few chunks of ice wrapped in a washcloth.

Ralph lies on her back, presents her white belly. 'Now I can say hello,' Sam says, and pets the dog.

'Ralph likes you. Then again, she likes everyone.'

'A girl Ralph?'

'Picked the name first, and she happened to be a she.'

'She doesn't seem to care.'

'I'd offer you my phone, but the lines are down.'

'I'm not sure who I'd call.'

'What about the person you're looking for?'

'I don't know him.'

'You don't *look* like a stalker.'

She laughs, rewraps the ice melting on her wrist. 'I'd make a terrible stalker. I'd make a terrible almost anything.'

'So, what *do* you do?'

'I write obituaries,' she says. 'God is my assignment editor.'

'Must be cheerful work.'

'It *is*, actually,' she says. 'Let's not forget, these people are being remembered.'

'Yes, but for what?'

'More often for good than bad,' she says. 'But you'd be surprised how many people have secrets.'

The teakettle whistles. I pour hot water over two tea bags. I place her cup of tea on the table beside her.

An icicle breaks from the tree near the window and shatters on the walkway. 'So,' she says, 'am I anywhere near Old Farm Road?'

'I don't know.'

'Well, if you live here and *you* don't know . . .'

'Some streets don't even have signs.'

The sun has set, so I turn on a few lamps. 'I didn't realize how late it was,' she says. 'Do you know a place where I can stay?'

'Plenty of places down-island, but I'm not sure how you'd get there.'

'Anything walking distance?'

'You'd have to crawl.'

'Not quite what I planned,' she says.

I try to think of a solution, but there isn't one, or rather, there's only one. 'You could stay here.'

'That's nice of you,' she says, 'but I don't know.'

A loud crack outside frightens the dog, who runs in circles, tail between her legs. I look out the window. A tree limb has fallen onto the front porch and now blocks the door.

'Maybe that's a sign,' she says. She thinks about it for a moment. 'Let me make a call first, okay.'

'Phone's down.'

She takes a cell phone out of her pocket. 'I'm still getting service.' She presses a few buttons on her phone.

'Would you mind telling me your full name and address?' she says.

'Harry Weiss, 122 Woods Road.'

Her call goes through on the third try. She says, 'This is Sam Leslie. March 14, 2008. I'm in Martha's Vineyard. There's an ice storm, and I had a mishap with the car. Bloody nose, sprained wrist, could be worse. Staying at 122 Woods Road with a man named Harry Weiss. He's six-something, thin build, brown hair, beard, fortyish, has a German shepherd.'

She closes her phone, puts it back in her pocket. 'No offense,' she says. 'It's not that I don't trust you.'

'Neither Ralph nor I take offense.'

She sips her tea. 'I was just thinking,' she says. 'The man I'm looking for – maybe you know him.'

'I doubt it.'

'He disappeared five years ago.'

'So he's missing.'

'No,' she says.

She leaves the washcloth on the table, walks across the

room. She squats in front of my bookcase. 'Hey, look at this!' She holds up the book so I can see. 'This is him. I'm telling you – this is a sign.'

'What does he look like?'

'Not sure,' she says. 'None of his books has an author photo.'

'I haven't opened that book in years,' I say.

She starts flipping through the book, but I walk over and take it from her. 'I'm sorry, but I probably wrote some personal things in the margins.'

'I do the same,' she says. 'But hey, don't you think this is a sign? That I'm looking for him and I end up here and I find his book on your shelf?'

'It was a bestseller,' I say. 'You could probably find it in many homes.'

'True,' she says. 'But that's not what he would say.'

'How do *you* know?'

'Because I've read all his books.'

'I mean, how do you know what he would say *now?*'

'I don't,' she says. 'That's another reason to find him.'

'So, you don't believe in coincidence.'

'Do you know who Paul Winchell is?'

'No.'

'He was the voice of Tigger in *Winnie the Pooh*,' she says. 'He was also the first person to patent an artificial heart, assisted by Dr Henry Heimlich – yes, *that* Heimlich. I have too much information inside my head, I'm telling you. The point is, Paul Winchell died one day before John Fiedler, who was the voice of Piglet.'

'And this means . . .'

'Lawrence Welk's trumpeter and accordion player died on the same day.'

'Tragic,' I say.

'Jim Henson and Sammy Davis, Jr.,' she says. 'Orville Wright and Gandhi. Antonioni and Bergman.'

'If enough people die on any given day . . .'

'Adams and Jefferson,' she says. 'On the Fourth of July.'

'Coincidence,' I tell her.

'I don't think so,' she says.

'You don't sound sure.'

She touches her nose, checks her finger for blood. 'Something too easy to believe isn't worth believing.'

'I'm not sure you'd make it as a preacher.'

'The best preachers express the most doubt,' she says. She unties her boots with her uninjured hand, kicks them off. 'I've made a mess of your floor.'

'Ralph has done worse.'

The dog is sleeping by the door; her ears stand up at the sound of her name, but she doesn't open her eyes.

'Hey, what do *you* do?'

'Same things every day. I walk Ralph. If it's not too cold, I take her to the beach. I listen to music. I try to remember to call my mother. I read poetry. I don't like novels, certainly not long novels, because I don't like to become attached to things. I just started reading a book of six-word memoirs.'

'I know that book,' she says. 'An entire life reduced to six words.'

'Never done doing over my do-overs. That's one of my favorites.'

'That could be mine,' she says.

'Tried and tried. Wasn't quite enough.'

'Amen,' she says.

'Now I know I know nothing.'

'Sad, but true,' she says. 'So, what would yours be?'

'Hello, goodbye. Every story. Why pretend?'

'Too sad.'

I dry the floor where Sam had been sitting. Ralph stretches as I wipe around her. 'I could stomp my foot right next to her face and she wouldn't flinch. I love that about her. She doesn't know cruelty.'

'What would her story be?'

'Do I seem the kind of man who writes his dog's life story?'

'Yes.'

'I'm so happy you're here. Really.'

'I'm happy to be here, too. Not happy *why* I'm here, but.'

I laugh, despite my intention not to. 'Sorry, but that was Ralph's life story.'

'Well,' she says, 'I *am* happy to be here.'

'I don't get to laugh much.'

'I bet I can guess what you do for a living.'

'I don't do anything for a living anymore.'

'You're too young to be retired.'

'Apparently not.'

'Okay, let's see. Baseball hat, bushy beard, cords. You're a rich, eccentric entrepreneur. Some kind of Google person who showed up to work every day in sneakers and jeans and made a killing.'

'Sorry.'

'All right, then you worked in the music industry. You said that you listen to music, right. You were a record producer, something like that.'

'Nope.'

'Dog trainer.'

'No.'

'A horror writer, like Stephen King. You write spooky novels set on Martha's Vineyard, but under a pseudonym. Harry Weiss is your pen name. What's your real name?'

'Come on.'

'It's possible.'

'I was an artist,' I tell her. 'But not a very good one.'

'Must have been good if you're retired.'

'Just because people buy what you're selling doesn't mean it's any good.'

'Did you paint?'

'I can't paint or draw to save my life. I used to make sculptures out of found objects – junk people throw away or sell in garage sales. Old letters, baby shoes, bowling trophies.'

'Can an artist retire?'

'Sure.'

'Isn't that just who you *are?*'

'I don't believe in it anymore.'

'Don't believe in what?'

'I used to believe I could save things.'

'Do you have any of your work here?'

'I gave it all away. The older I get, the more I give away. Speaking of which, can I give you some food? You must be hungry.'

'I don't think I could chew,' she says. 'My jaw, my entire head, is sore.'

'I could make soup.'

'Thanks, but I'm more tired than hungry. I left New York early this morning.'

Freezing rain is falling harder now against the windows. I look outside: telephone wires hang lower, the hammock touches the ground.

'Any idea when this is supposed to let up?' she says.

'Not until tomorrow,' I say.

She winces as she moves her injured wrist in circles. 'I know it's early, but do you mind if I try to get some sleep?'

'I can sleep on the couch,' I tell her, 'and you can have my bed.'

'I'll be fine on the couch,' she says.

I bring out a blanket and pillow and tell her that if she needs anything I'll be in my bedroom.

I open the door to my room and ask Ralph if she wants to come in with me. She opens her eyes but stays beside the couch. Sam is already under the blanket, the only light a lamp above her.

A few minutes after I close my bedroom door, I hear Ralph crying, so I open the door to let her in. But she only wants the door open. Her herding instinct is strong; she's anxious unless she's able to see everyone in her pack. Sam, at least for tonight, is our pack's new member.

Before settling down in the hallway, Ralph comes into my room, walks over to the box, smells the socks and sweaters inside.

She does this every night.

I'VE FORGOTTEN SOMETHING, lost something, made a terrible mistake I can never amend.

Then she's in my doorway, asking if I'm all right.

I'm sitting up in bed, trying to catch my breath; it sounds as if I've been running away from something. I'm sweating through my shirt. Slowly I remember where I am, who the woman standing beside my bed is, and that I've had a bad dream.

Then I remember that my dream wasn't a dream.

I lie down, turn away from her. She sits on the edge of the bed, touches my back. 'Sounded pretty bad,' she says.

'Sorry I woke you.'

'I was awake,' she says. 'I don't sleep very well.'

A sudden urge to tell her the truth; much easier in the dark. But I say nothing; in the morning she'll be gone. If she comes back, as she very well might when she realizes where she's been, I won't answer the door.

'I can leave you alone now,' she says. 'I just wanted to make sure you were all right.'

I don't want her to leave; it feels nice to have another body on the bed. 'Tell me your six-word life story.'

She swings her legs up onto the bed and leans against the head-board beside me. I sit up, and we face each other in the dark.

'Daddy issues. Brother died. Got help.'

Rain against the window; the drip of ice melting from rain gutters and trees. 'Six words aren't enough. You should get seven.'

'Daddy issues. Brother died. Still getting help.'

'Much better,' I say. 'The story continues.'

'A sad story that never ends is happier than a happy story that ends.'

'Every story has the same ending.'

'Depends what you mean by ending.'

'It is finished. The end.'

'I hate when stories end with those two words,' she says. 'When I was a kid, I used to cry at happily-ever-after. Because, you know, they *lived* happily ever after, they weren't *living* happily ever after.'

'You were greatly upset by grammatical contradictions.'

'They lived happily – fine. I can accept that. But as soon as you use the past tense *lived*, you can't say *ever after*.'

'You have a nice voice.'

'I can't sing.'

'Everyone can sing.'

'I can't sing well.'

'Try a few notes.'

'Trust me,' she says.

'Then tell me a story.'

'Happy or sad?'

'Tell me about your father.'

'That wouldn't be a good bedtime story.'

'Okay, then your brother.'

'Unhappy ending.'

'Then tell me about getting help.'

She's lying on her side now, her head propped on one of my pillows. 'My marriage was not good,' she says. 'To be honest, it was much worse than not good. It wasn't safe where I was, you know. I wanted to leave, but. And then one day this book came in the mail, and I was like where did *this* come from. It was called *Everyday Miracles*, and there was a note inside from the author – not just to anyone, but to *me*. *Dear Samantha, it's not an accident that I've sent you this book.* And when I read the book, everything just clicked. It was as if he'd told me my real name. I'd been walking around for thirty years thinking I was this person named Samantha when really I was someone else. I wrote him a letter a few years later, told him his book changed my life.'

'Did he write back?'

'He told me it was *me*, not him. It was *my* intention to be free of my husband, so I attracted the book to me.'

'Is that what you believe?'

'Yes.'

'That would mean you intended to fall on your face.'

'Do *you* believe what's in his book?'

'That book was a gift. I got it a long time ago.'

'Have you ever tried it out?'

'I don't remember much of it.'

'I'm not trying to convert you or anything.'

I hear Ralph get up and shake herself out, then walk across the kitchen to her bowl. 'I've always loved the sound of her drinking.'

'It's relaxing,' she says. 'It's making me sleepy.'

'Me, too,' I say, and I lie beside her, close my eyes.

Hᴇʀ ᴄᴀʀ ɪs against a tree, its back wheels sunk in slush. The tree bends over the road, the tips of its branches touching down on the other side, creating an icy arch we stand beneath. It's sunny and warmer, and the ice is melting into a messy soup. I step gingerly across the ice, but my boots break through to the mud beneath. Ralph has come along for the ride; she sits in the back of the station wagon, hesitant to jump out.

'Before she was old,' I say, 'nothing could have stopped her from slopping around in mud.' I whistle for her to come, but she cries. She doesn't want to come, but she also doesn't want to disappoint me. 'There was also a time when I never wanted her to get dirty.'

'She's a dog – she's supposed to get dirty.'

'My wife used to say that.'

'Well, she was right.'

'She was right about a lot of things.' I wipe mud from my boots, then tiptoe into more slush. 'I used to be a lot more anal.'

'I can see that.'

'I don't like when things get ruined.'

'They're work boots,' she says. 'They *want* to get beat to shit. That's their reason for being. You don't want to deny them that, do you?'

I stomp in the slush, splattering my pants and the sides of her car.

'Better,' she says.

I whistle to Ralph, tell her to come. She cries. I bend down and slap my knees. 'Come on,' I say, and now I'll be sad if she doesn't come. 'Where's your boy? Where's your boy, Ralph?' She moves closer to the edge, looks down at the bog beneath her.

And then I say it.

'Where's your girl? Come on, Ralph. Where's your girl?'

Her look changes; she jumps from the wagon and runs in circles, then back and forth from one side of the road to the other.

'It's okay,' I tell her. 'I'm sorry. It's okay. Come here.'

She comes to me and I pet her; she gets down on her belly and slaps her paws in the slush. I toss some ice and mud on her back; she runs away, runs back.

'I shouldn't have said that,' I say. 'That was cruel.'

'She's forgotten already.'

'Maybe *girl* is just a word now. Every once in a while I'll say that just to make sure she still reacts.'

'She looks pretty happy right now.'

'Mud,' I say, 'is the secret to happiness.'

Sam picks up some mud and spreads it on her nose, then

spreads some on mine. My instinct is to wipe it off, but I don't.

I want to say, *She would have done exactly that*. In fact, you did exactly that on our honeymoon, and I wiped it off, so you put more on my face, and I wiped it off again, and you kept putting mud on my face, on my hair, on my clothes, until I gave in and let you cover me.

'You get in, I'll push,' I tell her.

The wheels spin mud onto my clothes, my face. Ralph barks at the sound, chases flying mud the way she chases snowflakes and breaking waves – things that disappear as soon as she catches them. The car doesn't move; it looks as if it will never move.

'Well,' I tell her, 'you might be on the Vineyard for a while.'

'No problem,' she says. 'As long as I find Old Farm Road.'

Ralph is on her back, covered in mud; she's so content she doesn't get into the car when I tell her to.

'Maybe she wants to walk back up the hill,' Sam says.

'She might want to, but she's too old.' I snap my fingers at the dog. 'Come on – get in. Let's go,' I say, and she comes.

'Maybe I should walk up,' Sam says. 'I don't want to get your car dirty.'

'I'm the one who's filthy,' I say. 'Besides, making a mess isn't the worst thing in the world.'

Only after she's in the shower do I remember that they're in the bathroom. I can't let her see them.

I knock on the door, and she tells me to come in. I open

the door slightly. 'I'm really sorry,' I tell her, 'but I need to grab something in here.'

'No need to be sorry,' she says. 'It's your bathroom.'

I don't remember which magazine I put them in, so I take the entire rack.

I spread the magazines on my bed and flip through them until I find the checks – five or six royalty checks with my name and address on them. I haven't needed to cash or deposit them. The house and car were paid for years ago, and I have no major expenses. I'll probably end up signing them over to my mother, whom I've been trying to convince to move into a retirement community. She'll never be convinced; she'll die in that house, just as my father did. I suppose I'm trying to convince myself as well, as I would hate to know strangers are living in the house where I grew up, the place where all of this – this story I'm trying to tell and thereby understand – began.

I hide the checks in my bottom drawer, beneath my socks.

She comes out of the bathroom towel-drying her hair. She's dressed in her muddy clothes.

'Not sure how much good a shower does when you forgot to pack a clean pair of jeans.'

'I can drive you to town,' I tell her. 'I'm sure you can find a pair.'

'You've done enough.'

'I don't mind,' I say. 'I haven't helped someone in a while. This kind of help is easy. Tea, a place to sleep, a shower, a ride.'

'What's the hard help?'

'Saving people,' I tell her. 'Not like someone who's been in an accident – first aid, CPR, things like that. I mean in a deeper way.'

'Are you saying my soul needs saving?'

'Of course not. If anyone's does—'

'I'm joking,' she says. 'I'm just joking.'

I shouldn't have stopped when she asked me to, but I couldn't justify not stopping, and now she's asking this man, this jogger, if he knows where Old Farm Road is. An older man, gray beard, black tights, muscular legs; probably runs every day, no matter what, even the day after an ice storm.

He looks the wrong way, and I'm relieved, but then he points behind us and says, 'It's back the other way, about a quarter mile. First left after the chocolate shop.'

'Are you sure?'

'Positive,' he says, trying to catch his breath. 'My sister used to live on Old Farm Road.'

Sam looks at me.

'We just came from there,' I say. 'I know it's not Old Farm Road because I live there.'

'Well, maybe it's the second left after the chocolate shop,' the man says. 'I haven't been there in a few years.'

'What about Woods Road?' she says.

'That's near where I live,' he says. 'About a half mile in the direction you're heading.'

'Thanks,' I say. I roll up the window and drive. The main roads are in remarkably good shape so soon after the storm, but patches of ice remain. The car skids, and I gently pump the brake. Brief panic, I pump once more, and the tires grip the road again. The road bends, and I take the curves with caution. A salt truck, its tires chained, passes us heading in the opposite direction.

'I don't think he knew what he was talking about,' I tell Sam.

'Maybe we should go back and try the road after yours,' she says.

'We're already heading into town,' I say. 'Let's get your jeans first.'

'Pull over here!' she says. 'Hurry, pull over!'

'What is it?'

'A police car,' she says. 'I can ask for directions.'

'Sorry,' I tell her, 'but I can't stop.'

'Why not?'

'My car isn't registered.'

'Then let me out,' she says. 'They won't see your plates.'

'I'm sorry, but I can't.'

'Please,' she says, and I say nothing.

She unbuckles her seat belt, puts her hand on the door handle.

'What are you doing?'

'I'd like to get out of the car now,' she says.

'Buckle your seat belt.'

'Stop the car.'

'Not until you buckle.'

She does as I ask, but I don't stop.

'There's no reason to be afraid,' I tell her.

'You don't live on Woods Road,' she says.

When I don't respond, she says, 'What's your real name?'

'It doesn't matter.'

'It matters to me,' she says. 'It matters that you gave me a fake name and address.'

'How do I know your real name is Sam?'

'I can show you my driver's license,' she says. 'Let's see yours.'

'I don't have it with me.'

'That jogger saw us,' she says.

'I'm not going to hurt you.'

'That's what people say before they hurt you.'

'I'll bring you back to your car, okay.'

'I want you to bring me to the police.'

'What will you tell them? That I made you tea and gave you a place to stay?'

'Why'd you lie about your name?'

'I'm a private person.'

'Is your dog's name even Ralph?'

'Yes.'

'Don't laugh at me,' she says. 'I'm frightened.'

'I'm sorry.'

'Here,' she says. 'Pull over – into that lot.'

'Can't we just keep driving?'

'You're scaring me,' she says. 'If you don't pull over . . .'

She grabs the wheel, and the car begins to skid. I lose control, and we swerve into oncoming traffic.

You don't believe until it happens, you don't believe even *as* it's happening, that your skull can break a car windshield. Surely the glass will break the skull, not the other way around.

Surely your face will shatter. Surely your teeth will break, your jaw, your neck, your spine. Surely you won't walk away from this, you will be carried. Surely you will never walk again. You brace, close your eyes. Your body stops breathing. You hear it before you feel it. The loudest crash you've ever heard, and then you feel it. The window comes at you. The wheel, the dashboard, everything comes at you. You bounce back in the seat. A sharp pain in the ribs. You struggle to breathe. Your eyes remain closed, you squeeze them closed, this is all the energy you have, you won't open them no matter what, you don't want to see. Someone is moaning. Someone else. You can't remember who. What you want, more than anything, is one breath. You wait. You've had the wind knocked out of you before, you've fallen on a soccer ball, you've been punched in the stomach, you know how it seems as if you'll never breathe again, but you always do, and this will be no different. You try to breathe, but nothing. You try again. Nothing. And then you stop trying. The dark gets darker. Silence. Nothingness.

Part Two

Everyday Miracles

YOU KNOW, I always tried to avoid the dark. I sought out light; I created it any chance I had, whether day or night, but especially night, with a push or turn or flick of a switch. I knew where every source of light was. There was a standing lamp beside my bed – still there today, four decades later, used only when I visit my mother in Queens. At night I'd bear the dark until my parents turned on the TV. I hoped the sound would drown out my movements in bed, my reach for the lamp, the click of the switch. But my mother always heard. She would call up for me to turn out the light, and I would, or I would turn the switch twice in rapid succession so that it sounded like one click. Some nights she would come upstairs and turn off the light for me.

In the dark, anything could happen. My eyes never quite adjusted. Some nights I would get up to use the bathroom, or pretend to use the bathroom, and would leave on the night-light above the sink. This small light from down the hall was just enough to allow me to see the paneling that covered my walls. I tried my best to find friendly faces in the wood. You could find any kind of face you wanted, and it took great concentration to ignore the scary faces – wide eyes, mouths open in fear or disbelief. Some nights my mother called up for me to turn off the bathroom light, and I would tell her that I felt sick, and would lie on the bathroom floor, and sometimes in the morning I *was* sick, as if I'd created the illness with my mind.

Desperate, I stole my father's matches and hid them in a pair of purple striped tube socks I never wore. I coughed to cover the sound of the match struck, then counted down the seconds before the flame reached my hand.

There was a light on my bedroom ceiling, controlled by a wall switch by the door. There was a bright hallway light seldom used. There were two lamps in my parents' room set on nightstands on either side of their bed. There was an overhead light, but long ago the bulbs had blown and my father hadn't bothered to replace them. There were three lamps in the living room, and the light from the TV, and the almost constant glow from the embers of my father's cigarettes. Through the small square window in our front door came the moon and, on clear nights, the stars. In the dining room were a chandelier and a row of lights inside the breakfront that held my parents' good china, seldom used. There was a light above the kitchen table beneath which I ate and did homework, and a small stove light, perhaps my favorite, because it was kept on always. No matter how dark my room, I could, as a last resort, imagine that halogen stove light, below it a clock suspended at 2:22, a time to which I attributed special, almost magical meaning, its significance unclear to me until many years later, when I met you on February 22. It was bright the night we met – lightning outside, stage light inside – and it was meant to be, I remember thinking: everything had been leading to that moment.

There was a light in our yard, and a light in each neighbor's yard, a row of lights I could see over the fences dividing our properties, and beyond the farthest yard were the lights of Manhattan, what those of us in Queens called the city, even though we were the city, too.

There was the problem of the basement light. The switch was at the bottom of the stairs; you had to go down into the dark to feel for it (it always seemed to be moving), and when you were finished changing the laundry, you had to turn off the light and run up the stairs before something pulled you back into the dark.

I was often in trouble for turning on lights that didn't need to be on, or for leaving on lights I'd been told how many times to make sure I turned off.

But you already know all this about me. You don't know everything I'm about to tell you in this book, and neither do I, but you know all too well about my complicated relationship with light and dark. Many nights I fell asleep beside you, whether I was reading or not, with a lamp still on. When you complained, and you had every right, I bought an alarm clock whose face glowed just enough for me to see the outline of the chair by the window, the dog stretched on the wood floor near the heating vent, the shape of you beneath the covers. I want to tell you now, and I mean it, this isn't loneliness speaking, that you were light enough. A few nights we lost power and the clock face went dark. If I could have those nights back, I would not check the circuit breaker, I would not look outside to see if the rest of our block had lost power, I would not find a flashlight and leave it on on my nightstand. I wouldn't get out of bed at all, wouldn't leave your side. I would get under the covers with you where it was darkest, where it was brightest despite the dark.

THE WEEK BEFORE Christmas meant extra light in the house: a small tree in the window, a flashing wreath on the door.

I was seven years old. Lucky seven, my father had told me.

My mother sat with me, rubbing my back until I fell asleep.

Later, I woke alone and blind in the dark. I was floating deep in space, a million light-years from home.

I snuck out of my room, tiptoed across the hallway, testing for creaky parts before committing my full weight, and sat on the stairs. My parents were watching *The Bishop's Wife*, an old Christmas movie about an angel. My mother liked Cary Grant movies because he and my father, with the exception of my father's mustache, looked alike. Through the banister I saw the angel — he might as well have been my father — help a blind man cross a street, cars braking just before hitting them. Then he saved a baby from getting run over by a truck. He could appear and disappear at will; he could fill a glass with wine using his mind; he could decorate a Christmas tree in a few seconds. I decided then, before falling asleep, that I wanted to be an angel. When I woke, the angel was making a typewriter type without touching it. I fell asleep again.

Later, I'm not sure how much later, I woke on the stairs: the front door opened, then closed; a man's low voice, not my father's.

Then my mother crying.

I moved down a few steps to see better.

My father stood facing the door, his arm around my mother. Smoke rose in a thin line from his cigarette. Some nights he'd wake from sleep just to smoke. The smell, especially during the night, soothed me. My mother tried to make him quit; she asked me to help by stealing his cigarettes and running water over them, but I didn't want him to quit. It was difficult to imagine his face without a cigarette between his lips.

When I saw the man, I'm not sure I understood that he was real. Maybe he's an angel, I thought. But then I saw that he was holding a knife. He wore a flannel shirt but no coat. Short red hair, a wide nose, face covered with freckles. I was afraid of freckles; I thought they were contagious. My mother had freckled hands, and when she touched my food I wouldn't eat.

The man wasn't taller than my father, but was much bigger; he was breathing heavily, his chest heaving as if he'd just run up the hill to our house.

My father stepped in front of my mother; he kept smoking his cigarette, but never touched it with his hands. The smoke went in through his mouth and out through his nose. I wasn't sure what he'd do when the cigarette ran out; that was when he always lit another one. He smoked between bites of roast beef; he sipped beer between inhale and exhale.

The man took a step toward my father, who remained calm. He spoke gently, as if to a child. 'This is my wife,' he said. 'She's scared, as you can imagine.'

The man said nothing; he held the knife at his side, against the leg of his jeans, blade pointing down. He kept squeezing the knife's handle.

'She doesn't know what I know,' my father said, 'which is that there's no reason to be afraid. It's just that you walked into the wrong house. It's been a long night, and you're lost.'

My father puffed on his cigarette and said, 'What you want to do is put that down.' I knew he meant the knife, and was glad he hadn't said the word. 'You won't need that here,' my father said.

The man raised the knife; he looked at it as if unsure how it came to be in his hand. He blinked a few times, then stepped forward and laid the knife on the coffee table.

'Now what you want to do,' my father said, 'is go down two blocks to the pay phone and call someone who can pick you up.' He reached into his pocket and gave the man a dime. 'Here you go,' he said. 'Good luck getting home.'

The man nodded, put the dime in his pocket, opened the door, and left; he didn't bother taking his knife.

My father didn't rush to lock the door; that's what I would have done. He didn't call the police until the next day, and only when my mother insisted.

I came down the stairs and asked them who the man was.

'He was lost,' my father said.

'What did he want?' I said.

'We live in a sick world,' my mother said.

'Everything's fine,' my father said.

'It's a miracle you wake up alive,' she said.

She started shaking. My father tried to hold her, but she pushed him away as if he'd done something wrong, as if he hadn't just saved us.

The next night, at bedtime, my father asked me if I was afraid to go to sleep; I said yes. 'Nothing to be ashamed of,' he said. 'But I want you to know something.' He turned his head away to breathe out smoke. 'When you're afraid of something,' he said, 'it tends to find you.'

I waited for him to say more, but he didn't.

'Why did he do what you told him to do?'

'The mind's powerful,' he said. 'I saw him put down that knife, then he did. I saw him leave, then he did.'

'How do you know God didn't do it?'

'God did do it,' my father said. 'But where do you think God lives?'

'Where?'

He tapped my head with his finger. 'Right here,' he said.

WE LIVED SURROUNDED by the dead: a mausoleum behind our garage, rows of gravestones as far as you could see. Our house backed up against the cemetery where Harry Houdini was buried. Each Halloween, on the anniversary of his death, dozens of people would gather at his grave and wait for him to rise from the dead or contact them from the other side — to give them a sign that he still existed somewhere, in some form. When my father told me this, I was both thrilled and terrified that the dead might rise, that resurrection might not be Jesus' exclusive miracle. My mother, a devout Catholic who believed that magic was sacrilege, told my father to stop filling my head with nonsense.

'Look who's talking,' he said.

My father, with a quiet, childlike wonder, saw the world as a strange, magical place; my mother saw the world as a place to fear. My mother carried her cross while my father pointed out how beautiful the wood was. I've spent most of my life trying to figure out which one of them was right. It's entirely possible, of course, that they both were.

But for a while my father won.

His name was Glen Dale Newborn, and we lived in Glendale, Queens, and so I believed that the neighborhood had been named for him. I believed, too, when I was a boy, that Glendale was the entire world, that there was nothing else, so the world had been named for my father.

My mother's name is Rose, and I think now that the world was named for her, too. Pretty petals, but watch out for the thorns. Red hair, pale skin, as short as my father was tall, five feet to his six, yet she seemed taller than him, taller than anyone I knew. I was tall, too – eventually even taller than my father – but I hunched to make myself smaller.

Years later a fellow self-help author got at that. He told me, 'On every page of your books there are two things battling for space – faith and doubt. Your faith, as it comes through in your words, must be stronger than your reader's doubt. Your faith must be stronger than your own doubt. Just as long as you never forget that doubt is faith's friend, the very thing that makes faith stronger.'

A motivational speaker motivating a motivational speaker.

'It's always two stories battling for space in your mind, in your heart,' he'd say, as if he knew my parents and my childhood intimately.

The story my mother would have had me believe was that my father, though she loved him, was a little strange. She never used the word *crazy;* she knew I would have rejected that word. But that he was strange *was* true; I know that now, though I should have known – and probably on some level did know – then.

Even so, I believed every word he said.

My earliest memory, as remembered for me by my mother, was the time my father went away. For how long, I can't be sure, especially since it's not really my memory, only what I've been told. I was four and didn't stop crying when my father was gone except to sleep. So my mother says. My father went fishing and there was a storm and he couldn't get home.

I had never known my father to go fishing. He didn't own a pole, a tackle box; he didn't even *eat* fish.

So the questions left to me now, years later, long after he's gone, questions to which I have no answers: Where did he go if not fishing? Where does one go when one goes away?

Add to this story the story my mother told me about my grandfather, my father's father, dead long before I was born – drowned, as I've been told, and even my father never denied this.

My grandfather was an alternately devout and lapsed Catholic who decided he could walk on water. Whether he made this decision during a period of devotion or not is unknown. He *was* out fishing, so the story goes, and walked off the boat into choppy waters and disappeared into the sea.

Whenever my mother wanted to use the word *crazy* for my father – if she looked out the window and saw him showing me and my friends magic tricks, coins from behind our ears, a dollar bill folded again and again and again, then gone in his palm – she'd use it for my grandfather. She'd tell the story of how he believed he could walk on water, how foolish, and one was to understand – I was – that the same might be said about my father: that he was a good man, a good provider, but had misguided beliefs about how the world works. By which my mother meant: my father didn't care much for church, didn't see the point of grace at table, and meant by the word *God* something entirely different from what my mother, from what most people, meant.

When my mother was upset with my father, her temper heightened by his unwillingness to raise his voice and engage her, she'd say, 'They're going to send you away to you know where.' Or, 'Careful, you'll end up like your father and the rest of the Newborns.'

I wasn't ever sure what my mother meant. Maybe other Newborns had tried to walk on water and drowned. Maybe they'd all gone crazy, and my father was next and, after him, me.

One is supposed to learn from stories, whether true or not, especially stories about one's forebears, but years later I tried to walk on water.

I was seventeen and trying to save my first girlfriend, who had no intention of being saved. It's likely she didn't need saving; she's probably doing just fine now, whatever that means. She was two years younger, fifteen going on forty. She drank and smoked too much. She would sit on the edge of the subway platform and wait for the train, her legs dangling over the edge.

My father was gone by then, and she saw me as tragic, someone like her – her father was also gone – and that's why she liked me. She thought we were all in this mess of a world together. We'd get high on my father's grave, and I'd find myself telling her that happiness wasn't as much a bunch of B.S. as she liked to believe. She'd laugh and tell me I was funny, then she'd fall asleep in the cemetery grass, and I'd wake her before dark and walk her to the train.

She was perfectly named Gail. She's a passing wind in this story, a gust across the page, here only because she's part of a pattern in my life, a desire to save, and because she was there the day I tried to walk on water. Not the ocean, but the lake in Central Park, beneath the arch of the Bow Bridge. Pretty wimpy, I know – hardly a test of faith – but it *was* cold.

Maybe it's misleading to say that I *tried* to walk on water. I didn't believe I could; in fact, I was certain that I couldn't. The urge rose up in me suddenly. I said nothing to Gail. I didn't jump or dive; I walked out of the rowboat and immediately sank. So, the laws of physics worked; they applied to me. This was good news. I swam to the base of the bridge and waited. I was shivering, jumping in place, shaking my arms to get warm. It was an exhilarating fall.

Dear Wile E. Coyote,

Your problem isn't Road Runner; your problem isn't that you can't walk on air. Your problem is that you don't believe. You've been left in the dust too many times; you've been blown up too many times, your coat turned to ash; you've been flattened by too many trucks; you've failed and failed again, and that's what you believe.

You've accepted your role as Road Runner's foil – he gets what he wants, what he already has, freedom and speed and a few more pecks of birdseed set out by you, a trap deep down you know will never work. You know the outcome every time before it arrives; one might say you create it. You will always be thwarted; you will always be chasing, always one step too slow; you will always be hungry.

Who knows, maybe that's a good thing – never quite reaching your goal, never quite reaching the finish line, never catching the bird you must believe it's your fate never to catch. I'm pretty sure you wouldn't eat Road Runner even were you to catch him, wouldn't even harm him, wouldn't ruffle a single feather. I'm not sure you'd know what to do with him except set him free, pretend you'd never

*caught him, and go back to your chasing, the only thing you've come
to know how to do.*

*I tuned in every Saturday morning, hoping – even though I'd
already seen every episode – that you might stop chasing Road Runner
and let him come to you, that you might start acting as if you'd already
caught him, as if you already had everything you could ever want,
king of the desert, knock on a cactus and out comes a tall glass of
water, a fat steak. I kept hoping just once you wouldn't look down
and see the air beneath you, the fall to come. Or that you'd look but
believe anyway that you could fly.*

SATURDAY MORNING HAD a feeling; *was* a feeling. The feeling
when I heard the truck, trash can lids crashing onto the
ground, the roar of the compactor, the sight of my father
pulling up, smoking a cigarette without ever touching it with
his hands.

Spray-painted in red on the side of the truck was an
angel smoking a joint. Most of the tags were illegible, but
I could make out a few – Curious Feet, Atom Bones, Iz
the Wiz.

My father waved to me on the stoop, and the men he
worked with said, *Hey, kid*, and I ran to the curb and watched
the compactor crush trash – bottles and boxes, rotting food
and old shoes, a vase, a rug, a broken vacuum cleaner – all
of it gone.

Every day my father brought me something he'd found in
the trash: a blue button that must have fallen off a sweater,
a bee-keeper's mask, a white clown shoe, a transistor radio,
rubber balls, beer caps, matchbooks. Whatever he brought

home I saved in a trunk. The tongue from a baby shoe, the felt headband from a fedora, a blue tassel from a red fez. Birthday cards and breakup letters. Magic wands and handcuffs. A holy card of Christ on the Cross.

One day my father brought home a silver watch he found at the bottom of a trash can. 'A gift for you,' he said.

I wound the watch, but the second hand didn't move.

'It's broken,' I said.

'Well,' he said, 'we'll have to fix it.'

He laid the watch in my palm and told me to close my hand carefully, as if the watch were an egg.

'Close your eyes,' he said, 'and see the watch working. See the second hand moving.'

I felt him put his hand over mine. He tapped my hand a few times, then said, 'Move. Come on – move!'

He had me say it with him. 'Tell the second hand to move,' he said.

'Move,' I said.

'Say it like you mean it.'

'Move,' I said.

'Like you really believe.'

'Move!'

'That's more like it,' he said.

'Move, move, move,' I said, and each time he tapped my hand.

'Okay,' he said. 'Let's take a look.'

I opened my eyes, then my hand: not only was the second hand moving, but it was bent up toward the glass.

'Sometimes that happens,' my father said.

He told me it was probably a good idea not to tell my mother, given how she felt about such things.

My father brought home other dead watches, and together we brought them back to life, but the first one was always my favorite. The watchband was too big, so I carried it around in my pocket.

The games we played – magic, my mother said – became a kind of religion, which is to say they brought me joy cloaked in a mystery I couldn't quite put into words. If given the choice of discovering God or my father as a fraud, I would have been better able to handle the debunking of God. If God were exposed as a figment of humanity's imagination, no more than wishful thinking, a coping mechanism, then at least I wouldn't be the only fool. But my belief in my father was mine alone, and I alone would have borne the disappointment should his powers have turned out to be mere tricks.

The day after Halloween, my father took me to the cemetery. I was ten. He had wanted to take me to Houdini's grave the night before, at midnight, but my mother had said no.

Now, after a late-morning storm, trees dripped with rainwater; the grass soaked my sneakers and the tips of my father's brown work boots.

We removed dead flowers from gravesites and propped up others, still alive, that had fallen. We passed a stone so old its name and date were unreadable; the stone had turned black. My father touched it; I was afraid he might catch death.

The stained glass of a mausoleum had blown in. We stopped, and my father looked inside. I was tall but not tall enough to see, so he lifted me.

Inside was a chair made of stone, nothing else. I imagined someone sitting in the chair, alone, forever watching over the dead. Then I thought: No one will ever sit in the chair. The names of the dead were engraved on plaques on the walls.

We continued through mud puddles until we reached a large monument with three steps leading to a statue of a weeping woman. I thought at first that she was Mary mourning Christ, but then I saw the bust: it wasn't Jesus but a man wearing a bow tie, his hair parted down the middle.

'You were named for him,' my father said. 'But don't tell your mother – she doesn't know.'

My mother had wanted to name me Cary, after Cary Grant. My father said kids would make fun of me for having a girl's name, and besides, Cary Grant's real name was Archie. My mother said Archie would remind people of the comic book. My father suggested Harry, but my mother knew it was for Houdini, so my father said what about Eric, and my mother liked it.

'She still doesn't know it was his real name,' he said.

We sat on the steps, and my father showed me a trick. He never would have called it a trick; that's the word most people would use.

He told me to empty my mind, close my eyes, and stare into the darkness beneath my eyelids. Then he told me to think of a number between one and ten, and to concentrate on the number, to visualize it, to tell him the number with my mind, to want him to know.

'Ready?' he said.

I tried to think of nothing but the number. I wrote it over and over on the blackboard in my mind. 'Ready,' I said.

He closed his eyes, touched my head with his, took a few deep breaths.

'Got it,' he said. 'Seven.'

'How did you do that?'

'I didn't – *you* did.'

'Try again,' I said. 'This time, *any* number.'

'Easy,' he said. 'Just do the same thing. See the number. Want *me* to see it. Really concentrate.'

I closed my eyes tightly and in the dark saw three 2's blink brightly in white and red lights.

Then my father said the number.

I liked numbers, equations, problems. I believed – and was comforted by the belief – that every problem was solvable, that every question had an answer. I spent much of my time solving math problems, then checking my answers in an answer key. It was satisfying to be able to make a check next to the questions I'd answered correctly, and to see how many I could get right in a row, and to see by how many right outnumbered wrong, and to be able to understand, when I'd erred, where my thinking had gone wrong, and to remember my mistakes so that I wouldn't make them again.

When I ran out of math problems – when I'd finished all the workbooks in the house, even those for grades I was years away from reaching, I'd grow restless; my mind would form, in the absence of answerable questions, unanswerable ones. *Why* questions, my mother called them. Why would a good person go to hell if he missed Mass and was struck by a bus on his way to Confession? If God was God, why did He need to send His only Son to earth to suffer a painful death just to save the rest of us from our sins? Why not an easier way? She'd answer up to a point – the point at which she couldn't, or had grown weary of my asking – and then she'd give me chores to do – fold the laundry, sweep the yard. My father would indulge me as long as I wanted, but rarely gave me answers. More likely he'd say, 'That's a great question' or 'Beats me' or 'What do *you* think?'

HAD I NAMED years then, twenty years before you started that tradition, I might have named it the year of the blackout or the year of the Son of Sam or the year of making things disappear. I might have named it the year of hearing voices. I might have chosen any number of names had the year's name, in retrospect, not been so painfully obvious.

I might have called it the year I had to start a second, then a third box to hold all the objects my father brought me. Little gifts, little nothings, other people's junk.

He brought me discarded postcards I'd read and reread before sleep, trying to imagine the lives of the people who had written them. At least once a week he brought me a postcard from San Diego, San Francisco, Santa Fe, small towns with the strangest names: Surprise, Arizona; What Cheer, Iowa; Come by Chance, New South Wales; Truth or Consequences, New Mexico; Hell, Michigan; Paradise, Pennsylvania; Ecstasy, Texas. Most of the notes were cheerful, overexclamatory, but in some, usually near the end, I detected a hint of sadness; these were the ones I tended to reread most. A man named Steven told a woman named Lee about a play he saw in Chicago called *When Three Become Two*, how it made him miss her, how he'd keep his promise, but in his PS, which was written in tiny cursive, he mentioned the despair he felt on the Skydeck of the Sears Tower, not because it was windy and he could feel the tower swaying, but because the sky was clear and he could see across Lake Michigan to Indiana, where he knew she was. It was, for a while, my favorite postcard. I had rotating favorites, which I'd bring to school and keep inside my books and read throughout the day; I'd daydream during class, wondering what Lee looked like, what Steven's promise had been.

There was a Rita who wrote from Richmond that she was considering giving up, that she had tried and tried, but her prayers hadn't been answered. There was a John in Austin who'd had the best day of his life with a girl named Linda he'd just met, and a Jon without an *h* in Vancouver who'd lost his wallet and had to sleep in a park and was about to hitch his way to Walla Walla, he might miss the funeral, please give his apologies to the kids. In my mind Rita hadn't given up, John had married Linda, Jon had made it to Walla Walla for the funeral, and all these people knew each other, and they knew Steven and Lee, and somehow everything and everyone were connected, we were all part of the same story, and I wanted it to have a happy ending. I imagined that if I brought the right postcard to school, if I reread it often enough and sent the person who had written the note my best wishes and played out in my mind a happy ending for whatever story I had created, then all would be well.

But the next week my father would bring me a new post-card from Salem or St Paul or Baton Rouge, another note filled with exclamation points but with a passing sadness or regret, a parenthetical or PS that said, though not always directly, help me, love me, don't leave me, come back, don't give up, don't let me give up, I'm sorry, I'll try harder, do better, be better.

It was the year of hearing voices.

My father brought me a transistor radio he'd found in good condition, batteries included. In bed at night, I would roam the AM dial until a voice compelled me to stop; it could have been a word or phrase that stopped me, or just the tone or conviction of the person's voice.

'The chaos around you has been put there by design.'

'You're the boss, you're the chief. I see bright skies for you. But you're standing in your own way, man. Give up that negativity – dump it.'

'Doesn't it seem true that we wouldn't get into so many tight spots if we asked for God's help a little sooner?'

'She set fire to the garage because she believed Satan was inside.'

'You're lucky there isn't a bullet in your heart.'

'I am protected and guided by the Divine at all times. Let us step into the Light together.'

I fell asleep with the radio pressed to my ear. Some nights I woke afraid someone was in the room with me; I would lie still, trying to locate the voice – closet, attic, under the bed.

'One son put him in the grave,' a man's voice said. 'The other wants to raise him from it.'

I felt the radio under my pillow, brought it to my ear, and waited, but there was only silence. I thought the batteries had died, but when I tried other stations, my room filled with voices again.

'She's a happy, satisfied camper with the Lord,' a woman said. 'She doesn't ever want to be without Him.'

My father was teaching me how to make things disappear that year, but I wasn't very good at it, not at first. Whatever he made disappear, I made him make reappear. Marbles, pens, paper clips, bottle caps, anything I asked him to.

He closed his hand around a matchbook, blew on his hand, and showed me his empty palm.

'Where did it go?'

'Back where it came from,' he said.

'Where did it come from?'

'Where everything comes from.'

'But *where?*'

'Nowhere,' he said.

'How can something be nowhere?'

He shrugged.

'Fine,' I said. 'Make it come back.'

He closed his hand, blew on his fist. When he opened his hand, the matchbook was there, as if it had never been gone. I opened it and counted the matches; there were eight where there had been nine.

'There's a match missing,' I said.

'I guess it didn't want to come back.'

'Why not?'

'Maybe it was burned out,' he said.

'Not funny,' I said.

He struck a match to light his cigarette. Seven where there had been eight.

'Can you make bigger things disappear?'

'Like what?'

'People.'

'Who?'

'The Son of Sam.'

He breathed smoke out of his nose. 'I can work on that, see what I can do.'

He was the man in my dreams who took me away, who took away my mother and father; he was the voice I'd hear faintly in the static between stations; he was the creak I'd hear on the attic steps; he was the wind rattling my bedroom window; he was a shadow in the basement when my mother sent me down to fold laundry; he was dead leaves blowing in the backyard; he was the crow cawing on the clothesline; he was the man who walked by our house three times one night, then rooted through our trash; he was the man sitting in a black car across the street from the cemetery when I walked past in the early-morning dark to deliver the *News;* he was the front-page headline I promised myself I wouldn't read but kept reading; he was the man in my closet; he was the man sitting alone in the back of church who kept looking at me; he was the man talking to himself while feeding pigeons in the park near school; he was footsteps in the school bathroom as I sat in a stall between classes; he was silence and any sound that broke it; he was why my teacher's husband came to school each day to pick her up; he was why women were cutting their hair and dyeing it blond; he was why my mother pushed her dresser against her bedroom door each night; he was why I had nightmares about my father pushed into a trash compactor; he was why I waited by the window for my father to come home from work; he was why I kept asking my father, kept pestering him, could he make a person disappear.

One hot night in July, as I was about to go to bed, I asked my father if he could make the whole world disappear.

'Why would you want to do that?'

'Just asking.'

He put out his cigarette in an ashtray about to overflow. 'I suppose,' he said, 'if you put your mind to it.'

And then the world *did* disappear.

My father was gone; the couch he was sitting on was gone; the coffee table on which he'd been resting his feet was gone; the entire room was gone. I couldn't see my hands when I waved them in front of my face; I couldn't see anything. My mother cried out from the basement, where she had been folding laundry. 'Glen,' she said, 'I'm down here in the dark!'

'We're all in the dark,' my father said.

I was relieved to hear their voices, was relieved to feel the floor beneath my feet. I was still there; my mother and father were still there; the world was still there, even if I couldn't see it.

My father opened the front door, and it was all darkness. Streetlights and porch lights were out. Small circles of light moved across the ground: our neighbors on their stoops with flashlights.

I felt my way upstairs and brought down my radio: that was how we knew for sure that it was a blackout. Later, when we realized there was nothing we could do to turn darkness into light, someone brought out a boom box, and someone else brought out a card table and a bowl of chips, and someone else brought out a cooler filled with beer, and it turned into a block party. My father was able to convince my mother to come outside and dance with him. I knew people by their voices or the smell of their cigarettes or perfume. You could be invisible as long as you didn't speak, as long as you avoided the glow of flashlights. The dark, as long as we were all in it together, felt safe.

Use the box your new pair of sneakers came in, the one that's been sitting empty in your closet the past few weeks. With a black Magic Marker write *wish box* on the lid. Cross out *wish* and write *creation*, because you're making things, not asking for them. Go through your old newspapers and cut out a police sketch of his face. Glue it onto a piece of construction paper, and above the sketch write in black Magic Marker *caught!* Concentrate on the headline you've created; know that it will be true. Don't doubt, not even a week later, when two more people are shot in the head while kissing in a car in Brooklyn, the woman killed, the man blinded. The male victim's name is *violante,* which looks and sounds like *violent,* and you wonder what that can do to a person, having to say such a name so many times, having to spell it, having to write it on exams and forms, a violent word. You believe, even as a boy, that names have meaning, have power, and you wonder how his life might have turned out differently had his name been *violet,* had he not parked his car in a neighborhood called *gravesend.* Before he left his house that night, his mother said, 'Be careful, you know what's going on.' And later, when he was with his date, swinging on park swings, she got nervous and wanted to go back to the car. This is further evidence that it's best not to be afraid. Animals, even human animals, can smell fear. Resist the urge to open your *creation box* to make sure the Son of Sam is still inside. If you look, that would be a sign that you don't believe. If you show faith, it will be rewarded two weeks later when your father shows you the front-page headline: *caught!* Now you may open your *creation box* and show your father. He won't be surprised; he'll pat you on the back and say, 'Nice work – you got him!'

Three months later, on Halloween, I wanted to be the Invisible Man. I wanted to be like during the blackout but better: others couldn't see me, but I could see them: their private selves, who they were when they believed no one was looking.

I wanted my father to make me disappear, even though I was afraid to be nowhere, wherever that was, the place everything came from. That morning, while my father shaved (he smoked even while shaving), I asked him if I could make *him* disappear, and he said, 'Sure, but only if you believe you can,' and I asked him if he was afraid to be nowhere, and he said no, and I asked him if he'd come back, and he said, 'If you bring me back,' and I said, 'How do I bring you back?' and he said, 'Same way you make me disappear,' and I said, 'When you come back, will you tell me about nowhere?' He shifted his cigarette so he could shave the unshaven side of his face without burning his hand. 'I'll tell you everything,' he said. 'As long as I don't come back with amnesia.'

I put on a trench coat and fedora for my costume and had my father wrap my face and hands with bandages. The idea was to take off my clothes and unwrap the bandages and not be there. Or *be* there, but have everyone believe I wasn't.

Before I left for school, I took a photograph from the album in my mother's closet: me and my parents when I was five, my first day of school. I cut out my father, folded what remained, and put it in my pocket.

During the day, I kept the photograph on my desk. I imagined his chair by the front door empty; I imagined morning without him leaning over the sink to shave; I imagined my mother in bed alone; I imagined a garbage truck coming down our street with a man who was not my father on the side of the truck, a man who was not my father emptying cans and whistling for the driver to move up; I imagined my father's ashtray empty on the coffee table.

My classmates kept saying I was the Mummy, even though I'd told them I was the Invisible Man.

'But we can *see* you,' they kept saying.

Twins named Tara and Tina came as each other, but no one could tell if they'd really come as themselves.

A boy with one arm – he'd been born that way – came as someone who'd survived a Jaws attack.

The walk home took twice as long; I went out of my way, and out of my way again, to avoid kids with shaving cream that could have been Nair, but still got egged, my trench coat a too easy target.

I wouldn't meet you for another twenty years, and eventually I told you most of these stories, but here's one I never told you or anyone, not even my audiences or readers. Only my mother knows, and I'm not sure she has ever forgiven me. Sometimes, even now, I need to remind myself that it wasn't my fault, that it had nothing to do with me. I try to convince myself the same about you, about everything.

We stood in my room, listening.

My father kept coughing – so much that he put out his cigarette without finishing it, something I'd never seen him do. I told him to be quiet.

My mother was on the stoop, a coffee can filled with pennies in her lap.

I cared too much what other kids thought of me to go door to door with a sack. I didn't even like candy; years ago my mother had killed that joy by cutting chocolate bars into pieces in case there were razor blades. My father, to tease her, would eat before she cut. 'You'll be sorry when your tongue falls out,' she'd say.

My mother liked to shake the can, her attempt to entice, unaware that the last thing kids wanted was pennies, that they would make fun of her, would call her the penny lady.

Silence would be our warning that she was coming, that she'd run out of pennies or that there were no more trick-or-treaters.

She wouldn't have liked what we were doing. She would have said, *What did I say about magic, about putting silly ideas into your son's head?* She would have said, *You'll be sorry.*

It was difficult to concentrate while listening for the sound of pennies. If a minute passed in silence, we paused, waited for her to shake the can.

I told my father to get in my closet.

'So that's where I'm going to disappear from.'

'Yes.'

'As long as wherever I go, I can breathe.' My father coughed again, and for a moment I wondered if he would ever stop. 'I'm really coming down with something,' he said.

'Try to be quiet,' I said.

He walked into the closet and stood with his back against my school shirts. Before I closed the door, he said, 'So long. See you soon.'

'Later,' I said.

I closed the door, sat on my bed, shut my eyes tightly, and imagined the closet without my father.

And then a sound: high-pitched, a girl just pinched. A sharp intake of breath.

I was angry that he'd broken my concentration. 'Be quiet in there,' I said.

He made a sound like when he gargled in the morning, then banged – or seemed to have banged – on the closet door, as if asking to be let out.

We'd have to begin again. I couldn't properly imagine him gone when he was making noise.

When I opened the door, he fell out.

My father's eyes were open, but he wasn't looking at me. A joke, I thought. A Halloween trick. To scare me, to scare my mother.

I heard the front door open, then close; my mother's footsteps.

'She's coming,' I whispered to him. 'Get up – hurry.'

My mother came up the stairs; I could hear her walking across the hallway to my room.

'Get *up*,' I said.

'What are you two doing in there?'

I flicked his ears, pulled his hair, pinched the skin on his hand.

I stood, kicked my father gently. 'Come *on*,' I said.

My mother tried to open the door, but he was in the way. 'Let me in,' she said, and pushed.

I pushed back, but could hear anger in her voice, so I gave my father up. 'He's teasing me,' I said.

My mother pushed her way in.

I expected her to say, *Now you know how it feels to be teased.* Or, *Glen, will you please, once and for all, grow up.*

But as soon as she saw him, she got down on her knees

beside him and shook him. 'Glen,' she said. 'Glen.' She shook him again, harder. 'It's okay,' she said. 'You can get up now, you can get up,' she said.

Then, to me: 'What happened?'

She didn't wait for an answer. She shook him *too* hard. She slapped his face, his chest, got on top of him, looked into his eyes. She shook him some more and kept saying Glen until *Glen* sounded strange, a word I was hearing for the first time, a word in another language.

'He's teasing,' I said.

She ran down the stairs, then back up. She kneeled beside him, put her mouth against his ear. 'I won't leave you,' she said. 'I won't leave, don't worry.' But as soon as she said this, she ran down the stairs again.

I could hear her out on the street, calling for help. One of our neighbors was a nurse; she had saved a neighbor choking on a cherry pit in the middle of the night.

I kept watching. Not his eyes – I couldn't look into them – but just above them, near enough to see if they moved.

A neighbor whose name I didn't know – an older man who drove a brown Cadillac and smoked a cigar on his stoop every night – ran up the stairs with my mother. Other people came – strangers, the fathers of children I knew but weren't my friends. The man who smelled like cigars got down on the floor with my father and kept saying *Glen*, that sound that was no longer a word. He slapped my father's face; he pressed his finger to my father's neck, his ear to my father's chest.

MY MOTHER DIDN'T want to leave.

I stood facing a soda machine, turning over in my hand two quarters the nurse had given me. I could see the reflection of my mother and the doctor. He looked down at her, his hand on his chin. She was yelling, but in a whisper. They didn't do enough, she said. He was too young for this to happen.

I saw a nurse give my mother a pill and a small paper cup, the kind you use to rinse after having a cavity filled. My mother pushed it away. She wanted to speak with whoever was in charge. The nurse put her hand on my mother's shoulder.

When my mother stopped crying, she accepted the pill and the paper cup, then sat down.

The machine swallowed one coin, then the other. I pressed a button that sent them back to me, and I kept doing this, even though long ago I'd decided orange. I didn't want to have to turn around; I could look at my mother's reflection, not at her. I inserted the coins and pressed the orange button.

The can making its way down through the machine and into the receptacle was as loud as I believed my own heart was. I pulled off the tab and took my first sip; everything was too loud. I drank too quickly, and it was more than half gone. When it was all gone, I'd have to face her, I'd have to say something or nothing, and then she might say it — that it had been my fault, how many times had she told me, this was God punishing me for not doing what I'd been told, for doing what I'd been told not to do, this was my cross, hers too, this was permanent, irreversible, did I know what that word meant, it meant the rest of our lives.

The cab ride home, the two of us without him. My mother beside me on the backseat.

Two boys threw eggs at the cab. One boy was shirtless and had tiny nipples; the other boy wore a red bandana, which was something I'd asked for the previous Christmas because it looked like you had a wound under it and I thought it was romantic to have a wound, people would consider you tragic and brave, but instead my mother got me a herringbone-tweed cap other kids made fun of.

The eggs hit the window where I was sitting, but I didn't flinch. The streets were dark but for jack-o'-lanterns still lit in windows and on stoops. Then streets I recognized, streets close to ours, houses I knew. Our house. The brown car my father drove, *had driven*, which my mother didn't know how to drive, which would sit in front of our house for five years; I would start it once a week, twice a week in winter, until I was old enough to drive.

A magic wand was stuck in our tree. Wind blew candy

wrappers along the sidewalk. In the street were a glittery princess slipper and a cracked vampire mask. On our front door was a shaving-cream smiley face and below it the words, *I'll be back.*

The dark house, the click of a lamp turned on. A closet opened, my mother's coat hung on a hanger, the smell of mothballs. Her footsteps, then mine, up the creaking stairs. My mother in her room, what had been their room, and me in mine, where it had happened.

Even in the dark I could see the outline of the closet door. I got out of bed, turned on the light, and put my hand on the knob.

It was all a trick, I realized – the ultimate illusion. My father was *that* good. Better than anyone, even Houdini. A trick to make the heart stop. A trick so good that it fooled the men who'd come to the house and breathed into his mouth and pushed on his chest and put a mask over his face and pressed a plastic ball that sent air into his body; so good that it fooled the doctors and nurses at the hospital.

I imagined him laughing as he stood up from the operating table, where they must have pronounced him dead. I imagined him tiptoeing into the hallway, down the stairs, and outside to a cab. He could have gotten home before us. He'd disappeared, and now, if I focused my thoughts, he would reappear.

I stood with my hand on the knob, listening for his breathing.

He might wait until morning, I thought.

He might wait until the wake or the burial – a knock from inside the coffin as it's lowered.

He might wait years.

Until then, he would be the voice in the static between stations; the creak on the attic steps; the rain against my bedroom window; the wind that blew leaves across the backyard; a blue jay on our clothesline; footsteps, shadows, silence; any sound that broke silence.

IT WAS THE year of rules.

So was the next year, and the next. With every year came more and more rules, refinements of old rules.

You couldn't break one, or else.

The first rule, the most important, was *Think positive*.

Every thought was positive, negative, or neutral, and you had to be careful.

With practice negative could become neutral and neutral positive, and with more practice, negative could bypass neutral and become positive.

The negative *It's cold and snowing and someone will throw ice at my face* became the neutral *It's cold and snowing*, became the positive *Thank you for morning sunlight reflecting off the white world*, became a mantra you could repeat all day, became a song, *Thank you for sunlight, thank you for the white world*, all day to keep out the negative.

Negative made my lips tingle, made my arms and legs weak, made me fear falling.

That was how I knew I needed to change my thoughts or else.

The first time I felt my lips tingle: Rockaway Beach, an August morning, my tenth birthday. The steady sound of waves breaking, a lifeguard's whistle, the cries of seagulls as they swooped down to scavenge bread crusts, crumbs clinging to muffin wrappers. The ripe smell of seaweed. Sea wind blew sand onto my legs. Waves, louder and closer, sprayed my face with ocean dew.

I opened my eyes: skywriters wrote words that faded before I could read them. A fat boy ran past with a jellyfish impaled on a stick.

My mother covered her pale legs with a towel. But the towel didn't cover her feet; they were starting to burn.

She'd had a severe sunburn once, had stayed in bed three days. The way she'd moaned, I'd been afraid she might die. My father had made a game of peeling her skin – whoever peeled the biggest piece won.

Now my father dozed with a hat over his eyes. My mother suggested we move our beach chairs away from the water; my father told her to stop worrying so much. My mother said, *The water's rough, it's coming closer*, and I felt the tingling in my lips as if I'd tried to eat that jellyfish. My mother moved her chair and told me to do the same. My father didn't move; he said nothing when the water reached his feet, not when it rose to his ankles, not when a wave knocked him from his chair. He lay on his back on the sand, and the water rolled over his head, back out, over him again, and I wanted to speak, but my mouth didn't work, and the water rolled in and out, my father could have been a body washed ashore.

You could make a negative memory positive by revising it: we all moved our chairs back; the water never reached my father.

Thank you for morning sunlight. Thank you for the sound fall leaves make when I walk through them. Thank you for the sight of my breath in cold morning air. Thank you for the long eyelashes of the girl sitting across from me on the bus, so long they look fake. Thank you for when she blinks.

She pulled the bell cord and stood: the other side of her face was pink with burn scars; only one eye had lashes.

Years later, in Atlanta, a woman with facial burns asked me to sign her copy of my third book, *There Are No Accidents*. She had lost her house in a fire. Within a year, she had lost her job and her marriage.

I wasn't thinking the right thoughts, it was nothing but negativity and anger and self-pity, and your book got me back on the right path. I feel beautiful again, I really do. Thank you, thank you for everything.

I signed her book, *For Sharon, with best wishes and admiration.*

I wrote in my notebook about the girl on the bus. I described her eyelashes and tried to think of them from time to time, especially when I was trying to turn a negative positive.

But it was impossible to think of her eyelashes without thinking of her burns, you couldn't have one half of her face without the other, and eventually I tore that sheet from my notebook and decided it was best not to think about her at all.

I slept with the notebook under my pillow. I brought it to school. I hid it in my closet with my father's ashtray and his last pack of cigarettes.

There were four sections: Rules, Signs, Proof, and Positive Thoughts.

I didn't want my mother to find it.

Composition, not spiral, which could unwind over time and cut you. Pencil, not pen, in case I made a mistake.

I pressed hard, and sometimes it was impossible to erase a mistake completely; sometimes the eraser was dirty and made things worse, and I had to buy a new notebook and copy everything from the old one.

A week after the day it had been a year, a windy November morning, my mother tied a yellow ribbon around the tree in front of our house. Many of our neighbors did the same – dozens of yellow ribbons, their long strings flapping in the wind. I knew why – I'd seen the headlines in the papers I delivered – but I liked to pretend the ribbons were for my father, so that he'd return.

I walked to the bus stop, and it was yellow and more yellow, and I thought how nice it would be to be kidnapped and held hostage, to be taken away for a while, to be feared dead, to have so many people missing you, and then to return.

It would be the closest one could come to coming back from the dead. It would be like dying without dying.

Four hundred forty-four days later, two hundred twenty-two times two, the hostages came home.

One by one they walked down the airplane steps waving. Some of the men had long beards, and I decided then – I was in high school – that when I was able, I would grow a beard. A beard meant you'd been away for a long time; a beard meant you weren't allowed to shave; a beard – and Jesus was proof of this, too – meant you had suffered.

One by one they emerged from the plane, but it was never him.

Another rule was, don't step on a crack while delivering newspapers, don't allow the shopping cart's wheels to touch a crack because *electricity counted*.

I had to push down on the cart's handle to wheelie the front wheels over each crack, then lift the handle so that the back wheels cleared the crack, then step over the crack. If I touched a crack, I had to back up – clearing the crack in reverse – and try again.

It was slow going, but the time saved not having to do a do-over was worth the time it took not to make a mistake in the first place.

I had to get up earlier than the birds. There were dark circles beneath my eyes, which were almost as tragic as a beard.

Eventually it became muscle memory. I almost never stepped on a crack.

This wasn't about not breaking my mother's back; it was much bigger than that. It was about keeping the earth in its orbit around the sun and the galaxy in its trajectory through the universe; it was about everything that could go wrong not going wrong, disasters large and small I tried not to think about.

Another rule was, don't read headlines. Headlines were almost never positive and more likely negative than neutral.

Another rule was, if you make a mistake and read a negative headline, rewrite it positive.

Woman Saves Children, Self. Three Rescued from Brooklyn Fire. Plane Crash Kills No One. Headless Body Not Found in Topless Bar.

Thank you for morning sunlight. Thank you for the sight of my breath in cold morning air. Thank you for everything this day and every day forward going well for me and for everyone. Thank you for the license plate that just passed with my father's initials and his date of birth – GDN 519 – thank you for that wink, just when my body was tingling and a wave was just about to take me under.

There were signs, winks from the universe that I wasn't alone, that I was following the rules, thinking positive thoughts.

One morning a garbage truck passed as I pushed my cart beside the cemetery gate, not more than a hundred yards from my father's grave. Fat-lettered graffiti on the side of the truck read: *It's all in your head.*

Later the same day, I sat in a bathroom stall at school, not because I had to go, but because I had to get out, had to leave class: the boy sitting next to me was picking his nose, and his desk was touching the floor, and the floor was touching my desk, and my desk was touching me. My lips tingled and my arms went weak, and when I raised my hand to ask to use the lavatory – for years I'd thought it was *laboratory* – it was as if I held a medicine ball – we'd tried that in gym that week – and the teacher said *fine*. I could tell it wasn't fine – I asked to be excused more than any other student – but went anyway. I sat on the toilet seat, but then I realized that the other boy's desk touched the floor, and the floor touched the toilet, and even when I stood on the toilet, I might as well have been touching that boy, and I looked to the side and saw written on the wall, *It's all in your head, dude*.

That night, in bed, I heard the cop from the cop show my mother watched: *Snap out of it! It's all in your head!*

Some days – I still remember them – it seemed as if the world heard my every thought. I wanted a seat on the bus – I didn't like to touch the hanging straps – and there was a seat. I wanted someone else to pull the bell cord – I didn't want to touch it – and someone did. I wanted the clouds to part and they parted. I didn't want to go to gym and the teacher was out sick. I thought of a song and the song came on the radio. I thought of a bluebird and a bluebird alighted on a low-hanging branch on our tree.

One day, on my way home from high school, a squat man

wearing an army jacket was walking toward me. His jeans were baggy and too long. He was talking to himself, but was looking at me.

An image in my mind of the man hitting me – just a flash. I had to pass him to reach the subway. I didn't want to cross the street, only to have to cross back, even though that's what my mother had told me to do to avoid *people who don't look right*.

As I walked past the man, he came at me as if that had been his intention all along. He punched my face, then pulled my jacket over my head so I couldn't see. He threw me to the ground and kicked me, then took my jacket and walked away talking to himself.

People stopped to look, but no one went after the man.

An older man with a gray broom-handle mustache – he was hosing the sidewalk in front of a florist – asked me if I was all right. He reached into the pocket of his apron and gave me a handkerchief.

The taste of blood running from my nose; the lovely smell of flowers.

Another rule was, *Don't be afraid*.

Another was, *Whatever you're afraid of will find you*.

Part Three

Gloria Foster

Donald E. Stephens Convention Center, Rosemont, Illinois, 2000

IT'S NOT AN accident that I'm standing on this stage. It's not an accident that each of you is sitting exactly where you're sitting. Believe me, there are no such things as accidents. We have complete responsibility for all that we're experiencing in our lives. We create everything, even so-called accidents. Coincidences are never coincidences. Nothing is random. Nothing means nothing.

This is good news. There's a reason behind everything, and that reason is you.

Synchronicity is just the universe winking back at you. The universe is saying, 'Pay attention. This means something. This is what you've been thinking about, what you've been asking for.'

When you're aligned with abundance, you can create accidents on purpose. You can count on everything and everyone you need to show up at the perfect moment. Don't hope and pray for the right person to enter your life. Don't hope and pray for lucky breaks. There's no such thing as luck except the luck we create.

I encourage you, every morning when you wake, to make the following commitments to yourself. I promise to pay attention today. I believe that everything means something. I believe that the universe is constantly winking at me, reflecting my internal state, giving me a chance to cancel and erase any negative thoughts and feelings I may be having. I commit today to being open to serendipity — to expecting it, in fact. I believe that everything I need will present itself to me. I believe that I will meet the exact people I need to meet at this moment in time. I believe in perfect timing. I believe in creating happy accidents.

Now, I acknowledge that there are people who don't believe any of this. Some people believe that the worst that can happen, will. And so it should be no surprise when the worst does happen. They read the paper and begin their day looking for tragedy. They watch the evening news and end their day thinking the world is a dangerous place. Their dreams are dark, filled with anxiety. I don't judge such people, but I really do feel sorry for them. Because they don't have to live in such fear. Please hear me: I don't deny that tragic things happen in the world. But by focusing on tragedy, we attract more of the same.

Each of you has to answer the following question, the most important question you'll ever answer: Do you believe the universe is friendly or unfriendly? If you believe the universe is unfriendly, then that's precisely the kind of universe you'll live in. There's plenty of evidence if you'd like to make that case. On the other hand, if you believe that the universe is friendly, then that's precisely the kind of universe you'll live in. A universe in which like attracts like, in which thoughts become things, in which you are not powerless, in which you deserve to feel as good as you'd like to feel, in which there's no doubt or fear or competition or worry or jealousy or hatred or blame or desperation.

A universe in which there's always enough, in which there's no such thing as exclusion. A universe in which one happy thought leads to another leads to another. A universe in which there are no limits. A universe in which miracles aren't miraculous because they happen all the time.

WAKING DOESN'T FEEL like waking, more like being reborn: the world is still here, waiting for me.

My body aches everywhere, but I don't care. A bag drips clear liquid into my arm. Inhale and the room swells; exhale and I see tiny white horses ride a wave of steam from my mouth. I try to breathe them back into my lungs, but they gallop across the room, disappear into the air.

Hanging from the ceiling above me is a cord. It's so clear to me: if I pull, the world will turn off. I try to will my hand to move.

A tall woman with red hair stands at the window, her back to me. She's breathing on the window, using her finger to write words on the fogged glass. I try to speak to her, to ask who she is, where I am, what happened, but I can make no sound.

Dawn or dusk, I can't tell. I look through the window to see if the world will become lighter or darker.

With my thoughts — old habit — I try to communicate with her. Turn around, I think, and she does.

'Gloria,' she says.

I look past her and see that this is the word she's been writing in her breath on the window.

She must have been telling me her name. But I don't know anyone named Gloria, not that I can remember.

The arm she wasn't writing with is in a sling. The bandage on her nose wraps around her head. She has a black eye.

'Gloria,' she says, her voice an echo.

I blink twice, deliberately, trying to start a code she might learn to recognize: one blink for yes, two for no.

I want to ask her if I'm critical, if I have information she needs before I die. Perhaps someone tried to murder me, tried to murder both of us. I wonder, for the first time, if she's my wife, and then I remember that I have a wife, and I begin to cry I'm so happy, and my ribs ache with my shaking, the most wonderful hurt I've ever experienced, until I realize the error of my verb tense, not have, *had*, and now the hurt is just hurt. My fear has changed: I'm no longer afraid to die, but to live.

Memory returns: I live alone on Martha's Vineyard, this woman came to find me, there was an accident, I couldn't breathe, and then—

Gloria. She wants to know who Gloria is.

I don't know, I think. Isn't that *your* name?

I blink twice, but she doesn't notice. I blink twice again.

'When you came back, you said Gloria. You told me to write it down. It was the only thing you said. I wasn't sure if it was a name or if you saw God.'

Came back from where?

89

As if she can hear my thoughts: 'You're going to be fine, but for a few minutes you were gone.'

And then I remember. Not who Gloria is, but why I said this name, though I have no memory of having said it.

Here, *there* seems only a dream. Yet there, *here* seemed like a dream.

Dream or not, I heard the name. Gloria.

My father's voice.

Impossible, yet it was my father's voice that said this name.

Even if I could speak, I wouldn't tell her everything, this woman who came to save me.

'I know who you are,' she says. 'I told you – my accident wasn't an accident. Neither was yours. I think it has something to do with Gloria.'

'Ralph.'

But that's all I have in me – one word.

'She's fine,' she says. 'I've been taking care of her. I hope you don't mind, but I've been staying at your house. It's been a week.'

I try to wet my lips, but there's no saliva in my mouth. She gives me an ice chip from a cup on the table beside the bed.

'Two cracked ribs,' she says. 'Punctured lung. That's what caused the real trouble. Concussion, too. You have a terrible headache, I bet.'

I blink once.

'Do you remember my name?'

I blink twice.

'Sam,' she says. 'Sam Leslie.'

Night through the window: it had been dusk when I woke, not dawn. I close my eyes and listen to drugs drip into my arm.

When I open my eyes again – it could be five minutes or five hours later – the cord above me is gone. Sam is gone, too. I watch my breath, but now the horses have the torsos and faces of men. Quickly I breathe them back into my body. The next time I exhale they are children riding the wave of my breath all the way to the window across the room, where the name Gloria is still written.

I IMAGINE THE house, her in the house, without me.

She wakes in early-morning darkness, her face sore. Ralph waits bedside, wagging her tail as eagerly as possible for an old dog.

She rolls to the edge of the bed, wincing at the pain in her arm, and presents her face for the dog to lick. Then the dog lays her head on the mattress, waits to be scratched.

She sleeps in her underwear. Perhaps – because she packed only a few items of clothing – she sleeps nude.

Jeans, a sweater, one of my coats, a walk with the dog, cold but sunny, down the road and into the woods, hard dirt trails, the satisfaction of watching the dog empty her bladder and move her bowels wherever she wants, her graceful way of squatting, the steam her pee makes at the base of a tree carved with your initials, a sentimental gesture of our last year together.

Back home – after a week, the house feels like home – to feed the dog. She knows by now the dog won't eat alone, won't touch food unless someone else is in the room, so she makes tea (no coffee or coffeemaker) and spoons some yogurt onto a bowl of granola (she seems the yogurt type). Her car has been towed from the mud. I imagine that she has gone grocery shopping, milk and bread and eggs, a jar of peanut butter; I imagine that she has explored the Vineyard, knows where to buy the *Times*, where the best bookstores are; I imagine that she has bought a new pair of jeans.

The sound of the dog drinking makes her thirsty. She swallows two pills for pain, then undresses for a shower.

Careful not to soak the bandage on her face, she washes with her back to the water. Her sprained arm is pinned to her side as if by an invisible sling. Right-handed, she shaves her legs with her left, using an old razor I shave my neck with once every few weeks. Her red hair wet looks darker.

When she opens the bathroom door, the dog is waiting with her shoe. Thank you, thank you, good dog, and on to the laundry room, where yesterday's clothes are clean and dry.

Dressed but barefoot, she sits cross-legged on the rug, her back straight against the couch, and closes her eyes. Her daily practice. She follows her breath, in and out through her nose, and any thought that finds her – her brother lying on the bathroom floor, the note he didn't leave, how she could have saved him, the strong sense she has, stronger than ever, that accidents are not accidents, that something important is going to happen – she recognizes only long enough to say goodbye, then lets it go, emptying her mind, even if only for a few seconds, before a new thought finds her, then she lets that one go, returns to the breath, and after a while there's nothing *but* the breath, and she's gone.

She comes back only when the phone rings.

An older woman says she's sorry, she must have dialed the wrong number.

No use trying to meditate again; twenty minutes is enough for today.

The phone rings again. It's the same woman; this time she asks for me. 'Is Eric there? Is my son there?'

'Don't worry,' Sam tells me when she comes to see me later that morning. 'I didn't tell her who I am.'

'Who *are* you?'

'What do you mean?'

'I mean, what would you have told her had you told her the truth?'

'That I'm a friend.'

'Did you tell her about the accident?'

'No.'

'That's probably for the best,' I say. 'What did you tell her?'

'That I was the maid.'

She picks up the pad on the table beside the bed, looks at what I've written, looks at me.

'What happened when you died?'

'Nothing.'

'Where did you go?'

'Nowhere.'

'Tell me the truth.'

'It was like sleeping.'

'Is this her last name?'

'Whose?'

'Gloria's.'

'Who is Gloria?'

'I've been waiting for you to tell me.'

'If you don't know, then why are you here?'

'What do you mean?'

'If there's no such thing as an accident, then why are you here?'

'I was trying to find you.'

'Okay, but that was for you. What are you here to do for me?'

'Walk your dog.'

'What else?'

'Get you into an accident.'

'If you believe that I was supposed to get into that accident—'

'I got that from *you* – from your books.'

'I don't believe that anymore.' I press the button that sends more morphine into my blood. 'You're the teacher now, I'm the student. Tell me why I was supposed to have that accident.'

'What was it like?' she says. 'I mean, did you see the light, or what?'

I press the morphine button, press it again, press it again. 'What's the point of all this?'

She looks at the paper in her hand. 'Gloria Foster,' she says.

SHE WALKS THE dog, cooks for me, brings me my toothbrush and a cup to spit into. She offers to wash me, and I'm grateful, but I ask her instead to help me to the sink, where I clean my face and hands and chest with a washcloth. She rereads my books, takes notes in the margins. A refresher course, she calls it. Every time she forgets, and begins to read a passage aloud, I remind her not to.

'Funny how you're right next to me – I mean, it's *you* – yet I'm sitting here reading your books.'

'I'm not the same person who wrote those words.'

'I like the old you better.'

After a pause: 'That was a joke, you know.'

My doctor has given me orders: two weeks of bed rest; no driving for a month; no exertion, no stress. Expected: headaches and nausea. Possible: dizziness, double vision, tinnitus, depression, mood swings, memory loss, sensitivity to light, and poor judgment, though I'm not sure how I'll decide if my judgment has been poor. If I experience a headache that lasts longer than a day, or doesn't respond to meds, or becomes severe, I am to call. If I experience memory loss or confusion, I am to call. If I have difficulty breathing – beyond the difficulty to be expected with a cracked rib – I am to call immediately. Otherwise: rest, rest, rest.

My car is totaled, so Sam drives hers to the market every day for the paper. The third day I'm home, she's gone three hours. I assume she's taken a trip to a bookstore or to buy another change of clothes, but she returns holding a stack of paper. She went to the library to use the Internet. She found over three hundred Gloria Fosters in the United States.

'Did God tell you the middle name?'

'God didn't tell me anything.'

'Did the same angel or ghost or voice that told you the first and last name happen to mention a middle name, even a middle initial?'

'I told you what I know.'

'No location?'

'No.'

'Not even a state?'

'No.'

So she asks the old me for help. She sends out her intention – using a step-by-step process I wrote about in *Everyday Miracles* – to receive the information she needs in order to find Gloria Foster. For three days she meditates an hour in the morning and an hour in the evening, expecting a message to come to her. How it comes doesn't matter; could be something she reads, something a stranger says in passing, a phrase or even a single word that enters her thoughts as if someone else put it there.

In Sam's case, it comes as a brief but vivid dream; she's certain it contains the information she's been asking for.

A row house with a cemetery behind it.

'That's *my* house,' I say. 'The one I grew up in, in Queens. My mother lives there.'

'Gloria Foster lives in *this* house.'

'How do you know?'

'My brother told me.'

'Your dead brother?'

'He was walking in the cemetery,' she says. 'It was him, but how he might look now if he were alive. Heavier, the same wavy hair. Still handsome.'

'What did he say?'

'He kept throwing rocks at this house, but the rocks turned into dandelion clocks. They hit the back of the house, and the snow scattered like light.'

'And you take that to mean Gloria Foster lives in that house?'

'You don't have to believe what I'm saying,' she says. 'I should tell you, though, that I'm going to find her even if you don't want to.'

'Just because a man you don't know said her name when he came back to life.'

'I know you.'

'You know *him*.' I point to the book on her lap.

'Okay, then I know him,' she says. 'Maybe I'll take *him* with me. Either way, I'm going to find her.'

'Even though this has nothing to do with you.'

'My brother was in that dream,' she says.

'Your brother is dead.'

She pulls the bandage off her nose, slowly at first, then one quick yank. Her eyes water.

'I'm sorry,' I tell her.

'Dead or not, this has something to do with him.'

'Fine, but what does it have to do with me?'

'Your books helped me so much, and then you were gone. There were rumors that you no longer believed what you'd written.'

'So what.'

'But what you wrote is true,' she says.

'And you're going to make me believe again.'

'I just know that we need to find Gloria Foster.'

'Why *we?*'

'You're the one who said her name,' she says.

'Now that you have the name, you don't need me anymore.'

'Come on,' she says. 'Doesn't part of you still believe?'

'Believe what?'

'That the law of attraction works. That our intentions really *are* powerful.'

'I didn't intend any of this – a car accident, cracked ribs, you.'

'Sometimes you don't realize your intentions until they manifest.'

'If intentions worked, my wife would still be alive. So would your brother.'

'Everything happens for a reason, even though the reason may not always be apparent.'

'Stop quoting me.'

'The universe is always listening to us.'

'Please stop.'

'Your words, not mine.'

'His.'

'He's *you*.'

'He's not me.'

'Okay, but he's still inside you.'

That night she wakes me from a restless sleep. I can't lie on my side or stomach; my ribs hurt too much. On my back, my breathing is shallow.

I stare at her, but can't remember her name. Red hair, freckles, black eye, broken nose.

'I know where she is,' she says.

'Let me guess,' I say. 'Another dream.'

'My brother,' she says. 'He showed me the name of the cemetery.'

'Hold on,' I say. 'I'm hearing everything you say twice.'

She gives me a pill from one of the bottles on my night table; I work up enough saliva in my mouth to swallow it.

'I don't trust dreams,' I tell her.

'I'm asking you to trust *me*.'

'When are you leaving?'

'*We* are leaving in the morning,' she says.

What I don't tell Sam is that all night you've been singing to me as clearly as if you were lying in bed beside me – the song you were singing when we met, the one I play most often now that you're gone. It's been much easier not wanting anything, not thinking too much, not believing in anything but what's in front of me, and now this woman and her dreams and her dead brother and you singing to me in my sleep.

'This is all going to turn out to mean nothing.'

'Nothing means nothing,' she says.

'If you quote me one more time, I swear.'

'Sorry,' she says.

'I'm tired,' I tell her. 'I'm just tired.'

'I'll do all the driving.'

'I don't think I've ever been more tired.'

'You can sleep the whole way if you want.'

I turn away from her and close my eyes, hoping to fall back into my dream of you. I listen for your voice, but it's gone.

Part Four

It's On Its Way

Sun Valley Wellness Festival, Sun Valley, Idaho, 1998

IT'S GREAT TO *be here with you on this beautiful day. In fact, there's no place in the world I'd rather be.*

All it takes is a single happy thought. Then another. Then another.

I like when it's sunny, when it rains, when it snows. I like when it gets dark early, when it stays light late. There's something beautiful about every moment of every day. All you have to do is make the decision to see the positive, to filter the world.

You need to live as if.
    Let me repeat that: You need to live as if.
    As if you already have everything you want. As if the universe is listening. As if it, whatever it is, is on its way.
    Anticipate what's coming. Live in a perpetual state of expectation.
    If you want love, expect love. If you want health, anticipate health.

If you want good news, prepare for it. Celebrate whatever you want as if it's already arrived.

When you expect something, it's on its way. When you fear something, it's on its way.

All that you desire is behind a door. All you need to do is open the door and receive it.

Imagine you're trying to get from Point A to Point B. You're moving along, you're doing fine, picking up speed, you'll get there in no time, but suddenly there's an obstacle. What do most people do when an obstacle is in their way? They slow down. They go around the obstacle. Fine. But what happens when there's another obstacle, and another, and another? You have to keep slowing down, and eventually you get frustrated, you get tired, you come to expect obstacles.

Now, let me ask you all a question: Wouldn't it be better to get rid of those obstacles?

The first step in getting rid of obstacles is simple: Name them, expose them, get them out in the open.

So, take out a piece of paper and fold it in half.

On the left side of the page we're going to list the ten obstacles that keep the door of abundance closed.

1. *Impatience*
2. *Doubt*
3. *Negativity*
4. *Fear*
5. *Competition*

6. *Worry*
7. *Jealousy*
8. *Anger*
9. *Blame*
10. *Desperation*

Take a good look. See if you recognize any of the obstacles that have stood in your way.

Be honest. Today is a day for being real. Today is going to be one of the best days of your life. Trust me.

Now, on the right side of the page we're going to make a new list. Ten keys to keeping abundance flowing into your life.

1. *Patience*
2. *Faith*
3. *Positive thinking*
4. *Fearlessness*
5. *Being happy for others*
6. *Confidence*
7. *Kindness*
8. *Joy*
9. *Self-responsibility*
10. *Gratitude*

Circle that last one, gratitude.

Underline it. Put a star next to it.

Don't ever underestimate the power of thank you. Don't complain, don't judge, don't blame, don't compare. Just say thank you. Over and over, to everything: thank you, thank you, thank you.

Some days nothing seems to be going your way. But the truth is, if you greet even those days with one thank you after another, the universe hears this. The message you're sending out is: Everything always goes my way, even when it seems like it's not. I'm going to celebrate now, because I know that it, whatever it is, is on its way. Nothing can derail me from this certainty. There are no obstacles in my way. If something seems like an obstacle, it's really not. This is what the universe hears every time you say thank you.

Don't sweat the details. Don't worry about how or when. Miracles aren't rational. Just know that it's on its way.

But things haven't always worked out, you say.

I know, I know.

Please, listen to me: Don't allow the weight of the past to pull you down. Don't allow your past to define your future. It's time to retell your story beginning with your next thought.

Now is all that matters; nothing else exists.

Right now I feel good about blank.

I want us to begin today by filling in that blank. Take the next ten minutes and write this sentence as many times as possible. Think of all the things you feel good about and let the universe know how grateful you are.

One happy thought, then another, then another. One thank you, then another, then another.

Right now I feel good about . . .

Right now I feel good about . . .

The universe is listening. Trust me.

I WAS HEARING the song everywhere; it was following me.
Late one December night, after a talk, I couldn't sleep.
I got out of bed and turned on the TV. I hoped to find *It's a Wonderful Life*, the movie I've seen more than any other. My affection for the film had to do with its idea that everything happens for a reason, that life is a meaningful chain of events. You save your brother from drowning and he becomes a war hero. Rather, your brother becomes a war hero *because* you saved him from drowning. *Post hoc ergo propter hoc*. After this, therefore because of this. You hear a song because you turn on your TV at 2:22 a.m. You turn on your TV because you can't sleep. You can't sleep because you wake from a dream that your father, dead almost twenty years, is tapping on your hotel room's window. You have this dream because sleet is falling against your window and because once, when you were a boy, you made your father disappear and he never came back. You hear the last ten seconds of a song, the end of the credits of a movie, and it's enough to make you fall in love with the voice.

A few weeks later, back home, you hear a teenager at the market — a girl with dyed-red hair, a nose ring, and sad, brown eyes — singing the same song off-key. You're tempted to ask her the name of the song, the name of the singer, but don't. Instead, you trust that you'll hear the song again, that eventually it will lead you to the singer, and when that happens, you'll write about it in your next book, tell the story to audiences across the country, how you met the love of your life by expecting miracles, by trusting the power of intention and the law of attraction.

During the next few months you keep hearing the song. A man hums it as he hands you the bagel you ordered. A woman in scrubs sings the refrain between cigarette drags outside a hospital as you walk past. A woman on the subway sings a verse while you sit beside her pretending to read.

And then one February night you duck into a Chelsea bar to avoid sudden rain and lightning, and you hear the song. But this time it's her. Not a recording, but her actual voice. You see in your peripheral vision a woman onstage; she's singing a song about hello and goodbye. The lyrics are sad, but you'd never know by her happy, ethereal crooning, and her smile. It's like listening to two songs at once. You want to move closer, lean in. But you don't want to look. You're not ready for her to be anything more than a voice. Despite what you wrote in your first book, you're a little afraid each time a miracle happens.

You move closer to the stage and look. A woman seated on a stool behind a microphone, guitar on her lap. Brown curly hair, green eyes. Thin gray sweater single-buttoned over black T-shirt, dark jeans, thick brown belt, brown boots. You look away, and she's only the voice.

When a fight breaks out at the bar, she keeps singing. A drunk man in a suit tries to push his way to a much larger man who's laughing, arms at his sides, as if daring the other man to hit him. Unable to reach the larger man, the man in the suit throws his beer bottle, which hits someone, not his intended target, and soon a dozen people are shoving and throwing punches or trying to prevent the fight from escalating. Two bouncers with compact bodies of veined muscle aren't enough to control the crowd, and through it all she keeps singing with eyes closed. She doesn't open her eyes despite the crowd pushing its way toward the stage. The world around her could blow up and she would keep singing.

You move closer, and it seems you're the only person listening, she's singing to you alone. She opens her eyes, sees you, smiles, closes them again, and now she's not only a voice, she's a face, but not yet a name.

'Hello,' she said, and offered her hand. 'I'm Cary Weiss.' She'd come to sit with me between sets, as if we'd arranged to meet beforehand.

'Hello,' I said, and we shook. 'I'm Eric, but my name was almost Cary – you know, like Cary Grant.'

'That's how I spell it – with a γ.'

'Weiss was Harry Houdini's real name, you know.'

'I didn't know.'

'Ehrich Weiss,' I said. 'I was named after him.'

'Are you a magician?'

'Not really.'

'An escape artist?'

'No,' I said. 'An author.'

'What do you write?'

'Books.'

'I meant what *kind* of books.'

'Actually, just one book.'

'What's it about?'

'A man keeps hearing a song, then meets the woman who sings it. I write about things like that.'

When it was time for her next set to begin, she said, 'I don't think I can do it.'

'Do what?'

'Get up there and sing.'

'Why not?'

'I feel sick,' she said. 'Happens every time. I keep a bucket backstage.'

'But you're great.'

'I should have been a veterinarian,' she said. 'In my next life I want to come back as a vet.'

'Do you not like singing?'

'I love singing,' she said. 'This happens when I'm *not* singing – when I've just finished a song, especially a song I've really nailed. I can hear the echo of my own voice, and I like it, and I think, That wasn't *me*, that couldn't have been *me*.'

'Are you afraid of success?'

'I don't want fame, if that's what you mean.'

'That's not what I mean.'

'I'm very happy,' she said. 'My friends tell me I'm the happiest person they know.'

'Being happy is good for you,' I said. 'Chapter 6 in my book.'

'Oh,' she said. 'So you write self-help books.'

'Book,' I said. 'Singular.'

'What's your book called?'

'*Everyday Miracles.*'

'I like that,' she said. 'Will there be a sequel? I mean, is it part of an epic trilogy or something?'

'I'm not a novelist.'

'Seriously, I'm going to get your book.'

'Sure, but will you read it?'

'Of course,' she said. 'I'll even write you a fan letter.'

She lived in a high-ceilinged two-bedroom apartment in Brooklyn; she used one bedroom as a studio, where she wrote songs. Running around the apartment, chewing newspapers, table legs, my shoelaces, anything in her path, was a German shepherd puppy, a female named Ralph. Huge ears, needle teeth.

A warm night for March, so we ate our first dinner together in a narrow, brick courtyard Cary shared with two other tenants. Rainwater from an early-evening shower dripped from the fire escape into my wineglass. We sat in silence – not at all an uncomfortable silence – waiting for each drop. I thought we might spend the entire night this way, and that would have been fine. *Drip*, a long pause, *drip*, a longer pause, *drip*, an even longer pause, the red wine at the bottom of my glass a shade lighter.

After dinner we played with Ralph. We threw a tennis ball for her to fetch, hid training treats in our pockets and made her sniff them out, played hide-and-seek, Cary in one closet, me in another, then both of us in the same closet, quiet in the dark, the smell on her breath of the cherries we'd had for dessert, her finger on my lips to tell me to stay quiet, Ralph scratching the door, crying for us to open.

When we opened the door, she jumped on us, licked my hands, latched on to Cary's jeans, and pulled. We ran through the apartment until the downstairs neighbor banged on his ceiling, then we looked at the clock and saw that it was late.

That was the year of hello. The song, the bar, an exchange of names, our first date, our engagement six months later.

It's a cliché to say that some couples just know, but we did. There was no drama, no doubt, no complications having to do with career or geography or religion, no recent messy breakups not yet fully cleaned up. It's also a cliché to say that we felt as if we'd always known each other, so let me revise that one: it felt like every date, every dinner, every movie, every kiss, every night we slept beside each other had already happened, as if we were living lives already lived. We joked about this almost constant déjà vu, the surprise – a good one – we felt every time we had that strange feeling that we'd done all this before, that we were characters in a story already written, one we'd read a very long time ago but had forgotten.

At the end of every year we made a list. Seven years, seven

lists. A way of naming the recent past; practice in short-term memory. There was the year we bought the house in Chilmark, where I now live alone. There was the year my second book was published, the year one of Cary's songs was used in a sweater commercial, the year I shaved my beard and immediately grew it back because I didn't like to see my own face. There was the year we watched every Woody Allen movie, the year I started running, the year we made our own bread. There was the year the towers fell, of course, a difficult year for entirely different reasons. There was the next year, the year of color codes for fear, but for us there were no codes, just fear, and ours had nothing to do with planes flying into buildings or anthrax or smart bombs – our fear, I should say mine, was a much more personal, a much more selfish fear.

After the year of hello was the year of silent Saturdays. Our first year of marriage – one of my favorites.

No talking. Just gestures and facial expressions and touch to know what the other wanted, what the other was feeling. There were gifts in silence: to put my finger to her lips to say *hungry*, to have to touch more, to make love without words and to lie, after, with only the sound of our breathing. Every Saturday every year until the last, when I didn't *not* want to hear her voice, didn't want her *not* to hear mine.

The last year, I couldn't not speak. It was *too* quiet. I would panic, would forget she was in the bedroom, would call out to her, and she would walk into the living room, her finger

Nicholas Montemarano

to her lips to say, *Silent day, did you forget?* and I would say, 'I don't want to do it anymore,' and she would mouth, *Are you sure?* and I would say, 'Say something, anything – it doesn't matter.' Then she would sing to me – not words, just sounds, humming – and that way I could hear her voice, but she could still say that she hadn't spoken.

WE CHOSE NAMES before we tried. Lucy and Vincent for Lucy Vincent Beach, our favorite place on Martha's Vineyard.

Cary was against it: she was content living in the present; she didn't want to pretend something was real when it wasn't.

To believe, I told her, is to make it real.

She smiled at me, rolled her eyes. Our differences, then, endeared us to each other. I believed in knowing; she believed in uncertainty. I believed in control; she believed in surrender. I believed in what could be; she believed in what was.

'But you wrote me a fan letter,' I joked. 'Chapter 6 cured you of your bucket problem.'

'I was flirting,' she said. 'Besides, I still have my bucket problem.'

'Sweetheart,' I said, 'you need to read my next book.'

In my mind, we already had twins, a girl and a boy, Lucy and Vincent. Born before they were born.

I reminded Cary that she had done something similar with Ralph. Her previous boyfriend didn't want a dog, and so for a year Cary pretended she had a dog named Ralph – a joke, yes, and to annoy her boyfriend, but also to win him over, to convince him that having a dog would be fun. She pretended to walk the dog; she set a bowl of water on the kitchen floor; she bought a collar, a leash, and a rubber bone.

The boyfriend didn't find this funny or charming, but aggressive. No surprise, they broke up, and a few months later a friend called about a litter of puppies. Cary fell in love with the first one she picked up, a German shepherd that looked exactly like the dog she'd been imagining.

'You see,' I told her. 'We really do see the universe the same way.'

'But I'd imagined a male dog.'

'Small detail,' I said. 'You wanted a Ralph, you got a Ralph.'

The first time we tried, Cary felt a sharp pain in her abdomen. She was the type not to make a fuss over pain, but it became so severe that I had to take her to the emergency room in the middle of the night.

She sat beside me, her eyes closed, and tried to take deep breaths. Every so often she winced, then returned to her breathing. She was good at living in the present even if it was unpleasant.

It was August, hot and humid. A sweaty young man, too skinny, hair in a ponytail, paced the ER, his shoulder bleeding through his white shirt. He had large, frightened eyes and the long, delicate fingers of a pianist. A short, overweight woman sat across from us, moaning. Her legs and arms were stubby, but her face was beautiful. She took off her shoes and socks, as if this might help. Her feet were dry and calloused, her toenails painted pink. A nurse had to call the woman three times before she looked up; it was as if she'd forgotten her own name. She took her shoes with her, but left the socks behind.

When a nurse called Cary's name – we had been waiting two hours – she turned to me and said, 'My sister was pregnant when she died.'

I didn't know how to respond; it was the last thing I expected her to say.

'When I told you the story, I left that part out.'

'It's not your fault,' I said.

'I just wanted to tell you,' she said, and together we went to see the doctor.

It was one of the first stories she told me about herself when we were dating. She bought her father flying lessons as a retirement gift; he had retired early, in his late fifties. After he earned his license, he planned a day to take Cary, her sister, Parker, and their mother for a flight over the Berkshires. But Cary woke that morning with the flu and couldn't get out of bed. She hadn't been that sick in years – not since the chickenpox in sixth grade. Her father said they could reschedule, but Cary said they should go without her; there was always next time.

Even had anyone remembered that she'd bought the flying lessons, that it had been her idea, no one would have blamed her.

At the funeral, Parker's husband – widower, rather – leaned over to Cary and said, 'She was pregnant. She told me a few days before.'

'Maybe we're not supposed to have children,' she said. 'Maybe it's something we have to accept.'

We were making a salad. I was peeling carrots, Cary was chopping lettuce. The knife against the cutting board, the pile of carrot peels in the sink, the whir and suck of the garbage disposal – we both had strong déjà vu. It was as if the conversation we were about to have had already happened, as if we were reading a script. I knew all my lines. I even knew that I was about to say something foolish, that I was about to make a mistake.

'You accept things too easily,' I said.

'Life's easier that way.'

'Your life, maybe. But this is *our* life.'

'It's my body.'

'I don't think you should give in so easily.'

'You heard the doctor.'

'Doctors don't know everything.'

'Things happen for a reason,' she said.

'But we've talked about having children,' I said. 'They have names.'

'That wasn't a good idea.'

'I saw them,' I said. 'They were real.'

'They were never real,' she said.

*

I couldn't bring myself to tell her what I really believed: that her guilt about her sister – about her entire family, but especially about her pregnant sister – was causing her endometriosis. Her guilt, unless she changed her thoughts, would never allow her body to become pregnant.

The doctor was recommending that her ovaries – each covered with a grapefruit-sized cyst – come out immediately, before the cysts could rupture. Her bladder, bowels, and uterus were covered with scar tissue.

We went to see a fertility specialist, who gave us an option other than hysterectomy: surgery to remove the cysts and scrape away the scar tissue, followed as soon as possible – whenever Cary recovered – with fertility drugs and hormone injections.

Cary was in the hospital four days, recovering from surgery; I slept on a cot beside her bed, answering letters from readers. During the first few nights, when Cary had a tube in her nose and was too weak to talk, she'd tap on the sides of her bed, and that was how I knew she was thirsty – I'd feed her ice chips – or wanted me to sit with her for a few minutes.

On the third day she was able to get out of bed and walk to the bathroom. I asked if she needed my help, but she said no; she walked past me holding her hospital gown closed.

She'd been in the bathroom ten minutes, so I went to the door; that was when I heard her crying.

I opened the door. She was looking down at the scar.

'Were we supposed to do this?'

'If we want children.'

'This doesn't seem natural,' she said.

We fought quiet fights. Sometimes I think I was the only one fighting. She was usually unflappable: when she was angry, she sang; when she was happy, she sang. No matter what, she went into her studio at home and sang: songs she'd sung a hundred times or songs she wrote as the words came out of her mouth. Some songs – beautiful songs that made me forget what I'd been angry about – she sang only once; I never heard them again. I'd ask her – my way of making up, of saying sorry – if she would sing a song I especially liked. 'The one about waking from a dream,' I'd say, and she'd say, 'I'm not sure which one you mean,' and I'd say, 'The one about dreaming – it goes like this,' and I'd hum the refrain as best as I could, and she'd look at me blankly as if she'd never heard it. 'I'm sorry,' she'd say.

I believed her.

Most people have it in them to be that aggressive, to refuse to give something so beautiful, something only you can give, a song no one else knows. But she didn't have that kind of aggression in her, or if she did, she was bigger than it. So I believed that she didn't remember; believed when she said that it really hadn't been *her* singing – it was something singing *through* her; it passed through her the way water and air and life pass through a body.

Those songs are lost; I can't remember them. She didn't mind losing them. Everything came and went, she said, and that made them more precious while they were here. Hello, goodbye, the only story we know.

We got to practice hello and goodbye: I was traveling to promote my second book, *It's On Its Way: Creating the Life You've Always Wanted*, and she was singing at some clubs on the East Coast. If we were gone at the same time, she took Ralph with her and they stayed with friends or in pet-friendly hotels. She'd call me in my hotel room and say *park* and *run* and *boy*, words to make Ralph bark into the phone.

'See,' Cary said. 'She misses you.'

'She's happy wherever she is,' I said.

If Cary was ovulating, we'd come home; we never wanted to miss a month. I'd fly home from Seattle even though I was speaking at a conference in Los Angeles the next night; Cary would drive home from Boston – she didn't fly – even though her next show was two hours away, in Northampton, where she grew up.

Every morning, after waking, and every evening, before sleep, I closed my eyes and meditated on the children we'd have. Lucy and Vincent.

I believed in miracles and had hundreds of letters as evidence: people who had read my first book then cured themselves – with only their thoughts – of diabetes, hypertension, multiple sclerosis, liver cancer. A man who was told he'd never walk again, a devout Pentecostal for whom even the laying on of hands hadn't worked, read my book, believed that he'd walk again, visualized it, acted as if it would happen. He removed the wheelchair ramp leading to his front door.

Two weeks later, when he hadn't walked, he still believed, and as evidence of his faith he gave away his wheelchair. The next day, he walked. 'I wasn't surprised,' he wrote. 'Everyone else was, even my wife, but not me.' A seventh-grade girl wrote that her hair had fallen out – she, like her father, had alopecia – and that her mother read my book and taught her some of my techniques. The girl made a creation box, and inside the box she put photographs of herself before she lost her hair, and she believed that her hair would grow back, she even gave away all the hats her friends had given her, and after only a few months of sending out her intention, of believing, her hair began to grow back.

These people, whom I had inspired, now inspired me: if I had helped them believe, then their letters could strengthen my own beliefs.

I worked on the nursery; I bought a box of diapers; I bought two pairs of baby socks, two tiny winter caps. Three months passed, five, eight, ten, more time than a baby would have lived inside Cary. The answer, whether from a pregnancy test or Cary's body, was always no.

No, to me, meant *not yet*.

To Cary no meant *no;* it meant *maybe never*.

And that was fine with her, she told me. If you accept whatever happens, she said, if you embrace what life gives you, there are gifts.

After a year of trying, the home pregnancy test said yes.

'That's what it *says,*' she told me.

'I knew it!' I said. 'I knew it would happen!'

'You never know,' she said. 'It could be a false positive.'

'Jesus,' I said. 'It's like you *want* it to be no.'

'No,' she said. 'It's just that I don't want you to get your hopes up.'

'My hopes are up,' I said. 'My hopes have *been* up.'

'That's what I mean,' she said. 'You like to be sure, but how can you ever be sure?'

'You're holding *sure* in your hand.'

'I don't mean *this*.' She laid the pregnancy test on the bed. I didn't want to touch it; I was afraid I might make the pink strip disappear. 'What I mean,' she said, 'is that you can't be sure you're supposed to be doing something until you're doing it. Maybe we're not supposed to have kids.'

'Will you please stop saying that.'

'I'm not trying to upset you,' she said. 'It's just that I don't *feel* pregnant.'

'But you are.'

'Maybe,' she said.

I was in Denver a few days later when she called. As soon as I heard her voice, I knew. I told her I couldn't talk, I was just about to leave for an interview, I'd call her when I got back to the hotel. There was no interview. I lay in bed, closed my eyes, and tried to will it untrue, what she hadn't said but what I'd heard in her tone, the way she said *hi*, her first word, a little too happy, but beneath her happiness, fear.

The phone kept ringing that night, but I didn't answer. I like to think this was an act of kindness, a desire to protect her from me, from the unkind words I wanted to say, but there was meanness, too: I wanted to make her wait; I wanted her to spend those extra hours worrying about what I'd say.

'I'm sorry,' she said, her first words when I answered the phone, a few minutes before midnight.

'Me, too,' I said.

'I really am disappointed.'

'Me, too.'

'I wish you were home.'

'I'll be there in the morning.'

'Are you angry?'

'No.'

'Are you sure?'

'I'm sure.'

'I don't believe you.'

'I'm not angry.'

'You are.'

'Jesus,' I said.

'I can tell,' she said.

'I'm not angry!'

'Tell me again,' she said. 'Say it like you mean it.'

THE YEAR HE felt the pebble in his shoe.

Smaller than a pebble – let's call it a grain of sand. The one fear he couldn't meditate or positive-think away. He could take off his shoes and socks, shake them out, wash his feet, but the next morning, after he dressed, it was still there, he could feel it, a little bigger than the day before: the grain of sand, his greatest fear.

It's easy for me – the man writing this – to look back and say that was the moment, but even *he* knew it then.

Valentine's Day, the dog's third birthday. Seventy pounds, fully grown, but the hyper tail of a puppy, slaps the floor if you look at her. Ready to jump on you, even though she knows not to. She sits at the window, crying. Sniffs at a thin crack in the glass.

The girl – as he calls his wife – wants to stay in bed, too cold to get up. She wants the boy – as she calls him – to make pancakes. She doesn't like to exchange gifts that can be kept, and so pancakes can be his to her. She likes best things that can be used only once. She likes one-night-only performances. She likes art made to change or die, art you can experience only once, Andy Goldsworthy's snowballs that melt to reveal leaves, pinecones, twigs, thorns. When she hears a song she likes, she turns up the volume, closes her eyes, shuts out everything else, but has no interest in buying the album. Her best songs, what she considers her best, she doesn't record; she plays them only at her shows.

'Use real syrup,' she tells him. 'And don't skimp on butter.'

While he's putting on a sweatshirt she adds, 'Anything but round. Some other shape we can say we're eating for the first and last time.'

She used to live on the second floor, but now they live on the first and second. They bought the brownstone; they rent the third floor to a med student and a pianist, lovers or friends or friends who want to be lovers, they can't tell. They have heard fights, and so they wonder. The med student, a woman, crying. After, silence. Then the piano. Then more silence.

The dog follows him down to the kitchen, takes a drink of water. He finds her chew toy, makes her lie down for it, throws it for her to chase.

Snow flurries overnight, white dust on the street. Not so much that he can't run later. His feet are cold on the kitchen floor. He doesn't own slippers, even though his wife assures him he'd look cute; he doesn't like dog hair on the bottoms of his socks. He stands in front of the stove, one foot warming on top of the other, then the other on top, as a circle of batter forms a pancake.

He remembers: not round. He reshapes the circle into a rectangle. Too easy, he thinks, so he thins the rectangle until it's a line. Boring, he decides, and divides the line near the bottom: a line on top of a dot. An exclamation point. Too enthusiastic, so he uses a spoon to curve the top of the line. A question mark. Perfect. She'll see it and tell him another knock-knock. She likes the dumbest ones best.

Knock-knock.

Who's there?

Boo.

Boo who?

Don't cry! It's not as bad as you think!

He hears the dog run upstairs. A game with the girl. She eggs on the dog to chase her room to room, through hallways, up and down the stairs. Ralph is faster than the girl and smarter than most dogs, so she wins. Catches the girl out of breath from laughing so much. He has played with them before, knows that involuntary laughter, that feeling, something chasing, closing in, right behind you. That rush of adrenaline even if what's chasing has no intention of harming you. Fear-laughter. Ralph doesn't know what to do when she catches them. All that effort, finally she has them, now what. She touches with her nose, circles, slaps her tail against their shins, looks for a tennis ball, needs something in her mouth. If she finds nothing, they'll bend down so she can lick their faces.

He can hear this game from where he stands, watching batter bubble in a pan. He moves his face closer to smell, then flips the question mark. He decides to make toast and scrambled eggs; he pours two small glasses of orange juice and starts a pot of coffee even though he doesn't drink coffee and messed it up the last time he tried to make it for his wife. She'll be happy with the gesture.

And then it happens. It began as a thought, a fear, a grain of sand, and then it happens.

He thinks to call up to her, as a parent might to a child, *Be careful up there, you don't want to get hurt.*

Immediately following this thought is an image of his wife on the floor, not moving, and immediately following this image comes the feeling in his body, a chill that has nothing to do with the cold floor or the cold outside, the snow falling more steadily now, maybe he won't be able to run, after all, and immediately following this feeling in his body he hears her fall down the stairs.

He finds her at the bottom. The dog is halfway down the flight, unsure what to do; even her tail, between her legs, knows that the game's over. His wife lies on her side, unmoving, against the wall. He imagines she's broken her neck. He rushes to her, touches her back, says her name. She moves her hand. The silence that comes before crying. It terrifies him when the sound comes. A child crying. He thinks, I would rather she be unconscious. A stupid, selfish thought. I can say that now because I'm no longer him. The man who shares my name, ten years younger, no gray in his hair or beard, puts his hands on her back, tells her not to move.

He remembers – perhaps I'm remembering now, for him – the first time he heard his mother cry. It scared him then, too – the knowledge that adults could cry. It was the year after his father died. An unexpected thunderstorm. His mother hurried out to the yard to take in the laundry from the line – sheets and pillowcases and his school pants and one of his father's old shirts she sometimes wore to bed – and in her hurry she banged her knee on the open screen door. She fell to the ground and cried the way children cry: high-pitched and breathless, her face red and shaking. The boy who shares my name ran to his mother, tried to touch her knee, where she was holding. She kept swatting his hand away. 'Leave me alone,' she said. 'Please leave me alone.'

This is that fear, but worse. His mother, he secretly knew, was a child. His wife, too – a child. But different from the child his mother was. His wife was a child who skipped and sang and pouted and played games with the dog and was unafraid to get dirty, to ruin her clothes and shoes. If she cried, she would cry quietly. Not this. This was the sound she should have made, but most likely did not, when she heard the news that her father had crashed a plane into the side of a mountain and her family was gone.

My only hope, as I tell this now, is that she doesn't hear him. My hope is that she's in too much pain to hear when he says, 'No more running through the house with the dog! No more! I *knew* this was going to happen!' My hope is that she doesn't hear, that she feels him rubbing her back.

He smells batter burning, sees smoke drifting in from the kitchen, the question mark has turned black, but he won't leave her, not until she stops crying.

'Stop crying,' he says.

THEY ARRIVED, AFTER all, Lucy and Vincent, but not in the manner I had intended. Red-haired twins, four years old, the girl too shy to look at us, the boy unblinking, studying our faces.

Impossible, these names. The beach we loved, where we threw sticks into the ocean for Ralph to fetch. Names we'd chosen for the children we couldn't conceive, the children I'd tried to will into existence. Names given to these twins by someone else. And now they had been matched with us.

Lucy and Vincent, dropped off at our door, ours for the time being.

Becoming foster parents had been Cary's idea. Everything, she said, was for the time being; everything was temporary; everything, eventually, had to be let go; so why not embrace this truth, why not welcome it into our lives. That everything changed, she said, that everything ended, made life worth living. 'I mean, could you imagine,' she said, 'if everything lasted forever.'

'I want you to last forever.'

'No thank you,' she said.

'So you actually *want* to die?'

'Eventually,' she said.

'Well,' I said, 'I don't want you to die.'

'That's sweet,' she said, 'but I have news for you.'

She must have noticed the look on my face; she grabbed my face and kissed me.

They walked into our home, Lucy hiding behind Vincent, each carrying a bag of books and toys. Their caseworker, a burly man with a deep but gentle voice, introduced us to the children. I crouched in front of Vincent and held out my hand for him to slap me five; he stared at it, so I put my hand on his head and told him how happy we were that he and his sister were there.

I leaned around him to look at Lucy, but she pressed her face into her brother's back.

'She's afraid of beards,' Vincent said.

'Well,' I said, 'at least Cary doesn't have one.'

Vincent smiled. From behind him, a muffled voice: 'Girls don't have beards.'

'Are you sure?'

'You're silly,' she said.

We showed them their rooms, their beds, the dresser they'd share. They fought over beds, even though they were identical, and over the bottom drawer. 'Stop being a dope,' Vincent said. Lucy started to cry, but before we could say anything – our first parenting moment – Vincent hugged his sister and said he was sorry, she could have the bottom drawer as long as he could have the bed by the light switch, and she said fine, as long as he stopped calling her a dope, and he said fine, as long as she let him be in charge of the light, and she said fine, as long as he stopped calling the doll she slept with Barker instead of Parker, and stopped making the doll make dog sounds, and stopped holding the doll above his head and dropping her and pretending she was falling from the sky, and he said fine, but I could see that behind his back he'd crossed his fingers.

Their mother, a heroin addict, came to see them every other week unless she wasn't doing well, code for: wasn't clean, wasn't going to meetings, wasn't going for counseling. She was thin and had long, dark hair; she wore the same black leather jacket whether January or June. Her name was Eleanor but people called her Rigby, she said, because of the Beatles song. We called her *Mom* to the twins, but rarely did she look comfortable in that role, not even when Lucy clung to her legs or Vincent sat in her lap. She read to them too quickly, the book shaking in her hands.

The first time she visited, after she was out of rehab and had been clean two months, she kept stepping outside for air. She had asthma, she told us, but when we looked out the window she was smoking. She saw me by the window once; she turned away and dropped her cigarette. When she came inside, she said, 'You can't give up everything at once. I mean, they expect you to give up everything.'

She was an artist, she told us. 'But now I have to get a schmuck job like everyone else.'

During her visits, in bits and pieces, she told us the bare bones of her story, at least its most recent chapter. The father of her children, also an artist ('a much better artist than me, I mean he was a *real* artist, he lived it'), OD'd when she was six months pregnant; the kids never knew him. 'Probably for the best,' she said, but during her next visit she said, 'I wish they could have known him. Not as their father, just as an artist.' The next visit, before she said hello, as if continuing a conversation she'd been having with herself on the subway, she said, 'He's going to be famous. You should see what he left behind. People in the art scene – they worship him. They won't let his work die.' We talked about the kids for a while – Vincent liked the peanuts guy at Shea Stadium; Lucy liked giraffes at the zoo; both were afraid of planes, of heights; Vincent was wetting the bed – but as soon as there was an opening, and sometimes even if there wasn't, she'd say, 'His name was Maynard Day, but everyone called him May Day,' or 'I guess it could be worse, I could have OD'd with him,' or 'They have his genes, so.'

I wasn't sure whether this last statement was consolation or concern.

Whenever we found Vincent sleeping beside Lucy, we knew that he'd wet his bed. The first time, when we changed the sheets in front of him and told him it was okay, he grew angry: he balled his hands into fists, shut his eyes tightly, and his body went rigid; his face turned almost as red as his hair.

'He didn't do it on purpose,' Lucy said.

'We know,' I said, and Cary said, 'It happens to boys all the time, even Eric when he was your age.'

'Nothing happened!' Vincent said, punching the air with each word. 'Leave me alone!'

So we didn't change the sheets in front of him, didn't acknowledge his bedwetting in any way. Sometimes Lucy brought it up in indirect ways; she'd tell Vincent, for us to hear, that when he got into her bed the night before he scared her, and would he please not touch her with his feet, which were cold.

'Fine,' Vincent said. Then: 'My father was famous.' Anything to change the subject. He was the more dominant of the twins, without question, and perhaps Lucy knew that his bed-wetting was her only leverage.

I was surprised one night, before bed, when Vincent came to me. He wanted to ask me a question, but not in front of girls. We sat on the floor in my office, and he asked me if it was true, had I really wet the bed when I was a boy.

'Yes,' I lied. 'Right around when I was your age.'

'Did you ever sleep over at someone's house?'

'A few times, sure.'

'When did it stop?'

'Oh, it didn't last very long.'

'How long?'

'Are you afraid it'll never stop?'

He nodded his head yes.

'Believe me,' I said. 'It will.'

'But how?'

'No water or juice before bed.'

'We tried that.'

'Okay,' I said. 'I'm going to tell you the secret method, but first you have to promise never to tell anyone.'

'Promise.'

'Double promise?'

'Double promise.'

'It'll take practice,' I said, 'but eventually it'll be easy. Not too many kids know about this. Here's what you do. You realize that wetting the bed is impossible. It simply can't happen. You couldn't wet the bed if you *tried*. Then,' I said, 'you want to lie in bed, close your eyes, and feel how dry the sheet is, you want to imagine waking in the morning with the sheet just as dry. You want to close your eyes and see it in your mind. We can practice now, if you want.'

He closed his eyes.

'Imagine how great it feels to wake in your own bed,' I said. 'Your sheets are dry, your pajamas are dry. Keep your eyes closed,' I said, 'and really feel what that'll be like. Pretty good, huh.'

He nodded yes.

'Now, before you fall asleep, I want you to keep imagining yourself waking tomorrow in a dry bed. If you find yourself getting worried, just say to that worry, "I'm sorry, but I don't want you right now," and go back to imagining what it's going to be like in the morning.'

'I don't want worry,' he said.

'That's it,' I said. 'That's the secret.'

'Easy,' he said, and in the morning we found Lucy in Vincent's bed.

'Dry,' he said, his first words upon waking.

Later, during breakfast, he said, 'Do you got any other secrets?'

'Who has a secret?' Lucy said.

'Me and him,' Vincent said.

'I want a secret, too,' Lucy said, and Cary said she'd tell her one later.

'So,' Vincent said, 'do you got any more?'

'That,' I said, 'is the only secret you'll ever need to know.'

But Lucy and Vincent had their own secret; they told me one February morning, the day after we returned from Martha's Vineyard. We'd taken them to Lucy Vincent Beach; Cary told them it had been named for them, and we carved their names into a rock.

We were home in Brooklyn, sitting by the window, watching squirrels leap from tree limb to tree limb, when a plane passed overhead; we watched it disappear into the clouds, reappear, then disappear again.

Lucy walked away from the window.

'She's scared,' Vincent said.

'You should be scared, too,' Lucy said.

'Well, I'm not.'

'Why are you scared?' I asked her.

'Because it's going to fall,' she said.

'I don't think it's going to fall,' I said.

She ran back to the window, looked up at the plane as it moved out of view. 'There are three people on that plane.'

'Probably more than that,' I said.

'Three,' she said. 'And it's going to fall, and they're going to die.'

'My father died,' Vincent said.

'Yes,' I said. 'I'm sorry.'

'Don't worry,' Lucy said to me. 'You're not on the plane.'

'Neither are you.'

'Yes, I am.'

'Lucy,' I said, 'you're right here.' I put my hand on her head as if to prove she was really there.

'Vincent's on the plane, too,' she said.

'Stop saying that,' he said.

'It's nice when you go up,' Lucy said, 'but then something bad happens.'

'Tell her to stop,' Vincent said.

'Lucy,' I said, 'your brother's getting upset.'

'It was a long time ago,' Lucy said.

'I don't want to talk about that,' Vincent said.

Rigby didn't confess until she'd been clean for eight months. If she stayed clean until the end of the year, and held on to her job – she was waiting tables at a Polish restaurant on the Lower East Side – she'd be able to regain custody of her children.

'The second time I was here,' she said, 'I put it in my bag.

Didn't look at the title until I got home. I was like, Shit, of all the books I could have stolen, I get a self-help book.'

'But why steal a book?' I said. 'Why steal anything from us?'

'Not sure,' she said. 'I'd been doing all these destructive things for years, and I'd had to give them all up, except smoking, and maybe something inside me was just like, man, I have to do *some*thing bad, even if it's tame like stealing a book.'

We were sitting in the courtyard, where she could smoke. She finished her cigarette, then lit another; she took a long drag, and ash fell from the tip before the drag was done.

'As soon as I saw the title,' she said, 'I threw the book under my bed. I don't read books like that – you know, here's how to fix your life in three easy steps.' After a pause: 'No offense.'

'None taken.'

'But listen,' she said. 'One night I was out of cigs, and I was looking around for an old pack. I found one under the bed, two stale cigs left, and there was the book. That was the first time I noticed your name. So I said, Let me read the first few pages. And, you know, I just kept going. I mean, at first I was like, this is *not* for me. But, hey, two days later I'd read the whole thing.'

It was the chapter about gratitude, she said. The exercise where you treat everything that happens to you, and everything that has ever happened to you, as a gift. 'It's the opposite of how I normally see things,' she said. 'Everything's a curse, everything's out to get me, everything's holding me back, everything's responsible for whatever lousy place I'm in. I was like, well, that's not working for you, so let's try this. Today, I told myself, everything's a gift, everyone's my teacher. Let's see if this guy knows what he's talking about.'

It was difficult the first few days, she told me. Especially waiting tables. 'A man asks three times for a new water glass,' she said. 'No hair in the water, no floaters, he just doesn't like the *glass*. Three times, and I was like God knows what this guy's here to teach me. Maybe patience, fine. Deep breath, here's your water, let me know if you need anything else. Same with the lady who talked on her cell phone while ordering, didn't say excuse me, just looked away as if I wasn't there – you know the type, has money to eat fancier but is trying to be cool by lunching at this Polish joint, wants to tell her friends back in Jersey about this great place. All these angry thoughts going through my head,' Rigby said, 'and I was like, wait a sec, I'm going to stop judging her, I'm going to assume she's actually a nice person, or maybe she's had a difficult year, a difficult life, and while she was yakking on her phone, making me wait, my anger reached a peak, you know, and then *poof*, it was gone. I could have stood there forever with my pad and pencil and been happy. I didn't need anything else, didn't need to *be* anywhere else. Then the woman got off the phone, looked at me, smiled, and said, "That was rude, I apologize," and I said, "That's all right, it was actually nice to stand still for a minute." She left me a huge tip, and I didn't even resent her for it. I have this thing,' she said.

'I hate when someone stiffs me, but I hate even more when someone overtips. It's like they're showing me up or something. I'm working on that.'

'I'm really glad you stole the book,' I said.

'Don't be *too* happy,' she said. 'For every moment I feel grateful, there are a dozen I still feel cursed.'

'You're doing the best you can,' I said.

'That's what I'm going to say to God when I die,' she said. 'I did the best I could.'

She lit another cigarette, took a drag. 'Not that that wouldn't be a lie,' she said.

She took another drag, and another. 'Not that I believe in God,' she said.

IN FALL, IN the day's first light, Cary would gather leaves to use as bookmarks. Just this morning, before I sat down to write this memory, I found a leaf in a book of poetry about garbage, a book my father might have liked had he liked poetry. I'm tempted to look for more, but I'd rather ration. I don't want to find that I've already found the last one. I prefer the possibility of surprise – a preference the man I'm writing about wouldn't have understood. Once dead, always dead, some might say, and so the leaf, and so the man who wrote the poem about garbage, and so my father. But some might say that the poet is alive through his words, and my father through my reading the poet's words, and my wife through the leaf, even though the leaf is dead.

Cary breathed beside me; the twins whispered in the next room; the dog twitched on the floor, chasing a dream squirrel she'd never catch.

I closed my eyes, inhaled deeply, and created my day: everything I could ever need, every person and experience to make my intentions manifest.

I had everything I wanted, so my intention was to keep: wife, children, career, faith.

I've heard it said that we keep nothing. I've heard it said that it's good to lose what we're most afraid to lose.

Peace and safety, I thought. Abundance and joy.

Sounds like prayer, but it's not. Prayer, at least the kind I practiced in my Catholic boyhood, felt more like begging. Felt more like *please*. Whereas this was a making, an act of creativity, of authorship. Prayer felt like turning the next page of a novel and hoping everything turned out all right. I preferred to be the author of my life.

Peace and safety, abundance and joy. A mantra during my run. My body grew stronger with each mile, an extra lap around the park, seven miles instead of five, the wind keeping me cool, fast up the final hill, I could have gone three more miles easy, could have run to my mother in Queens and back, and with this thought I remembered what day it was, why so few people were on the street. Thursday morning, but no one on their way to work.

After breakfast I took the children with me to the bakery. Most stores were closed, but not the bakery, not the butcher; in small ways the day revealed its identity. A Thursday that feels like Sunday except no church bells. Long line in the bakery, already out of pumpkin pie. A cheesecake, then. And a black-and-white cookie for the kids to share. They bickered over the vanilla side – Lucy complained that Vincent had taken too large a bite – and left me with chocolate, the consolation prize, if you ask me, of the black-and-white cookie.

It made sense that I might forget what day it was. After all, I woke *every* day giving thanks. For years Thanksgiving had been me and my mother, sometimes a widowed neighbor who was childless or whose children lived across the country. Every few years my mother would invite someone new (there was never a lack of people about whom my mother could say, 'She has no one'), and at its peak, the year I started college, we had eight guests, none related to my mother by blood but by tragedy. A few men, but mostly women she knew from church or the supermarket or the bus, the youngest a divorcee in her early forties, the oldest a ninety-year-old man who, until his recent stroke, had taught piano to children in the neighborhood. After I moved out, when I was eighteen, my mother sent letters updating me on Mr Keller's heart surgery or Mrs Grimm's daughter's car accident, as if I remembered these people, some of whom had joined us only once. My mother's letters, which arrived every month or so, even though I saw her just as often, gave the impression that she was writing to a son who lived in Rome or Paris rather than a subway ride away in Manhattan. My mother has lived in New York City all her life but has never, as of this writing, taken the subway; I might as well have been across the ocean.

Now, with Cary and the twins, my mother had no need for others; plenty of tragedy at the table already. There was my father, of course, there was always him, and to keep him company was Cary's family ('Father, mother, sister, wiped out, just like that,' my mother told people, seeking their faces for sympathy she could pretend was for her) and the twins themselves ('Poor things, their mother has problems, you know,' and she'd leave it for others to complete the rest of the story), and so my mother no longer invited others, though she'd watch at the window to see which elderly neighbors had been 'left all alone' and would make sure to visit them the next day.

Always a walk to the cemetery, never together. My mother would leave the house first thing in the morning, without me. Ten minutes later, from my bedroom window, I'd see her laying flowers at my father's grave. Those first few years, when the loss of my father was new, when my guilt was most unbearable, this was the worst, most subtle form of cruelty.

Too many thoughts in the shower, memories I didn't want. I stepped out and began towel-drying my hair, and only then did I realize that I hadn't rinsed out the shampoo, so I had to turn on the water and find the right temperature and rinse my hair, and when I stepped out of the shower again, I remembered that the towel had shampoo on it, but there were no more clean towels in the bathroom, so I called Cary, but she couldn't hear me, and I walked wet down the hallway and found a clean towel in a pile of unfolded laundry, and on the way back to the bathroom I slipped.

It was Lucy who found me on the floor. She pointed at me and laughed. I wrapped the towel around me.

She walked over to me; she wanted to know why I was crying.

'I'm not,' I told her. 'My face is wet.'

'That's crying.'

'Not always,' I said.

'Laugh big,' she said. This was a game Cary had taught her, a game Cary had played as a girl with her father.

'Okay,' I said. 'Do something funny.'

'Just laugh big.'

'Make me.'

'Laugh big!' she said, and stomped on the floor.

I closed my eyes, held my stomach, and pretended to laugh really hard.

She looked pleased. 'Now laugh small.'

I chuckled quietly, and this satisfied her.

'Cry small,' she said, and I made a sad face and sniffled and gasped a little, and she said, 'It's okay,' and I stopped pretending, and then she said, 'Now cry big!' I closed my eyes and covered my face with my hands and shook and made the sounds of crying – sounds anyone but a child would know were fake – and Lucy pulled my hands away from my face and said, 'No! It's okay! Stop crying! Please stop!' and I smiled to let her know that I was all right.

'Open sesame,' I said, and the kids knew what that meant; we'd played this game before.

We were in the center lane, eastbound on the BQE; we hadn't moved much in ten minutes. Below, in Calvary, the dead slept, whispering reminders where we were going. Any cemetery, not just the one behind my mother's house, felt like home.

'Any second now,' I said. 'Like the parting of the Red Sea.'

'What's the parting of the Red Sea?' Vincent said.

'A miracle,' I said, and traffic in the center lane, and only that lane, moved.

Vincent kicked the back of my seat. 'Again!' he said.

'No need to,' I said. We were going forty, fifty, sixty, and the other two lanes hadn't moved.

Vincent's laugh sounded like choking. He was so loud we didn't notice at first that Lucy was crying.

'Honey,' Cary said, 'what's wrong?'

'I don't know,' she sobbed.

'Are we moving too fast?'

Lucy managed to catch her breath. She said, 'I don't like miracles.'

'You seem really upset, sweetie,' Cary said.

'Yes,' Lucy said.

Cary reached back and held Lucy's hand, but said nothing. She believed in allowing children – adults, too – to feel whatever they were feeling. Crying was good. Tantrums were allowed, even encouraged. Difficult emotions were not to be fixed; they were to be witnessed. Our most important job as parents, she believed, was to listen.

We pulled off the expressway and drove through Queens. Lucy was trying to catch her breath.

The lights. A game that soothed me. Red to green, one after another, timed to my thoughts, timed so that the car would never have to stop. I imagined the car had no brakes. Green light, green, green, just in time. Then yellow – extra gas, through. 'Slow down,' Cary said, but I raced toward the next light, already yellow – a moment of doubt, then gas, through the red light. 'Eric, please slow down.' Cary touched my arm, and I turned to her. Then she yelled, 'Watch out!' and without looking I pressed the brake and the car skidded to a stop.

A girl, maybe twelve years old, had pushed a stroller into the street. Now she stood frozen in front of our car, gripping the stroller's handle; she was so close she could have reached out and touched the bumper. Blond hair, braces, red high-top sneakers. A young woman, short and thin enough to pass as a girl herself, probably the girl's mother, ran into the street, pulled the girl and the stroller onto the sidewalk. She glared at me.

I got out and said, 'I'm sorry, it was my fault,' but the woman seemed not to understand.

'It wasn't her fault,' I said.

The woman reached into the stroller and pulled out a baby; it wasn't moving. Then I saw that the baby was a doll. The drivers behind me were beeping their horns. The woman yelled something at me in Russian. I got back in the car and drove the final few blocks.

My mother was waiting by the window. She wanted to know what had happened, what was wrong; she had a radar for such things.

'Why does something always have to be wrong?'

'I can tell,' she said.

'It's like you *want* something to be wrong.'

'Don't start,' she said. 'It's too early to start.'

She kissed Cary, then the twins. 'Lucy's been crying – her face is all red.'

'She's fine now,' I said.

'So she *was* crying.'

'I don't like miracles,' Lucy said.

'Did you see one?' my mother asked.

She pointed to me. 'He made one.'

'Is that what he told you?' my mother said.

'No,' Lucy said. 'I seen it.'

'I seen it, too!' Vincent said. He stomped around the dining room. My mother's wedding china, used only on Thanksgiving and Christmas, rattled on the table. 'I seen it, too! I seen it, too!' he yelled. 'And then we almost ran over a baby!'

'What did you do?' my mother said to me.

'A girl ran into the street,' Cary said. 'No one was hurt.'

'Was he driving too fast?'

'Everyone's fine, Ma.'

This word, from Cary, softened my mother. Cary had taken it upon herself years earlier to call my mother *Ma*. My mother referred to Cary as her daughter. But when they hugged, it was the opposite: she was a girl and Cary was her mother. They swayed as if slow-dancing; my mother's eyes were closed. I put the cheesecake in the refrigerator, and when I came back they were still hugging. Cary's hands kneaded my mother's back, and they were both somewhere else, hugging someone else. I didn't feel jealous. If anything, I felt relieved that someone could give my mother that kind of love.

My mother busied herself stuffing the turkey. She brought out cheese and crackers, and juice for the kids. While we snacked she folded laundry, then went outside to sweep. I tried to help, but she said no, so I stood in the yard and watched her. Just the two of us, she became the mother I knew – nervously sweeping where she'd already swept, bending to dislodge a leaf pressed wet into the ground. Every leaf and twig had to be accounted for. A new leaf fell; she went to get it. She'd been getting pains, she told me.

'Where?'

'I don't know – everywhere.'

'Sounds serious.'

'Are you making fun?'

'No, but if you have pains everywhere.'

'I have arthritis – you know that.'

I grabbed the broom, stopped her from sweeping. She pulled the broom away from me. 'I can do it,' she said. 'Go inside and eat.'

'Where's your pain?'

'It's nothing.'

'Have you seen a doctor?'

'They don't know what it is.'

'So you *have* seen a doctor?'

'No, but they don't know.'

'At least let me hold the bag,' I said.

'I have it,' she said.

I reached for the bag; she looked up at me from where she was kneeling. 'I said I have it,' she said.

I went back inside and put a cracker into my mouth. Cary read to the kids on the floor. On the muted television behind them Tokyo burned in an old monster movie.

I went upstairs to use the bathroom. My father's razor was

twenty-five years old; his facial hair was still caught in the blade. Hanging from the showerhead was a waterproof transistor radio; a man was talking about the plane that had crashed in Queens a few weeks earlier. He was scared, he said. Everyone had been scared since September. Anything could happen at any moment. If you waited long enough, eventually the sky would fall.

In my father's dresser were old bottles of cologne shaped like ships, the black comb he used, a pack of cigarettes he never opened. I opened the pack and smelled. His underwear and undershirts, his black socks rolled into balls. No surprises. I'd seen it all before, in the weeks after his death.

From my room I could see the stone; it looked farther away and smaller than I'd remembered. Until I moved out, I looked out my window every night before sunset. I was afraid to look, but I did. I remember expecting to see him seated atop the stone, smoking cigarettes or shuffling a deck of cards.

'Are you looking for the man?'

It was Lucy in the doorway, Vincent behind her. He laughed. 'You were scared,' he said.

'No, I wasn't.'

'Yes, you were.' He opened the alcove in the hall where my mother stored pillows and blankets; he crawled in, beneath the attic steps. 'This is a great hiding place,' he said.

'Careful in there,' I said.

'Why?'

'Just be careful.'

Lucy sat on my bed. 'Were you looking for the man?'

'What man?'

'The man who looks like you.'

'I found something!' Vincent shouted. He crawled out holding a baseball card covered in dust. I didn't recognize the card; it must have been my father's. Sam Leslie, Brooklyn Dodgers, 1934. He was standing on first base, reaching up to catch the ball. No field behind him; he was playing baseball in the clouds.

'Can I keep it?' Vincent said.

'Sure,' I said, but he put the card on the dresser and forgot about it.

'He's in the closet,' Lucy said.

'Who?'

'The man.'

'Let's get him!' Vincent said.

He went for the door, but I grabbed him. 'Stay out of there.'

'You're afraid,' he said.

'Aren't you?'

'No,' he said, but then I could see he was.

'Go ahead,' I said. 'Open the door. See who's there.'

'I'm not afraid,' he said, then ran out of the room.

'Are you going to look?' Lucy said.

'Would you like me to?'

She shook her head no, and we went downstairs.

I helped in the kitchen while Cary played with the kids in the yard. My mother handed me a carving knife. I stabbed the turkey with a two-pronged fork made for a giant. The knife sliced through easily and thin pieces of meat fell onto a floral plate. My mother put her hand on my back and smiled at what I was doing. She found a small piece on the plate and lifted it to her mouth. She picked up another piece, but this one she brought to my mouth. I turned my head, but she followed my mouth with the meat. Like a child, I pressed my lips together. My mother pushed the turkey into my lips; I could taste it. I opened my mouth to speak and she forced the meat inside.

I spit it out, and her smile was gone.

'Not even one piece?'

'You know I don't eat meat.'

'This isn't meat – it's turkey.'

'I don't eat anything that used to have a heartbeat.'

'But you wear leather sneakers.'

'Let's not go through that again.'

She tried to take the knife, but I wouldn't let her. She tried again, but I pulled back. She winced, pulled her hand away. A thin line of blood formed on her finger. 'Let me see,' I said, but she walked away. The turkey that would have been mine she gave to a skinny black cat in the yard.

During dinner my mother kept licking her finger; she looked up to make sure I was watching. Vincent lowered his face to his plate and spooned corn into his mouth as if eating were a contest. Lucy moved the food around her plate warily. She flattened her mashed potatoes into a kind of canvas and made a picture: corn as stars, peas and pieces of yam and cranberry as leaves on turkey trees. Cary told my mother how good everything tasted. She seemed happiest on days she should have been, and probably was, sad. Holidays, when she must have missed her family. Her mother's birthday, her father's birthday, her sister's wedding anniversary. The anniversary of the day the plane had crashed.

Somehow she convinced my mother to allow her and the kids to wash dishes. It took great effort for my mother to remain seated at the table while others cleaned. Every few minutes Vincent would show himself drying a plate. My mother praised the good job he was doing, then said, 'Careful you don't drop it, honey. You don't want a piece of glass stuck in your foot.'

The kids brought in dessert plates and clean forks and the cheesecake. 'Come eat,' my mother called to Cary, and Cary said, 'Okay, Ma, in a minute,' and I could hear something in her voice, though maybe I'd been looking for it all day. A few more minutes passed, and I went in to check on her. The water was running; she was leaning over the sink, her face in her hands. She heard me behind her and quickly straightened; her eyes were red.

'What's wrong?'

'Nothing,' she said. 'Just a headache.'

'You've been crying.'

'No,' she said. 'I was rubbing my eyes, and my hands are wet.'

My mother came into the kitchen and wanted to know what was wrong.

'Nothing,' I said.

My mother looked at Cary, who said, 'It's just a headache. Let's go eat some . . .' There was a long pause; she seemed to be searching for the word *cake* as if she'd forgotten it. 'Let's go eat,' she said.

Vincent put cake on Lucy's nose and she left it there, and Cary put cake on her own nose, then I put some on my mother's face, and for a moment she seemed happy.

As we were leaving, my mother asked if we were taking the BQE home.

'Not sure,' I said.

'Don't take the streets,' she said. 'That neighborhood – my God, what's happened to it.'

This was an old movie; I knew all the lines.

I kissed her goodbye.

My mother kissed Cary and said, 'I grew up in Bushwick. Such a shame what's happened.'

'What happened?' Vincent said.

'Never mind,' I said, and we drove home through Bushwick.

Under the flashing light of a red-and-yellow bodega, boys drank from paper bags. One kid kicked a bottle from another's hands; the other boy picked it up and smashed it on the street. They wandered in front of our car; the light turned green. I waited while they argued. The light turned yellow, then red. It was as if we weren't there. Lucy slept in the back. Vincent was awake, his nose against the window. I pressed the button that locked the doors. One of the boys turned to the car and said, 'You *better* lock your doors.' He put his foot on the car's hood as if daring me to step on the gas. One of his friends removed his shirt, closed his eyes, and spread his arms as if Christ on the Cross.

Peace and safety.

Silently I repeated the words I'd begun my day with. I'd

been running them through my head from the moment my mother warned us not to take the streets, which was also the moment I'd decided that was precisely how we'd go. A battle between my mother's fear and my positive thinking, my confidence in my ability to create a safe drive home no matter what neighborhood we drove through. A battle between mother and son, but only son knew it was being waged. My mind filled with two and only two words until they became a sound more powerful than whatever the boys were saying. Peace, safety. Peace, safety.

The light turned green, yellow, red. They stood in front of the car passing a bottle. Green, yellow, red.

One of the boys, the tallest and maybe the oldest, a beard already, approached the passenger side of the car, where Cary was sitting; he pulled on the handle, then started kicking the door. Cary released her seat belt and moved toward me. Lucy was awake; Vincent's face was still pressed against the glass as if watching a movie. I stepped on the gas and the boys moved out of the way and we went through a red light, and one of them – his arms still outstretched on his cross – called after us, 'I never asked to be born, you know! I never asked to be born!'

S HE COULD SPEAK, but not the word I wanted her to say.
    I pointed to my beard. 'What's this?'
She pointed to her own face.
'Tell me what this is.'
'Face,' she said.
'What's this *on* my face?'
'Hair.'
'Yes, but what's it called?'
She was blinking back tears.
I held her wrist, rubbed her hand on my face. 'Say it,' I said.
She tried to kiss me, but I turned away.
'Please say the word,' I said. 'I know you know.'
I closed my eyes and imagined that when I opened them, the past few minutes would be revealed to have been a dream.

But the word was lost to her. She no longer knew *beard*. Just, *hair on your face*. She no longer knew *lamp*, which she called *light*, and *sweater*, which she called *thick shirt*, and *guitar*, which she called *music*, and *tub*, which she called *small pool*, and *bed*, which she called *home*.

Two more days of this – the words *day* and *night* were gone, too – and I took her to our doctor. She had difficulty telling him what was wrong. She used the words of a child or someone new to the language. The names for objects and body parts and feelings weren't enough; she needed to describe them, redefine them. How do you say *wind* without the word? How do you say *door*? How do you say *headache*? How do you say *dizziness*? You say, *What moves grass and bends trees*. You say, *What you open to move from one room to another*. You point and say, *It hurts up here*. You say, *The world has been moving*. But what if you've lost the words *trees* and *grass*, too? What if you've lost the words *room* and *world*? You say, *What I feel on my face*. Without the word *face*, you say, *The thing I can't see that touches me*. You say, *What keeps me out or lets me in*. You say, *It hurts here* and *Everything seems to be moving without me*.

E YES CLOSED DURING the ride from airport to casino hotel.
I had been to Vegas once before, after my second book
was published; the lights and sounds hadn't bothered me
then.

Now, even through my eyelids, I could see lights blinking
across the cool night air, the kind of flashing that causes
seizures in reflex epileptics.

I could not cover my ears, as the driver – a long-bearded
man short enough to have to sit on a cushion to see over the
steering wheel – was talking about a murder he had witnessed
a few days earlier, a woman who ran over her husband with
their car.

I opened my eyes; neon-lit faces flashed by, too close to
the car.

'Kept backing over him,' he said. 'A dozen times, at least.'
He shook his head, looked in the rearview for a reaction; I
closed my eyes again.

'Headache?'

'No.'

'I get bad headaches, but only at night, when I can't sleep.'

Illness is an extension of negative emotion. Any malady in the body can be healed faster than it was created.

'Haven't slept more than three hours straight in, oh, about twenty years.'

It's important not to absorb any negative energy you may encounter. Imagine a shield surrounding your body; this will not allow the energy to enter you.

'You sure you feel okay?'

'Yes.'

'Not making you carsick, am I?'

'No.'

'Because if I am, you should say something. I wouldn't take it personally.'

'You're not.'

'Mind if I smoke?'

'No.'

'Never mind. I can wait.' He pressed the horn three times in succession. 'Jesus, Mary, and Joseph. Guy's going to kill – Have you ever smoked?'

'No.'

'Bad habit, but I love it.'

The flick of a lighter, then the smell. 'I'm blowing it out the window, okay? Right out the window.'

'Actually . . .'

'Stupid,' he said. 'Stupid, stupid, stupid. I don't want to give *you* cancer. Me, that's okay, but you didn't ask for it.'

Three weeks without a sustained negative thought, and now this. I quickly replaced the driver in my mind with the image of a flower. I opened my eyes: a tall, skinny man, taller and skinnier than I was, an Indian giant, stood outside the cab, offering me roses wrapped in plastic. I reached into my pocket, but the light turned green and we were gone. I turned to see the giant standing in the street, blocking traffic, watching me. I had the silly thought, though I don't think it's so silly now, that I would never see that man again, that he would live the rest of his life, however many years, then die, and this encounter would have meant nothing to him. Had I been able to give him the five hundred dollars in my pocket, he might have remembered; it might have changed his life.

The car rolled along a street lined with palm trees and strewn with trash blown by December desert winds. A gust pressed a piece of paper against the windshield; a word written in black ink. *Cancer. Cancel. Concern. Concede.* I leaned forward to see, but the word was upside down and backward. The driver turned on the wipers, and the paper was lifted into the air and behind us in traffic.

If not for the colored lights on the trees, I would have forgotten that in five days it would be Christmas.

A series of loud pops that sounded like fireworks.

I must have jumped. 'It's all right,' the driver said. 'Just a car backfiring.' He laughed. 'Unless it's gunfire.'

Traffic stopped; I looked at my watch. Thirty minutes to check in and get to the radio show.

I had told Cary that I didn't want to go, especially given the circumstances, but she insisted. She was feeling fine, she told me; it would be good for me to get away for a few nights. 'There's nothing you can do for me,' she said. 'There's nothing anyone can do.'

'I don't believe that.'

'But I do.'

'I don't believe that *you* believe that.'

'I know you mean well,' she said.

'Looks serious,' the driver said. 'Three-car accident.'

'Are we far?'

'Five, six blocks.'

'I can walk.'

'You know where you're going?'

'No.'

'Straight ahead. Take it to the end.'

'That way?'

'Straight to the end. Can't miss it.'

I gave him a one-hundred-dollar bill but didn't wait for change. I closed the door before he could thank me, and began walking against the wind, the straps on my bag digging into my shoulders.

A boy, twelve or thirteen years old, dark eyes and long curly hair, blocked my way. 'Let me carry your bag, please.'

'No, thank you.'

'You'll only have to tip someone else.'

'Thank you, but no.'

'Why not?'

'I'm sorry.'

'Don't you trust me?'

'I'm sorry,' I said again.

'I won't run away with your bag.'

'Here,' I said. 'Let's carry it together.' I gave him one strap, I took the other, and we walked to the end of the strip, where the casino flashed its manic lights at us.

I gave him one hundred dollars.

'Thank you,' he said, but he sounded sad, as if my giving him so much money proved just how destitute he was.

'Now you have to give it to someone who needs it more.'

'I don't know anyone who needs it more.'

'There's always someone.'

'But what about me?'

'It will come back to you,' I said. 'It will double.'

'How do you know?'

'It will if you believe it will.'

'Are you a magician?'

'No.'

'Are you Jesus?'

'No.'

'Is this real money?'

'Yes.'

He stared at me for a moment, then turned and ran. I stood in front of the hotel, waiting to see if he would look back, but he never did.

In the lobby, people fed coins into slot machines, and the machines made their gleefully sad noise. After I checked in at the front desk, I took an elevator to the tenth floor, but there must have been a mistake: the entire floor was water. Gondoliers sang arias while ferrying tourists across indoor canals. I tried the eleventh floor, but there were no rooms;

it was a mall. People carried shopping bags from one brightly lit storefront to the next; children sucked on ice pops and chased each other in circles. On the ninth floor, a kind of warehouse space, hundreds of headless mannequins stood in rows, wearing sequined gowns.

I went back down to the lobby. I considered walking past the front desk to the street, where I might find the boy and the giant and buy them dinner, but a pale woman with frizzy red hair recognized me and asked me to sign her copy of my book. She said she was looking forward to my talk the next day. She had read all three of my books; they had changed her life, she told me: she had used the power of intention to cure her arthritis and chronic fatigue, and then she met the love of her life; they were getting married in the spring.

'Congratulations,' I said. 'Best of luck.'

'We create our own luck.'

I signed my name and beneath it wrote *Best wishes*, then gave her the book. 'Be well,' I said. 'Take care.'

She grabbed my hand, closed her eyes, and bowed. For a moment I thought she might kiss my hand. 'Thank you *so* much,' she said.

I tried to pull away, but she wouldn't release my hand. I pulled harder, and finally she let go; she opened her eyes as if waking from a dream.

'You're a living saint,' she said.

She stood there, waiting for me to say thank you, to confirm or deny her claim. 'Goodbye,' I said, and walked away.

On my way back to the elevator – my room, I discovered,

was on the twelfth floor – I walked past the sales area: dozens of merchants selling books, inspirational calendars, CDs, angel 'oracle' cards, crystals, rocks, jewelry, and something called Goddess wear: white and gray medieval dresses trimmed with black velvet ribbon; blue cotton gowns with matching shawls; a red velvet dress with bell sleeves; the kinds of outfits worn in fairy tales.

I continued past the elevator because I heard applause; it was coming from a large lecture room overflowing with people. I joined the others in the doorway. A small Japanese man, behind a dais onstage, was explaining how water molecules respond to human thought and emotion. His assistant changed the slide: what water molecules look like when you say the word *Hitler*. Click. Water molecules when you say the word *love*. Click. The words *fear, thank you, amen*. An asymmetrical pattern of dull colors or a complex and colorful snowflake pattern, depending on the words said or thought. The slides changed too quickly; I couldn't tell which were good, which were bad. They all looked both beautiful and frightening to me. 'The human body is made up of mostly water,' he said. Click. And I left to find my room.

I knew they were in my bag, but kept checking – twice in my room, again in the elevator, once again in the bathroom, a few minutes before the radio show was to begin. The pills had expired years earlier, the words on the label long ago worn away. A shrink had prescribed them when I was in my twenties. When he asked why I'd been feeling anxious, I told him the truth: that I believed I could make things happen with my mind; that I had to be careful what I thought; that I couldn't stop seeing the world in shades of dark and light, positive and negative; that my apartment was filled with junk it was my responsibility to salvage; that certain objects belonged with other objects; that there were too many rules, there were signs everywhere, everything meant something. He wore cardigans and round glasses that hooked behind his ears. He was eager to save me, we were alike that way, so I did my best to make him believe that he was helping me. He suggested that I was made up of many parts, some of which were trying to protect me, to prevent me from feeling pain. 'It's an impossible job,' he said. I nodded and agreed, but never quite believed him. Then one day, after a year, I didn't show up for a session, and never went back.

The pills, even with refills, would eventually run out. I had to wean myself off them. Four a day, then three every other day, then three a day, then two every other day, and so on. But even after I'd stopped, I carried the bottle with me everywhere. Wallet, keys, pills. My pants pockets faded in the shape of the bottle. Years later, after my first book was published, I decided to leave them at home. Unless I was able to take a cab to the airport, and a plane to Chicago, and another cab to the hotel where I was speaking, without the pills, I would be a fraud, and nothing I could say to the people who had paid to hear me speak would mean much.

True bravery would have been to flush the pills down the toilet. That I kept them in the back of my desk drawer was a sign of my belief that one day I would need them again. I might have said, then, that I had created my own reality: a man standing in a bathroom stall in a casino hotel in Las Vegas, opening, then closing, then opening a pill bottle, trying to decide if he could get through a radio show without being tranquilized. That I didn't take one – not then – wasn't bravery as much as fear: that someone would know, that the pills no longer worked, that I'd be letting down every person who'd read my books.

So, instead, I sat in a chair beside Mona Lisa Mercer – the woman who had organized the Change Your Life! conference, a best-selling author herself, the grande dame of self-help, nearing eighty but looking closer to sixty, with her smooth skin and long gray hair – and kept my hand in my pocket. Anxious, I could pinch my skin through the lining of my pants. We were in a small room near the lobby, maybe one hundred people in the audience. Angela Payne, a woman from the radio station, also an author, was going to interview us and screen calls. She was my age. Dark hair, dark eyes, long blue skirt, black boots. I'd noticed a flyer in the elevator advertising her book, *Stress to Success in Thirty Days*.

Mona Lisa Mercer reached over and held my arm; she looked at me with her blue eyes and said, 'You're not nervous, are you, sweetie?'

'No,' I said. 'Of course not.'

'Because I can tell when someone's nervous.' She leaned in closer, narrowed her eyes, lowered her gaze to my chest. 'Shows up as a yellow light in the area of the heart.'

'Well, maybe I'm a little nervous.'

'Be careful – you have a nice head of hair. Fear can cause baldness.' She looked up at my face again, released my arm.

'I'm joking,' she said. 'Fear *can* cause baldness, it's true, but not from just a little yellow near the heart.'

Angela Payne turned away from us to cough. 'I hope I get through this without a hacking fit.'

'Listen to me,' Mona Lisa said. 'Touch your throat.'

I touched mine, and she said, 'No, I'm talking to Angela, but you can do this, too, if you want. Angela, touch your throat and repeat after me.'

Angela put her hand on her throat.

'I am willing to change,' Mona Lisa said.

'I am willing to change,' Angela said.

'A cough means stubbornness,' Mona Lisa said. 'Every time a person in one of my workshops coughs, I stop what we're doing and have that person touch the throat and say, "I am willing to change." If she coughs again, I have her say it again.'

I touched the bottle in my pocket. As soon as I did, Mona Lisa said, 'Give me your hand.'

I released the bottle and removed my hand from my pocket. She held my hand tightly, looked at me, and said, 'Eric, I'm grateful that you're here today. I bless you and your work.'

'Thank you,' I said.

When the show began, Angela introduced me and Mona Lisa, then interviewed us briefly. She asked Mona Lisa to tell her listeners how she came to believe in the power of the mind to create as well as heal illness.

'I believe it because I've lived it,' she said.

'I wonder if you might tell a bit of your story,' Angela said. 'For those listeners who might not be familiar with it.'

'My story is the story of the universe,' she said. 'You'd have to go back to the Big Bang. It's all related, sweetie.'

Her story was well known: raped when she was ten; abused by her stepfather; pregnant at fifteen, the child given up for adoption; two failed marriages before she was forty; cancer at forty-five; her miraculous self-healing through nutrition, forgiveness, and enemas; a series of mega-bestsellers listing every ailment in the human body and its emotional cause. If you had a problem with your eyes, you were in denial – there was something in your life you didn't want to see. *When I see a child wearing glasses, I think: Something's going on in that child's home that she doesn't want to see.* Bladder problems came from anger. *From being pissed off, sweetie – this stuff isn't rocket science.* Migraines were created by people who wanted to be perfect, who were angry at being imperfect. *It's almost always alleviated by masturbation – the sexual release dissolves the anger and pain.* Sexually transmitted diseases were caused by sexual shame. *The anus is as beautiful as the eyes; you need to begin to relate to your rectum!*

'Everyone suffers from self-hatred and guilt,' she said now. 'This creates illness, which is a form of self-punishment. The good news is that releasing these emotions will dissolve even cancer.'

'Do you agree, Eric Newborn?'

'It can't be denied that the mind is powerful,' I said. 'Everywhere you go in the world you meet yourself – your own thoughts manifest.'

I looked out at the audience. A man missing both legs held himself up with bodybuilder arms, his stumps not even touching the floor. A woman with a nervous twitch shook her hands incessantly, as if about to roll dice. A boy sitting beside his obese mother kept squeezing his penis. I fingered the pill bottle in my pocket, looked for the positive. I went back to the amputee's arms – how powerful they were. But then he must have grown tired; he lay in the aisle and stared at the ceiling.

'When you're angry,' Mona Lisa said, 'hold your middle finger tightly and watch what happens – the anger dissolves. Right middle finger for a man, left for a woman – works every time.'

The first caller wanted to know about nutrition.

'Easy,' Mona Lisa said. 'If it grows, eat it. If it doesn't grow, don't eat it.'

The next caller wanted to know about a typical day in our lives, so I talked about segmenting, which I'd written about in my second book, *It's On Its Way*. You break your day into segments, one moment at a time: brushing your teeth, taking a shower, going for a hike, reading a book, eating a peach. You focus on the positive, the wondrous, and if you do this, you'll attract more of the same in your next segment.

'What if you happen to notice something negative?' the caller said. 'Say, you're on a hike and you see a dead bird.'

'You always have a choice,' I said. 'You can bless the bird's life, give gratitude that the bird ever existed.'

'We live in a "yes" universe,' Mona Lisa added. 'Whatever you send out into the universe, it sends right back to you. That's why I'm filled with gratitude every day. Actually, I'm not filled with gratitude. I *am* gratitude. I bless my home, knowing that only good comes into it. I bless my telephone and mailbox, knowing that only good news comes to me. I'm *pre*-grateful. I sit for at least an hour every day with my arms open. I begin every day by looking into the mirror and saying, "You are wonderful and I love you. This is one of the best days of your life." Sometimes I sing this to myself.'

The caller was gone. Angela said, 'What if that doesn't work?'

'Impossible,' Mona Lisa said. 'It always works – what you give out, you receive.'

'Does it ever not work for you?' Angela asked me.

'Depends what you mean,' I said. 'Does good always come to me? No. Does what I send out always come back? Yes, I believe so.'

'Bullshit!'

We looked into the crowd; it had been a man's voice.

Then we heard the voice again: 'I hope you all get cancer.'

A man walked forward from the back: glasses, thinning hair, shirt and tie, barefoot. 'What about the Holocaust?' he said. 'Did those people have too many negative thoughts?' He came closer, stopped where we were sitting. His hands were crossed in front of him as if he were praying; he blinked behind his glasses. His voice grew louder: 'What about September? Did every person in the Towers have too many negative thoughts?'

The crowd behind the man backed away, all except the amputee, who remained where he was, though now he was standing on his hands again.

Security approached the man from all sides; he put his

hands behind his back. 'I know the routine,' he said. He was handcuffed and taken away, but even as he was leaving he yelled to us, 'This is not how the universe works! This is *not* how it works! We are *not* responsible for our own suffering!'

Angela tried to make a decent recovery by saying, 'Our listeners might have been able to hear that. There was a disturbance here – a man with some difficult questions. I wonder if either of you would like to respond.'

With one hand I managed to remove the cap and reach into the bottle. Under the guise of scratching my beard, I put a pill into my mouth. I decided not to swallow, but the pill began to dissolve on my tongue, a bitter taste I remembered immediately.

'God bless him,' Mona Lisa said. 'That's cancer waiting to happen. I can only hope he lets go of his anger.'

'I wonder about his question, though,' Angela said. 'How does human suffering on a grand scale – something like the Holocaust or genocide or a terrorist attack – fit into your spirituality?'

'I'm sorry,' Mona Lisa said, 'but I have to be honest and say – Listen,' she said, 'this isn't a time for condemnation. The past is the past. Now is a time for healing.'

'Eric Newborn,' Angela said, 'any response?'

'Everywhere you go in the world,' I said, 'you meet yourself.'

Children went room to room that night, singing carols.

I lay in bed, shaken by what the man had said. But the pill, years after having expired, was working. Maybe it was just the placebo effect. Either way, the anxiety moved from my chest to my arms and legs, then floated up from my fingers and toes to the ceiling, a yellow shadow waiting for the drug to wear off so it could begin its descent back into my body while I was sleeping, or in the morning, or during my talk the next day, or when I returned home to Cary and what was growing inside her, the thing I had feared all along. It didn't matter when; it would hover above me patiently, and then it would descend.

The drug sang to my blood: an old song, but I knew the lyrics. Sad, but sung sweetly, that was all that mattered. The music moved outside me, then a knock on my door: children singing about a babe in a manger, stars brightly shining, our dear Savior's birth. The carolers wanted me to join them; they handed me the words, but I didn't need them: some things you never forget. I would like to say that I sang – it's true that my mouth moved and made sounds – but it wasn't my voice; it was the drugs swimming through my blood and nestling in my brain.

She'd been following me for years.

Always the same yellow dress; that was how I knew her. It had been two years since the last time – a talk in Chicago, I think. Dark skin, dark hair going gray, tinted glasses behind which I couldn't see her eyes. She had gained weight – at least fifty pounds, it looked like. She must have bought the same dress in a larger size.

She sat in the front row, as always. She had come to a half dozen of my talks over the years. Chicago, New York, San

Francisco, Portland. I forget where else. It doesn't matter; even when she wasn't there, she was there.

It might have been easier had she been someone to fear, like the man who had interrupted the radio taping the previous evening. Then security could have escorted her out of the conference room. But she was polite and soft-spoken and never took up much of my time; she was always considerate of the people in line behind her. The first time she approached me – I think it was in New York, because I remember that I didn't stay in a hotel that night – she asked me her question.

Why?

That was the short version.

The slightly longer version: Why was her son – a bright, optimistic young man, first in the family to be admitted to college, scholarship to Princeton – why was her son shot while driving to pick up his grandmother for Thanksgiving dinner? If our thoughts manifest, if that's how the universe works – she was willing to grant me this possibility – then why was her son shot in the head, why was he now unable to move, to smile, to blink yes or no, to respond in any way; why did his mother have to shave him, change him, prop him in bed in a position that at least created an illusion that he was still a sentient being? If there were no such things as accidents, then what were we to call what happened to her son?

Reading these words, here, I can see how they might translate as angry or bitter, but they were not when spoken. Her questions were always asked kindly, with a genuine desire to hear my answers, no matter what they were.

I wasn't brave enough to tell her that I had no answers, and so I told her that my next book would address these very questions about human suffering. It would be called *The Book of Why*, and I hoped to finish it in a year or so. I even told my editor about my plan to write this book.

But I couldn't do it. I had nothing to say on the subject that this woman – she never told me her name – might want to hear. Instead, I wrote more of the same; I dug deeper into what I already believed. Two books later, neither was the one I had promised her. I had tried to begin; I read about suffering, theories of why. But I couldn't tell this woman – couldn't write in a book and sign my name to it – that suffering was punishment, that God watches over the world, doling out his unique brand of justice, his infinite versions of hell on earth. My mother might be able to write that book, but not me. And I couldn't tell this woman that her son's suffering was part of God's larger plan, which was a mystery. Nor could I tell her, as some books claimed, that each soul chooses its path before human incarnation – it knows everything that will happen before it happens, and signs the contract – and that the point of being human is the evolution of the soul. Nor could I tell her, as I had told others, though not in these exact words, that suffering is self-imposed, that we are all guilty, and unless we become conscious of our thoughts, we will eventually think our way into all manner of woe. I knew that nothing I could say would change the fact that every day she wiped drool from her son's chin, and changed his diaper, and kept in a drawer beside her bed the photo of the dark spots on his brain, and looked at this photo each morning as if the verdict might have changed, as if the dark spots might have disappeared overnight.

She included photos with her letters; I've saved them all. Before and after – life behind her son's eyes, then none. She wrote to me: *My son must suck air through a hole in his Adam's apple. The doctor tried to cap it, but he can't swallow. Saliva and mucus close his airway.* She wrote: *Every day, after I brush his teeth and shave him, I put on a dab of cologne. So at least he smells like he used to.* She wrote: *His mouth hangs open all the time, he stares vacantly past me.* She wrote: *Sometimes I see his eyelids flutter and I think, There he is, he's in there somewhere.* She even sent me copies of his journal entries from the weeks leading to the shooting. *See for yourself, he was a very positive young man.* I couldn't argue with this after reading his words: *Most days, no matter what's happening around me, on the news, all that, I can still say that the world is a beautiful place.* In the margins she wrote: *This was my son. This was who he was. He didn't watch violent movies. He never played video games. He had no anger in his heart.*

I heard from her, on average, every few months. Sometimes five or six months would pass without a letter, and I'd wonder if something had happened to her or to her son. Other months I'd receive a letter a week. She never signed her name, never wrote it on the envelopes above her return address. Chestnut Street, Philadelphia, and I knew it was her. I answered her letters for a while, then stopped. Dear, and then the letter. No name. Always the promise to write *The Book of Why*. Sometimes the lie that I was well into it and soon would be finished.

After a while, her son wasn't enough: she sent me photos

of others. A boy in a wheelchair, restrained because he couldn't help chewing his own hand. A girl in Minsk, a victim of Chernobyl, her brain in a membrane outside her skull. A boy in the same institution, the legs of a monster, feet and toes swollen to unimaginable size. She wrote: *What child could have created this? What child could have dreamed this?* She wrote: *Think of my son, think of all of these people, as you write your book.*

There were three hundred people in the audience, but the room might as well have been empty except for her seat. The words that came from my mouth could not – not that evening – stand up to the scrutiny of her suffering. I had been shy as a boy, a bit lonely; I had been afraid of the dark; I had lost my father when I was young. We all go through life bearing our crosses, but mine were not hers. I would rather *she* come up onstage and speak; I would rather *she* write *The Book of Why*.

But I was being paid to talk about my most recent book, *There Are No Accidents*. I didn't know, then, that it would be my final book. Before this one, I mean. Though I don't consider this a book as much as a letter: to the woman in the yellow dress, to Cary, to Gloria Foster. I didn't know, then, that I would ever need to write another book; that I would write *The Book of Why*, after all, though not as an answer but rather as an unanswerable question. I didn't know, when I thought I knew it all, that I would join the chorus of askers.

To Steven, please, with a *v*, not a *p-h*.

If you could make it out to Mary – that's my sister.

Would you mind signing two? One's for my daughter. I've been trying to get her to read your books, but.

I didn't bring your books with me, but I just wanted to say thank you, I really loved them.

I saw you a few years ago in Boston. I don't know if you remember – I'm the woman whose son tried to commit suicide.

One hundred six pounds. People said I couldn't, but look at me.

I just wanted to tell you, I read the new book and it really works. People thought I was nuts, but now I'm married, I own a house, I've been sober ten months.

Can I have a hug?

What are you writing next?

That's Meagan with two *a*s. M-E-A-G-A-N.

Could you make it out to my full name – Jerry Stillwell?

I just wanted to tell you, there's a typo on page 222 of the new book – right here, see, it should be *hello* but it says *hell*, it's missing the *o*.

Are you working on a new book?

Would you mind writing a note for my aunt? She's very ill, she's barely holding on, but we haven't given up hope.

Actually, I've written a book – it's kind of like yours, but for kids.

Would you mind writing something personal – it doesn't matter what, just something, you know, personal?

Loved this one even more than the first two.

Big fan of your books.

Does this work for allergies – you know, like to dogs? I've always wanted to get a dog.

Big fan. I have both of your other books. I give them as gifts.

If you could just sign it, please. Don't make it out to anyone. My husband says it's worth more that way.

When will you be finished with your next book?

If you wouldn't mind, I really need a hug.

She was last in line, but eventually she would reach me. People handed me copies of my book, told me their stories, and I signed: *Best wishes, keep the faith, hang in there, don't give up, don't worry, it's on its way, expect miracles, sending you positive thoughts, Eric Newborn.* I was riding the natural high that often came during and immediately following my talks. If you say something with conviction, and keep repeating it, you will believe it. Now I loved, and felt loved by, everyone. I wanted to hug and kiss every person who handed me a book to sign. Everything was possible. Everything with Cary would work out. She would be fine. She would come around and see things my way. When I got home, I would keep trying. I would tell her exactly what she needed to do, how to get better. And then I'd write about it, and talk about it, and even though there had already been so much evidence that the universe listened, that something was out there and we could communicate with it, this – her miraculous recovery – would be the biggest, the most important piece of evidence.

But first I needed to convince her. Because I couldn't do it alone. Or maybe I could. The way I felt then, there was nothing I couldn't do, even heal the sick, even heal the sick who didn't seem to want to be healed. And I *would* write *The Book of Why*. I would begin in the morning. And I wouldn't be afraid to say what I believed, which was that *we* are in charge, there's no one else to take credit or to blame.

When the woman in the yellow dress reached me, I was prepared to tell her this, was prepared to promise her the book within six months.

But before I could say anything, not even hello, how are you, how is your son, she hugged me. She pulled me against her. She put her lips against my ear and whispered words I couldn't understand.

I didn't try to pull away from her.

She released me, kissed my cheek, then walked away, past the crowd still waiting to speak with me. I never heard from her again.

Turbulence woke me from dreams:

Churches filled with wingless black birds the size of humans, the tap of their feet up and down aisles made of glass, the faces of the dead staring up wide-eyed from below, the air heavy with incense, the metallic taste of holy water poured into my mouth from a stoup held above me by invisible hands, those same hands using an aspergillum as a tongue depressor, a voice telling me to say *ah*.

I clutched the armrests, took deep breaths to slow my heart. Fear despite another pill an hour earlier in the plane's bathroom.

My mother could read about the crash in the morning paper; she could shake her head and cross herself, could tell the mailman about it, could tell the neighbors, all before realizing that her son had perished – she would use this more dramatic word – and then there would be nothing left for her to be afraid of, yet she would still be afraid, she would still, at almost seventy, push her night table against her locked bedroom door, a barricade to keep out whatever happened during the night to make the morning news.

I wanted to get home to Cary, wanted to tell her that everything would be all right if she listened to me. There would be no more pain, no more sickness.

Around me, despite the turbulence, human mouths hung open in dreamless catatonia. Through a sudden drop the captain would later apologize for, twin boys fought with swollen thumbs for a video game. A man wearing silk pajamas and burgundy velvet slippers ordered drinks for everyone in his row. More heavy chop, and the man finished his new drink so as not to spill it. Everyone on the plane was gladly stuck in Vegas. If the plane went down, it would be my fault: I was convinced that I could think it down. And so I tried to think it up, as if the engines and the captain's training weren't enough.

Another pill, and I closed my eyes: soon the plane was a womb and I a child waiting safely to be born, and the turbulence, so bad that even the crew had to sit and fasten their seat belts, was my mother-to-be dancing, and the rain against the plane's windows was the lullaby she sang to her belly, to me.

Four hours later: home.

A cab from Queens to Brooklyn, past windows lit with Christmas lights. New snow fell softly on snow I'd missed while gone.

The yellow shadow of fear had hopped in the trunk with my bag, and now it followed me up the stoop, up the stairs. I tried to enter the apartment quickly, lock it out, but it slid under the door.

It was after two.

A lamp on in the hallway, a blinking wreath in the window. Ralph greeted me with a shoe, made circles around my legs. I crouched, and she dropped the shoe to lick my face. I scratched her ears, found the sweet spot; one of her back legs involuntarily kicked and kicked, her nails tapping the wood floor.

Cary had fallen asleep on my side of the bed, one leg above the covers, one below. I took off my coat and the rest of my clothes and let them fall to the floor, and then her warmth against my cold body. In the six years we'd been together – over two thousand nights – I had rarely fallen asleep first. She would say that she had the pleasure of falling asleep with me still awake beside her, my breathing a lullaby. And I would say that I had the pleasure of watching her sleep. Sometimes, in sleep, she would put my hands – I have cold hands – between her legs, where her skin was warmest, and I would press my stomach against her back, and here was another night like that. But now there was something else: there was the pleasure of the moment, the comfort of being warm inside when outside was cold, but no longer the feeling that an infinite number of such nights lay before us. Now there was a kind of pre-missing that made the moment more precious yet less peaceful, and I would never go away again, no matter how much someone was willing to pay me to speak.

Part Five

Wish You Were Here

SAM IS IN the driver's seat, reading my third book, *There Are No Accidents*. I ask if she wouldn't mind reading something else.

'I didn't bring anything else.'

'Never mind,' I tell her. 'The ferry will be in Woods Hole soon. Then you'll have to drive.'

I forgot to bring my pain medication. Breathing hurts, so I hold my breath. Ten seconds, twenty, but eventually the body has to breathe. My head is worse than my ribs. I try to keep my eyes closed, but when I do, light flashes beneath my eyelids. A car alarm keeps going off, the siren echoing in the ferry's hull.

Ralph sighs in the backseat, oblivious to our human drama. Her nose twitches; even in sleep she's trying to smell the sea air.

'Tell me where we're going.'

'The less you know, the better,' she says. 'Let's face it — you haven't been very positive about this trip.'

'How long until we're there, wherever *there* is?'

'Depends on traffic.'

'Ballpark.'

'Seven, maybe eight hours.'

'Were you really going to go without me?'

'Yes.'

'I thought you were bluffing.'

'No way,' she says. 'Something big is going to happen.'

As I empty my bladder into a clogged toilet at a rest stop in Connecticut, I decide that I'd be better off back in Chilmark – morning hikes with Ralph, throwing sticks for her to chase, a walk to the market. I decide that my father was a dream, Gloria Foster will be a dead end, and that this trip – this adventure, as Sam likes to call it – will serve no purpose.

But I have no plan – no place to hide, nowhere to run. There's no one I might call from the pay phone beside the soda machines. I'm not the type to hitch my way back to the ferry, or anywhere, for that matter, though I suppose I should have no reason to be afraid. Once the worst happens, there's nothing left to fear. I used to wonder why my mother didn't understand the freedom that comes with loss. Now I understand: there's always more to fear.

I look through the crack between door and hinge: a man helps his son wash his hands; the boy keeps pushing out more and more soap until it forms a pink mass on the sink. An older man, gray and bearded and hunched, cords and sneakers, splashes his face with water. A teenager – black trench coat, black eyeliner – bumps into the older man. 'Sorry,' the man says, even though he's done nothing wrong. The paper towel dispenser is empty and the air dryer is broken; he tries to shake his hands dry, gives up, leaves.

Me in thirty years.

So you think, so you shall be, the old me would have said.

Ask and it is given.

The old me would have tried to save the old man, would have straightened his spine, would have had him smiling, feeling ten years younger, all from showing him how to change his thoughts.

The old me would have tried to save the new me.

I stand in the stall for twenty minutes – not long enough to come up with a plan, but long enough to become nauseated by the smell.

Long enough for Sam to be waiting for me outside the bathroom.

'I was worried,' she says.

'Did you think I would abandon Ralph?'

She looks at me, confused. 'I just thought maybe you were sick.'

'I am,' I tell her. 'I think we should go back.'

She moves her face close to mine, and for a moment I think she's going to kiss me, and I'm so tired that I'll let her, though I'm not sure I'd have the energy or inclination to return her kiss. Up close, her black eye, not quite healed, could be the eye of someone ten years older. Quietly, almost a whisper, she says to me, 'I want you to listen to me. I promise you, I swear to you, that we're going to find her, and when we do, it will mean something.'

I have an urge to sit on the floor – to refuse to move or speak. Either that or bang my head against the wall.

'Mean what?'

'I don't know,' she says. 'That's what we're going to find out.'

'This is all about your brother.'

'Not all,' she says.

The old man I saw in the bathroom wanders from candy machine to soda machine, wiping his hands on his pants. He reaches into his pocket for change, drops the coins on the floor, bends to pick them up, can't reach, kicks them under the machine. I touch the change in my own pocket. More than anything, I want this man to have his soda. I don't want to know his story, but if only I could make the machine give him what he wants. As I think this, as I intend it, the man reaches out and presses a button, and the machine, even though the man has inserted no coins, dispenses a can of orange soda.

'I retired from helping people,' I say.

'I don't need anyone to save me.'

'How do you expect *me* to help you?'

'I just know you need to be there.'

'Tell me where.'

'Four more hours.'

'Tell me.'

'Fine,' she says. 'Pennsylvania.'

'Where in Pennsylvania?'

'Lancaster.'

'Lancaster?'

'Ever been there?'

'Once, when I was a kid – a weekend trip with my parents.'

'Anything weird happen?'

'Not that I remember.'

'Well, that's where we're going.'

'Do you have an address?'

'No.'

'A street?'

'Not exactly.'

'Then how will we know where we're going?'

'The house near the cemetery.'

'Do you know how many houses might be near that cemetery?'

'Yes, but the street – in the dream, I mean – was green. The cars, the houses, the hospital across the street. My brother stepped on the street and everything turned green.'

'So what?'

'So maybe it's Green Street.'

'This is what we're going on?'

'This is why I didn't want to tell you the details,' she says. 'For someone who made a killing teaching positive thinking, you can be really negative.'

'You haven't met my mother.'

'Well, don't be your mother.'

LANCASTER IS LARGER than I remembered. We came here when I was twelve, a few months before my father died, but we didn't come into the city; we stayed in the country – working Amish farms, a one-room schoolhouse, an amusement park called Dutch Wonderland. We stayed in a motel, my parents in the bed, me on the floor, and when I looked out the window – awakened by the same crickets that had lulled me to sleep – I saw rows of corn in the moonlight, and I remember thinking that I could live in a place like this, could learn to milk a cow and churn butter and plow a field, could do without electricity, could wear the same black trousers and suspenders and plain white shirt every day.

I hadn't expected to return. Certainly not with cracked ribs, my head spinning with post-concussion disequilibrium, a relative stranger bringing me and my old, arthritic dog to find someone named Gloria Foster, a name spoken by my dead father.

Then again, it *is* April Fools' Day.

We park downtown, across the street from a café called

Starving Artist, its front window boarded. A few doors down is a restaurant, Wish You Were Here. It's after three; the sky is dark with storm clouds.

I walk Ralph, who takes her time sniffing trees and poles, then buy her two hot dogs at a gas station. Years ago, I would have made her earn each bite – sit, lie, touch my finger with her nose – but she's too old to be made to work for something as essential as food, so I let her lie on the cold cement while I break off pieces and bring them to her mouth.

She drinks water Sam pours into my cupped hands.

Ralph climbs into the backseat for a nap, her head resting on my overnight bag. Never a good watchdog, she looks the part, and that's enough. The first drops fall, then the rain stops, a false start. But a few minutes later the sky opens and a sudden downpour sends us into the restaurant.

Too late for lunch, we order tea to go. Sam asks the waitress – blond hair, nose ring, pregnant – if she can tell us where Green Street is.

'Green Street,' the woman says, and looks up as if waiting for a divine answer. 'Green Street,' she says again. 'I don't think I know, but it could be in a part of the city I'm not familiar with. Hey, Mitch!' she says, and the cook comes out of the kitchen, a young man wearing a hooded sweatshirt, shaggy brown hair, a word tattooed on his wrist. 'Where's Green Street?' the waitress says. He steps closer and I see the word, and I think, Maybe we *are* in the right place, but he says, 'Sorry, never heard of Green Street,' and then I see that 'Cary' is Gary, perhaps his father or brother or best friend, someone gone – remembered every time Mitch flips a pancake or washes his hands.

'Can you tell us where the cemetery is?' Sam says.

'Which one?' Mitch says.

'Lancaster Cemetery.'

'It's on the east side,' he says. 'Do you know the city?'

'No.'

'Left onto Lime,' he says. 'It'll be on the right side of the street. Can't miss it.'

The sky lights up, and I worry about Ralph.

'Supposed to be a bad storm,' the waitress says.

Thunder booms, the waitress drops a glass, and then we're all on the floor picking up chunks and shards.

'You said Lime Street, right?' Sam says. She isn't paying attention, and I hear her wince – a cut on her finger.

'Shit,' the waitress says. 'I'm sorry.'

'It's not your fault,' I say.

'I have bad luck,' she says. 'Let me get the rest.'

'It's just a small cut,' Sam says. She squeezes her finger until a drop of blood blooms, then she sucks it.

'I'm telling you,' the waitress says, 'I have the worst luck.'

'You did say Lime Street,' Sam says.

'About a mile,' Mitch says. 'Just before the hospital.'

'Thank you *so* much!' Sam says, as if he has told her the secret of life, the reason we're all here, and as if the reason is good.

'Careful out there,' the waitress says.

We run across the street to the car, where Ralph is pawing

at the window. A gust of wind carries a newspaper down the street and pins it against the side of a church.

In the car, we catch our breath. We can't see through the windshield, even with the wipers on high. Ralph paces in the backseat.

'Damn,' I say. 'I didn't bring her storm pills.'

Sam puts the car in drive.

'You can't drive in this.'

'You heard him – it's close.'

'I thought we were looking for Green Street.'

'There is no Green. Lime *is* Green.'

'What do we do if we find the house?'

'We ring the bell.'

'I'm not ringing a stranger's bell and asking for Gloria Foster because your dead brother threw dandelion clocks at a house.'

'Better not to have a plan,' she says.

'And what if she *is* there? What will we say?'

'I suppose we'd say hello.'

The few cars I can see through the windshield have pulled over. Sam keeps driving. Five years ago I stopped being afraid of everything except living the rest of my life, and so the idea of a car crash – another one – shouldn't frighten me. But my fear, after the accident in Chilmark, has been reversed.

I still wonder if my father's voice was part of a dream brought on by physical trauma. The brain's way of coping with near-death, the body's defense mechanism against annihilation.

Maybe. That's my mantra, or I'd like it to be.

For the past five years I'd believed in not believing – in shrugging my shoulders at the idea of anything not in front of me. Ruled by my senses. More like a dog. A creature of the present.

Maybe it was a dream. But maybe it wasn't. Either way, you weren't there, so I *am* a bit afraid that Sam might drive the car into a tree.

I don't think a tornado would stop Sam from reaching the cemetery.

I have this thought, and the rain turns to hail. Ice bounces off the windshield. Ralph is shaking in the backseat, and before I can turn to comfort her, she jumps into the front, knocking the gear into neutral. Ralph paws at my face as if I'm a door she wants to break through. She keeps jumping from my lap into the back, then onto my lap again. She kicks my ribs, and I lose my breath. Hail the size of golf balls cracks the windshield. Sam shifts the car back into drive and steps on the gas. I can't see where we're going. The car skids across the road, spins, and comes to a rest.

It's parked perfectly, but facing the wrong direction. When I look through the side window, I see the cemetery gates.

I hold my side while taking short, puffy breaths. Ralph scratches the window and barks. She has never understood that the storm is outside, not inside.

Sam slaps the steering wheel, presses the horn. 'Do you see where we are? I mean, do you *see?*'

'Yes, I see.'

'Well, why aren't you flipping out like I am?'

'I *am* flipping out,' I say. 'Jesus – look.'

'Right at the cemetery,' she says. 'I mean, what are the odds?'

'That's not what I'm talking about.'

'I swear, I wasn't driving this car. Someone else was driving.'

'Listen to me,' I say. 'Do you see what's happening?'

Day has become night. The wind bends trees; a limb crashes down beside the car. The cemetery gate swings open, slams closed, swings open again.

Ralph is lying down, panting. I suppose fear could kill a dog her age. I get out of the car and open the back door. Hail pelts my face, my chest. I run in the only direction the wind will allow me to run; Ralph follows. I hear Sam yelling behind us. I run to the nearest house, catch my breath on the porch. Trash blows across the street. Sam runs toward us, trying in vain to shield her head from the hail.

'What the hell,' she says when she reaches the porch.

'Looks like you were right.'

'I can't hear you.'

'You were right,' I yell over the wind. 'Best not to have a plan.'

'What?'

'There is no plan!'

A young man is at the door. Short and muscular, shaved head. Blue cotton pants and shirt, work boots, a uniform – plumber, electrician. He's motioning for us to come inside.

'Hurry,' he says. 'Everyone's in the cellar.'

We run through a small living room – sneakers and shoes

on the floor, children's books, toys – and into a dining room, six chairs arranged in a circle, except there's no table, a setup more suited for a group therapy session than dinner.

Through a door and down a flight of stairs into a cellar lit by a single hanging bulb. Three more people down there – two women and a girl.

When I drop the leash, Ralph runs to the girl, who's sitting on the floor in the back of the cellar surrounded by storage boxes and dusty end tables and old cans of paint. She could be five or six, and has dark hair in pigtails. She closes her eyes and mouth as Ralph licks her face.

'Found them on the porch,' the man says. 'All hell's breaking loose out there.'

'I'm Eric,' I say.

The man shakes my hand. 'Jay,' he says.

Then he shakes Sam's hand. 'Sam,' she says.

We wave to the women, and they wave back.

'That's my wife, Evelyn.' He points to the younger woman sitting on an orange folding chair, smoking. Baggy jeans, white sneakers, Penn State sweatshirt. She takes a drag, then waves.

'That's our daughter,' Jay says. 'And that's my mother.'

'Welcome to our beautiful home,' his mother says. 'Let's hope it's still standing tomorrow.' She laughs – a loud, sudden *ha!* She's a fleshy woman in her fifties and has gray hair, short and spiky. She asks Ralph's name, and when I tell her, she says, 'Here, Ralph! Come here, boy!'

'Actually, Ralph's a girl.'

'How did *that* happen?' her son says.

'Long story,' I say.

The girl stands, comes closer. In the glow of the light she slaps her hand against her leg twice. She signs something to her father – too fast for me to see. Touches her head, makes her hands into fists, shakes her arms.

'Most dogs are,' Jay tells her.

I look at him, confused.

'I forget we need to translate,' he says. 'She says your dog's afraid of thunder.'

'She doesn't speak,' Evelyn says.

'She speaks,' Jay says. 'In her own way.'

'She sings,' the older woman says.

'She *hums*,' Evelyn says.

Jay's mother stands and offers Sam her hand. 'My name's Dinah.'

Jay reaches into a cardboard box filled with tools and nails and screws, and pulls out a flashlight. The light flickers before going out.

The girl hooks her index finger around her nose twice and pulls down.

'They'll be fine,' Dinah says.

'Never should have gotten her those damn dolls,' Evelyn says.

The girl moves closer to her grandmother and makes the same sign.

'Honey, they'll be fine.'

The girl starts to cry, and Ralph licks her face.

'I'll get the dolls,' Jay says.

'No you won't,' Evelyn says.

'It'll take two seconds.'

'You're always giving in to her.'

Evelyn sighs, lights another cigarette. 'Go up and get them, then. But if anything happens to you, so help me—'

'Jesus,' Jay says. 'I'm not flying to the moon. They're right upstairs. I'll get the other flashlight while I'm up there.'

'Careful,' his mother says. 'Listen to it out there.'

The girl rubs her chest, keeps rubbing it.

'All right, all right,' Evelyn says. 'And you,' she says to her husband, 'you better come back.'

'Don't worry.'

'Come here and give me a kiss.'

'I'll be right back,' he says, and goes upstairs.

'She loves those damn dolls more than us,' Evelyn says.

'She's five,' Dinah says.

'That's all she thinks about – the Foster children, the Foster children.' Evelyn drops her cigarette, puts it out with her sneaker. 'That's what she calls them,' she tells us. 'It's our last name, but it sounds like they're foster children.'

'Let her make up her stories,' Dinah says.

'I'm sorry, but she's my daughter and I don't like it.' I feel Sam looking at me as Evelyn lights another cigarette. 'Damn it, where the hell *is* he?' She bangs on the ceiling with a broom handle. We all wait to hear his steps on the floor above or on the stairs, but there's only the sound of hail against the side of the house.

'I can go up and see,' I say, but before I reach the stairs, Jay returns.

'It's pretty bad out there,' he says. 'A tree fell into a

house across the street. And we've got a mess in our front yard.'

Jay gives his daughter the dolls, and she hurries to the back of the cellar to play with them. Ralph follows, then lies beside her.

The girl points at me with both hands, then pulls her fingers back toward herself. She keeps making this sign until Dinah says, 'She wants you to play with her.'

I sit on the floor beside her. She gives me one of the dolls. She spreads her fingers and touches her chin with her thumb; then she touches her forehead with her thumb. She keeps going back and forth – chin, then forehead.

'She says she's the mommy and you're the daddy,' Dinah says.

'What are their names?' I say.

She signs letters, but I don't understand.

'Lucy and Vincent,' Dinah says.

My ears are ringing, I'm dizzy, and for a moment I forget where we are and how we got here. I close my eyes and breathe; my memory returns in fragments: Sam Leslie, car accident, Gloria Foster, Lancaster, cemetery, tornado, Lucy, Vincent.

I ask the girl her name.

'Tell him,' Evelyn says.

'Don't pressure her,' Dinah says.

'She can speak,' Evelyn says. 'She chooses not to.'

The girl starts humming – quietly at first. She looks at me, then quickly looks away; she combs a doll's hair with her fingers.

'What's that song?' I ask her.

'She loves to sing,' Dinah says.

'Hum,' Evelyn says.

'That song,' I say. 'What's it called?'

The girl touches her head and salutes – that's what it looks like. Then she waves.

'"Hello, Goodbye,"' Dinah says.

'Tell the man your name,' Jay says, but she keeps humming the song.

Part Six

Faith

Omega Institute for Holistic Studies, Rhinebeck, New York, 2001

NO MATTER HOW *far you've traveled down a wrong road, you can turn back. It's never too late to make a you-turn.*

Just remember these words: cancel and erase. If you catch yourself having negative thoughts, if you find yourself lost in doubt, just say cancel and erase, cancel and erase.

If you start to feel sick, at the first sign of a sore throat or fever, just say cancel and erase. If you feel a migraine coming on, cancel and erase. If you feel a twinge in your back, cancel and erase. If you're feeling rundown, by all means rest, quiet your mind, be kind to yourself, but also say and believe cancel and erase.

Illness, even serious illness, is one way our bodies communicate with us. It's the body's last-ditch effort to get our attention, to tell us that something's wrong. But what's wrong — listen to me — what's wrong doesn't have to do with the body but with the mind. The body is only the messenger. There's no need — please hear me — to kill the messenger. In fact, I encourage you to thank the messenger. And the best way to thank the body is to cancel and erase the thoughts that helped trigger the illness.

I know, believe me I know, that this isn't the most popular way of looking at illness. But I think there's a double standard when it comes to the mind-body connection. If you believe, as many people do, that the mind can heal the body, then why not believe the opposite — that the mind can also obstruct wellness in the body? If you believe that stress can weaken the immune system and cause high blood pressure, then why not believe that negativity and guilt and self-hatred can cause cancer? Let's not forget what cancer really is. Cancer is the body trying to kill itself.

I assure you, this isn't about blame. This is about hope. Think about it: if we cause disease with our thoughts, with our fear and worry and guilt, then it makes sense that we can cure disease with love and faith and forgiveness. This is good news. If you see this as bad news, if you're frightened or offended, I'm sorry you feel that way. I understand all too well why you would.

But here's the truth: Every one of you has the potential to heal. You are all miracle workers. You can cancel and erase any disease.

The first step is to put a hyphen between the first s and the first e in disease. *That way you'll know what the word really means. Every disease stems from dis-ease about something. Dis-ease is an illness of thought that becomes an illness of emotion and eventually manifests in the body. So if you can create disease, you can cure disease. If disease begins in the mind, then that's also where it must end.*

As long as you believe, as long as you know beyond any doubt, you can heal any illness. Let nothing interfere with your intention to heal. Eliminate all negativity. Don't allow in any energy that will weaken your resolve. Refuse to talk about the disease. Focus on reasons to feel good. Recognize only the health and perfection in others. Breathe in only wellness. Be grateful for every breath, for the blood flowing through your body. Give thanks to every beat of your heart.

Remember: As you think, so shall you be. That's not me, that's Jesus Christ. Some of you may know him.

Maybe Michelangelo speaks to you more than Jesus. He said, 'The greater danger for most of us is not that our aim is too high and we miss it, but that it is too low and we reach it.'

I'm asking you all to aim high, I know. But the stakes are high. Your very lives. And the quality of your lives. The greater the stakes, the greater the opportunity. Every obstacle, including disease, is an opportunity. It's a chance for faith to win over doubt, for peace and happiness to win over tragedy and suffering, for self-love to win over fear. It's your chance to cancel dis-ease and replace it with ease.

THE YEAR OF hats.

She didn't lose her hair, but wore them anyway. Baseball hats, knitted berets, a linen newsboy cap, a wool tam, a tweed mod cap. For Christmas, for her birthday, for no reason, people gave her hats. She had so many hats she could go a month without wearing the same one twice. I wore a hat, too – the same one every day. An old, shapeless Mets hat my father had worn proudly when they were the worst team anyone had ever seen.

It was also the year of sleeping while holding hands or touching feet – a part of my body had to be touching hers. It was the year of slowing down, of noticing things I might not have noticed had she not been ill. I recorded. I *pre-remembered*. At moments I thought, No, I mustn't, this way of thinking will manifest exactly that – her gone, my having to remember. But I couldn't stop seeing the present from the perspective of a future without her.

The world became smaller and larger. I noticed the quarter-moons at the bottoms of her fingernails, and on clear nights

I could hear the stars ask their question: Does your small life, your small suffering, mean anything under this infinite canopy?

It was the year of talking to stars, to empty rooms, to the face in the mirror. To her, when she wasn't home. Practice. How to tell her what I couldn't tell her. That she could heal herself, could think the tumor away, if she believed she could.

Sometimes I practiced losing her; I was angry with her for dying before she died. Then I'd catch myself and say how stupid to think this way, you'll make it come true, practice being alone and you *will* be alone. So I tried to imagine her old. Gray hair was easy, and wrinkles around her eyes and mouth. I imagined her changing for bed or getting out of the shower, her belly rounder, softer. She covered her breasts with her hands. I tried to see her at fifty, sixty, seventy, but I was faking it. Difficult enough to imagine her forty. No matter how much gray, no matter how much gravity might change her body, she would remain young. Stooped and three inches shorter, she would skip.

WHY SHOULDN'T YOU, of all people, have a soft leather chair. Why shouldn't you, of all people, rest with your feet up, the better to nod off as the drugs drip into your veins. Recline far enough and you're floating on a blow-up raft in your childhood pool in Northampton, Massachusetts, sixteen and tan, much too young to care about cancer, much too relaxed on this lovely June afternoon to care that your sister keeps switching the radio station. The neighbor's chocolate Lab comes into your yard through the open gate and at full speed belly-dives into the pool. Close your eyes. When you hear the dog's breathing close, extend your hand from the raft and wait for him to lick your fingers. Why shouldn't this previously lost memory return to you here, of all places, as you wade into sleep. Why shouldn't they have *Us Weekly* and *People* and *Time* and *Self* and *Sports Illustrated* and *Better Homes and Gardens* to read as you drift off. Why not celebrity cellulite, if that's what you like, or a review of the new Johnny Depp movie, or a close-up of a wide-eyed pole-vaulter about to clear the bar, a new world record, a split second before the flyaway. Better, maybe, to bring your favorite children's books – *Blueberries for Sal, Katy and the Big Snow, Leo the Late Bloomer* – and have your husband read them to you as you drift, a sixteen-year-old girl and a woman more than twice her age, both of you nodding off in this soft leather chair in a room of soft leather chairs, blissfully unaware of the soft but steady sound of a slow leak.

A MAN WHO looks like me wakes in the night to no one beside him. He fell asleep with his foot touching hers, his hand warm against her stomach, just beneath her breasts, and now nothing. Two pillows, not four, and he panics. He sits up in bed and thinks, My God, did it happen already? Did I lose her years ago and dream that last night she was here?

He turns on a light, waits for his eyes to adjust. No dog on the floor, no robe draped over the chair, no slippers beside the bed. No sign of her. Not her glasses on the night table. Not the smell of her or the shape of her body on the sheets. He looks at his boxer shorts, blue-and-white stripes, and doesn't recognize them. The memory of having bought them, lost, just as the memory of having lost her, lost. His hair is short. When did he have it cut? He feels for his beard – still there, but trimmed. He wonders, Could it be summer? When he fell asleep it was March; it had been snowing.

The man who looks like me walks like me down the hallway. His office, unchanged. His three books in cloth, in paperback, in German, Italian, Japanese. On his desk, inside a blue binder, notes for *The Book of Why*; he hasn't looked at them in months. A box filled with letters from his readers. It could be the present or the future. That makes no sense, it's always the present. What he means is, some future present. Maybe he fell asleep in 2002 and woke five or ten years later. His wife gone, their dog gone, the same unfinished book on his desk.

Her studio is the same. White paper on her drafting table. Her overlarge, childlike writing. She doesn't write in straight lines – not in lines at all. Her writing looks more like drawing. Circles and arrows and smiley faces and notes to herself in caps, NO SONG BELONGS TO YOU, words traced over and over until they break through the page, GIVE EVERYTHING AWAY. She liked to stand when she wrote songs. Already she's in the past tense. She *likes* to stand when she *writes*. Most days he surprises her with a glass of lemonade, finds her leaning against the table, her eyes closed, or sitting on a stool in the center of the room, guitar on her lap. She sang – *sings* – as if each note is a secret. He looks for a date, but she has never dated her work, has never owned a calendar. Her favorite sweater, blue and red with wood buttons, a blue hood, hangs on a hook by the door. Blue socks inside her clogs on the floor. Three children's school desks facing each other. She used to draw with the twins. Their doodles are still on the desk in crayon. At least they were real, the man who looks like me thinks. He can think about them in the past tense. She drew with the children, wrote songs for them, with them. They're gone now. Not *gone*, just gone from here. Back with their mother, who stole his first book, read it, and healed herself.

In his first book he wrote: 'Nothing is impossible. We believe something is impossible because we've never seen it done. The best place to see something done – especially something you believe is impossible – is in your mind. Seeing is believing, believing is seeing. What you see clearly in your mind, you will believe. What you believe will manifest in the world.'

The man who looks like me walks like me to the bathroom. The door is open. The room, like the rest of the apartment, is dark. He needs to see his own face, needs to know how old he is, what year it is. He turns on the light and sees her on the floor, beside the toilet. A pillow beneath her head, another pulled into her chest. The dog sleeps beside her, opens her eyes to the light.

He looks in the toilet, wants to flush.

For her, not for him.

He wants to carry her to bed, but is afraid to disturb her sleep; it might have taken her hours to find this position. And so he lies beside her, on cold tiles, wraps his arms around her. The dog shifts, yawns loudly. He gestures for her to be quiet, even though she knows no sign for this command; he uses the sign he'd use for a human, finger to his lips. She looks at him, waits for her language. He gives her the sign that means lie down, but she's already lying down, so she stares at him. He closes his eyes, opens them. Closes his eyes again, opens them a few minutes later to the dog still staring. The ceiling light hums; he should have turned it off before lying beside his wife.

It will become the night they all slept on the bathroom floor, during the week she was the sickest she'd ever been, during the month she lost fifteen pounds, during the year they put chemicals into her body to kill what was killing her. The winter before the spring she would trust him, do it *his* way, even though it wasn't his body, wasn't his life or death, though it felt that way to him.

She wakes in the night, though the light's on and the blinds are drawn, so it could just as likely be day. The man who looks like me guesses he's been asleep for an hour, tops, so let's say night.

'How are the children?'

He can't tell if she's confused, as he was, about time. Maybe he's still confused. Maybe he's more confused than he was when he woke and walked around the apartment. Maybe the children are sleeping in their room; maybe they're not past tense, after all.

She asks again, clearly, 'How are the children?'

'They're fine,' he says.

Gone, he should have said. *Not here.*

He stands, lifts her to her feet. 'I'm going to bring you to bed.'

'Will you tuck me in?'

'Of course.'

'Will you stay?'

'Yes.'

How slight, he thinks as he walks her down the hallway, his arm hooked around hers. How almost nothing she feels, her body the body of a child. Her feet make no sound on the wood floor.

The children are gone, he wants to say. *You wanted practice letting things go, and you got your wish.*

It takes great will, but the man who looks like me doesn't say this. Perhaps he knows a man who looks like him will write it years later, in a book. Will confess, among other confessions, his desire to be cruel to his wife or to whatever caused her disease: bad genes, bad thoughts, suppressed guilt, a God who insists on writing his own story no matter the suffering of his characters.

Her feet. He doesn't want them to die. Not soon, not ever. They lie beside each other under a blanket her sister made. Head to feet. He rubs warmth into her feet, kisses her toes, the blood flowing through them. If she could live but he could only kiss her feet, never her lips or face or hands or belly, he would take it. If she could live but they could never speak, every day a silent day, he would take it. If she could live but they could never see each other, if they could speak but only with a door between them, he would take it. If they couldn't speak or see each other but could only write letters, he would take that, if it meant she could live. If they couldn't see each other or speak or write letters or send e-mails, but he could hear her sing, he would take that, if it meant she could live. Even if they could never live together, even if they could never speak or write or send e-mails, if he could only watch her, a woman walking to the market, a woman playing in the snow with her dog, a woman blowing bubbles in the park, a woman living a life without him, falling in love with someone else, singing her song where he can't hear it, he would take that, as long as she could live. If she could live, if she could keep on living, but only in another body, a body he couldn't love – a man's, a child's – he would take that. As long as she could live, he would agree not to know her. He would agree – and this would be most difficult – never to have known her. All this – bargaining, really – as he falls asleep with his lips against her feet.

She wakes once before light, asks again, 'The children – where are they?'

'They're fine,' he says. 'They're somewhere sleeping. They're dreaming about you.'

'I was dreaming about them,' she says. 'They were much older. So were you. You had a gray beard, but I was a little girl.'

Last week of April, first warm days of spring. One night we huddled under blankets, the next we opened windows and slept shirtless under the white noise of a ceiling fan. Overnight, the cherry trees on our street bloomed. A good sign, Cary said. We set two chairs by the bedroom window and read. Every few pages we stopped to look at the trees, then every few paragraphs. Then we put our books down, moved our chairs closer, and dozed in the morning breeze.

We ate lunch – bananas and cheese sandwiches and fig bars, things Cary could stomach – while we walked up and down our block, the pink blossoms already falling like snow, covering the ground, the hoods of cars. We found them on our back and shoulders and in our hair; we found them that night on our pillows. One blossom was pressed against Cary's back the next day when she undressed for the doctor.

When we came home from the hospital, our neighbors were shoveling. The sound made me afraid it was winter again; we didn't want to relive the past four months, didn't want to have to get through what we'd already gotten through.

But then I looked; the snow was pink.

'So pretty,' Cary said. 'Even on the ground.'

'They get slippery,' I said.

'Such short lives,' she said. We sat on the stoop and watched our neighbors – people we knew by face and by dog but not by name – bag cherry blossoms as more fell.

'Mayflies,' Cary said, excited to have remembered this word. 'Mayflies live only a few minutes, just long enough to lay their . . .'

I waited while her brain searched for the word. 'Long enough to lay their . . .'

'Eggs,' I said.

'Yes,' she said. 'That might be nice.'

'I'd rather live to be a hundred fifty.'

'Much too long,' she said. 'There's something . . .' She paused, her mouth open, waiting for the word. 'Beauty,' she said. 'There's something beauty about a short life.'

'Beautiful,' I said.

'Yes.'

'Tell that to a giant tortoise.'

'Next time I see one.'

We sat watching our neighbors stuff bags into trash cans set curbside for morning pickup. Then we went inside, where the rest of the day – the part we still had to live – stretched in front of us.

When faced with sadness, play a game; that was her way. The word game – the one she'd made up. No names for things, and try to guess them. Easy for her – she'd lost so many words. It made her laugh to see me have to try so hard.

She seemed so happy, you'd never know the news had been bad that morning.

'Hey,' she said. 'At least it didn't spread.'

Before my face could betray me, I pulled her against me. I stroked her hair and imagined it gray. I was hugging an old lady; we'd been married fifty years. No kids, but so what. Young couples would stare at us as we walked by, holding hands, and say, 'Let's be like them.'

After a few minutes, I felt her begin to pull away; it was the only time it had ever been her. It was something she took silly pride in: she was never first to break a hug, not even when college kids were giving free hugs in Prospect Park and there was a long line. Such a good hugger, they asked her to join them for a while, and she did.

She pulled away again, and this time I let her.

She hadn't lost *tree*, so even she had to work at that one. She called them the earth's whiskers. Pass to me. The earth was the universe's cloudy eyeball. Pass to her. Cloud: what breaks your fall. Fall: the time of rakes. Rake: a cartoon blow to the face. Face: what a blind lover feels. Blind: to see better, to smell better. Smell: to breathe colors. Breathe: to be still, to do nothing. Nothing: anything other than everything.

Enough, I said, but she wanted to keep going.

'I don't like this game,' I said. 'I can't tell when you're playing.'

'I know *clogs*. And *dog* and *hair*.'

'What makes the sky wet?'

She shrugged.

'Rain,' I said, and she repeated the word, *rain, rain*, a child learning a new language.

'What about the thing you're reading?'

'You're right,' she said. 'We shouldn't play.'

'Book,' I said.

'Are you mad at me?'

'No,' I said. A reflex, the right answer, even if not true.

'It's no one's fault,' she said.

I kneeled in front of her chair. I kissed her hands – each finger, front and back. My mouth never said, *Of course it's no one's fault*.

Behind her, the sky had turned dark. Cherry trees swayed in the wind and lost more blossoms. The sky flashed bright, and already Ralph was shaking at the door. I looked at Cary and waited.

'Lightning,' she said.

Then a long, low rumble across the sky. Ralph stood on her back legs and scratched the door.

'Something and lightning,' she said.

'Begins with a *t*.'

She closed her eyes, opened them, shook her head no.

'It's all right,' I said.

'Timber,' she said. 'Timber and lightning.'

'That's right,' I said.

Ralph scratched at our closet; we opened the door to show her it wasn't a way out. She put her paws on the sill; we opened the window to let her smell the rain and see the flashing sky, but still she wanted out. She stood in the corner and started to pee – whether from fear or a full bladder, we weren't sure – and I said, 'Let's give her what she wants.'

Ralph ran down the stairs, back up to hurry us, back down. When we opened the front door, she pulled me out. Down the stoop, quick to the curb to pee, then around the corner, faster now, trying to outrun the storm. She kept pulling me. We ran past people trying to right umbrellas blown inside out, or covering their heads with newspaper. We were as soaked as if we'd showered in our clothes.

I let Ralph lead, though I don't believe she had a plan. A crack of thunder set off car alarms and she froze. We were four blocks from home, rain falling as heavily as rain falls. Cars stopped at green lights, then pulled over with their hazards on. Ralph blinked, a statue but for this slight movement.

'Come on,' I said, and yanked on her leash.

She didn't budge.

I pulled again, as hard as I'd allow myself for fear of hurting her, but she was too scared and too strong.

'Now what?'

'You look silly,' Cary said, catching up.

'I can see your nipples.'

'So what. I can see yours.'

'I'm sorry,' I said. 'This was a bad idea.'

'I'm having fun.'

'Do I say "I'm sorry" too much?'

'I've already forgiven you for anything you'll ever do to me.'

Ralph was so wet she looked like a different dog – smaller, sadder, ears pinned back, tail between her legs. I pulled her leash again, but she spread her legs for leverage and stayed.

A flash of lightning followed by a single boom; the storm was directly overhead.

I'd met a man in Toronto – he had me sign a copy of my first book – who'd been struck by lightning twelve times and claimed he could see the future. He told me, even though I didn't ask for such information, that weather would play an important role in my life. I suppose you could say that to anyone and it might as likely be true as not. 'Watch out for strong weather,' he kept saying, as if warning his former self, before the first strike.

'You take her front, I'll take her back,' I said.

Ralph weighed seventy pounds; we had to keep stopping. Then three people, strangers, also soaked, helped us carry her. We must have looked either foolish or heroic, but my vote is for the latter, five wet humans carrying a petrified German shepherd through the streets of Brooklyn during a thunderstorm.

It was still raining when we got home, but the storm was moving away: three Mississippis between lightning and thunder, then four, then five.

We gave Ralph some dog Valium, and she lay on the first floor, at the bottom of the stairs. We sat by the window upstairs and watched the sky light up in the distance. By the time the storm ended, it really was night.

Tomorrow, I kept thinking, we'll have to talk about it. The next four months couldn't be like the past four. No more chemo, even though the oncologist had recommended just that. No more killing yourself to save yourself.

Before we turned out the lights, Cary called Ralph up to her dog bed, but she didn't come.

'Hey, buttercup,' she called.

We didn't hear her move.

Cary went to the top of the stairs. 'Hey, don't you want to sleep up here with the humans?'

'She must be exhausted,' I said. I went to the stairs and looked down. There was something about her legs; they were limp, and bent at awkward angles.

'Ralph,' Cary said. 'Come up.'

She waited. Then: 'Ralph, come here.'

'Ralph!' she yelled, and it made me jump. 'Come *here!*' she said.

I watched Ralph's chest, but didn't see it move.

'Eric,' Cary said, and sat on the stairs. 'Eric,' she said again.

I walked down, saying Ralph, louder with each step, and I didn't know what I'd do, didn't know how I'd turn and look up at Cary and—

A few steps before I reached the dog, she opened her eyes and blinked at me, confused as if still in a dream.

'God,' Cary said. 'She wasn't moving.'

'I know,' I said.

'It's crazy, but I thought—'

'I know,' I said.

Dear Mr Newborn,

I have read your books with great interest, and have found them useful in many ways. But, with all due respect, what about babies? They get sick, they die. They're born with disabilities, deformities. A fetus doesn't know what disease is. How would you explain birth defects and stillbirths in the context of your books? I ask because my sister recently lost her son at two weeks; he was born two pounds twelve ounces. She noticed me reading a book called There Are No Accidents, so you can understand why she asked to look at it. Just reading the table of contents made her angry. She asked me some of the questions I've just asked you, and I had no answers for her. I hope you can find the time to respond to this letter and tell me what I should tell my sister. Thank you for your time.

Sincerely,

Dear Eric Newborn,

I'm writing with thanks to tell you nothing you don't already know. The law of attraction works, it really does, I don't care what *anyone says. I know that now – there's no doubt. I have suffered from epileptic seizures since I was a girl, my first one when I was five years old. It was a difficult way to grow up, as you can imagine, the shame, it was hard to make friends, let alone a boyfriend. My mother was always afraid I would have a bad seizure and stop breathing or fall down the stairs or have one while crossing the street. I took this affliction through high school and college, never had a boyfriend except my wonderful husband (who passed away over six years ago now from a heart condition he was born with, we always knew it was possible he could die), so I thought it would always be with me, I accepted it as 'just who I was.' Medications and side effects and sometimes getting depressed, especially after I lost my husband, who was one of very few people who truly understood (we never had children, so it was always the two of us). What changed everything was when my mother (she's still alive at eighty-nine!) ordered me a book of photography for my birthday. I have always had an 'artistic' side and like to take photographs especially in addition to some painting. But the wrong book came. The book was supposed to be* Miracle: A Celebration of New Life *by a woman named Anne Geddes. It has beautiful photographs of newborns (even though my husband and I never had children, I have always liked taking photographs of babies, I do have three nieces and two nephews) and a CD of music from Céline Dion, who is also on the cover. But that book never arrived, it was yours,* Everyday Miracles, *so you can see how the mistake was made, which I now think is not an accident, because your name is Newborn and the book is photos of newborns. I'm sorry for taking up so much of your time, I know I'm just one of many letter writers. The thing is, I read your book, something made me open it, and it spoke to me, especially the part about some things never happen because you don't believe they can, and it was like a voice in my head said this has to do with your seizures, you can make them go away if you believe it's possible. I stopped taking my medication (of course I didn't tell anyone, they would have called me crazy), but got afraid and started again. I tried a few times. And then one day I reread the part of your book about not being afraid of the 'worst' thing that can happen, not giving it power over you, and that night I took a walk to the lake (I'm a ten-minute walk from Lake Sunapee in New Hampshire) and threw my pills into the water and cried (I was glad no one saw me), and I haven't had a seizure since, eight months and counting. I've been meaning to write you for a while now. There is no need to write back, I just wanted to thank you, though of course you can, if you have time. Thank you again and again!*

Sincerely yours,

There are always two stories competing for space on the page, in our minds, in our hearts. Two stories, only one of which can be true. Or: two stories, both of which may be true.

Dear Eric Newborn, Dear Mr Newborn, Dear Eric (if I may), Dear Author, Dear Sir, To Whom It May Concern, Greetings, Good morning, Good day, Hello there, Hi, Hello . . .

I have a question about your chapter 'The Creation Box.' May I please ask you a question about your new book, the chapter called 'The Power of Feeling Good Now.' I have a quick question about the chapter 'There Is Nothing You Cannot Do,' about the chapter 'You Get What You Think About,' about Chapter 4, 'The Art of Allowing,' about the chapter 'Getting Unstuck,' about the chapter 'It's Not Selfish to Want Happiness,' about the last chapter, the summary, the end, the final sentence, 'God lives inside you.' I have a question about you, I have a personal question, if you don't mind, I'd like to ask you a slightly personal question. Excuse my question, which is rather personal, but what are you afraid of? Do you ever worry? Do you ever get depressed? Have you ever had a cold? Have you ever been mugged? Has anyone ever punched you?

I want to thank you, I'm writing to thank you, I've been wanting to thank you for changing my, for helping me start over, making me see the truth about, making me understand how the world really, how to have the life I've always, the house I've always wanted, the job, the peace, the health I've wanted, how to make my dreams come true.

I'm happy to report, happy to tell you, I'm so happy to share my good news that my heart is, my migraines are, my wife is, I can walk, I can sleep, I can breathe. Feel free to use my story, feel free to include me, feel free to use this, I give you permission to use me, you may want to put my story in your next book.

Dear Mr Newborn, how would you explain, but what about, I don't understand how, why would you write that, it doesn't make sense when you say, I wonder what I'm doing wrong.

Dear Eric Newborn, it's a miracle, it's nothing short of a miracle, I'd call it a miracle, there's no other word for it but miracle, it's truly miraculous, I have no choice but to call it a miracle.

Take care, Be well, Regards, Kind regards, Warm regards, Best regards, Best wishes, Best, All best, Wishing you all the best, Best of luck, Cheers, Namaste, Thanks, Many thanks, With gratitude, Peace, Love, Yours, Yours truly, Respectfully yours, Sincerely yours.

We LEFT THE morning after the storm, before we could change our minds. I should say, before *she* could change *her* mind.

It must have been the dog – how scared Cary had been when Ralph wasn't moving, wasn't responding at all. I'd been trying to convince her for months, we'd fought about it, I'd been an ass, well-meaning, but at times an ass, and what it took, in the end, I can draw no other conclusion, was the dog. Cary woke me in the night, told me she wanted to cancel her next treatment. 'I don't want to do this anymore,' she said. 'Let's just go away.'

As if it had been *her* decision. As if I didn't have anything to do with it. As if upon hearing her words, *Let's just go away*, I didn't pull her to me and hold her and tell her she was making the best decision, we'd do this together, I wouldn't let anything happen to her.

Dawn was gray and sluggish, the street strewn with trash from overturned cans and leaves blown from trees. A large branch lay across the roof of our car like something recently shot.

May in Chilmark is October in New York; we packed sweaters and hoodies and boots and raincoats. Shorts and skirts and summer dresses, too – who knew when we'd be back. Not for a long time; at least that was the plan, now that Cary had agreed.

I went through our dressers, our closets, the medicine cabinet, the pantry for perishables; didn't bother to fold or organize. Two suitcases, as much as I could shove inside, while Cary sipped tea by the window.

Ralph sat on the stoop and watched me load the wagon. When I finished, I told her to get in. She ran in the house, back out, back inside. Everyone had to be accounted for, and Cary hadn't come out yet, as if she wasn't quite sure.

It was to be the year of solitude, the year of just the three of us, the year of tuning out the rest of the world, no TV, no radio, no newspapers, as few other people as possible, the year in our bubble; it was to be the year of mindfulness, of simplicity, of hikes in the woods and walks along the beach; it was to be the year of quiet, the year of wellness. We'd live that way forever. Farewell to the rest of the world. Farewell to disease and planes crashing into buildings and the fear such murders birth.

DEW ON LEAVES and spiderwebs. Crunch of grass frosted by overnight lows near freezing. A five-mile run that began in dark and ended in light: the push of the final mile, Ralph panting beside me, my breath a few inches in front of my mouth. The sensation, at times, that something was chasing me; at other times, that I was chasing something I could never catch. Then the first steps after, the hard work done, a stretch against a tree, beard wet, chest and back chilled from sweat absorbed into my shirt.

A warm shower, then back in bed, only a few minutes, my wet head on Cary's shoulder, the sound of Ralph drinking water in the kitchen, birds outside the window, a dog barking in the distance, Ralph's answer, then up for breakfast: granola, grapefruit juice, toast, herbal tea.

That was when I heard a fly buzz. I followed the sound: into the kitchen, above the sink, between curtain and window. Not just one. Too many to count. Blind to the glass, or perhaps expecting a different result each time, they kept crashing into the window. Flies on our anniversary; not what we'd planned. We opened the window, lifted the screen; we tried without success to shoo them out. They seemed unfazed by Ralph's attempts to eat them. Perhaps they'd heard that Ralph had never caught anything living – neither cat nor squirrel nor deer – in her life. We found dozens more in the bathroom, in our bedroom. We opened our closets and they flew out at us; they landed on our jellied toast, on our hands. They were loudly fond of our ears.

We didn't want to kill them. We didn't like killing anything; we caught spiders and wasps and mosquitoes in jars and set them free outside.

Cary propped open the door. 'Leave open,' she said.

'Door,' I said.

'I'm saying it in my mind, but . . .'

'Forget it,' I said. 'It's just a word.'

'Play catch,' she said.

We bought baseball mitts and a hardball – an anniversary gift to ourselves. I taught Cary to throw using her legs, to stretch as if playing first base on a bang-bang play. Ralph ran back and forth between us, waiting for the ball to drop. When it did, she picked it up, chewed it, played keep-away. By lunch she'd broken through the cowhide; when we threw, yarn trailed the ball like a comet's tail. Tired, we gave it to her; she chewed her way to the pill, what had been there all along unseen, a new, smaller ball for her to play with.

We ate in season: green skinnies, little rollies, sweet reds, and leaf fans. Cary's words. I said *as-par-a-gus*, overenunciating each syllable while she studied my mouth, but the word was gone. I said *spring peas, spring, peas*, and she opened her mouth. *Cherries, cher-ries. Rhubarb, rhu-barb.* The words were gone; she knew them only by taste.

'More purples, please.'

'Blueberries,' I said. 'Blue-berries.'

'They're purple.'

'Purpleberries, then.'

For a month we had stayed away from Vineyard Haven and Edgartown. We missed our favorite bookstore and ice cream shop, but we preferred quiet. Twice a week at dawn we went to the market for milk and honey and bread and rice, and to a roadside stand for fresh strawberries and blueberries.

We never said the word; we tried not to think it by thinking about other things, whatever was in front of us: butter dripping off corn on the cob, dust visible in a slant of sunlight, mouse bones by the shed.

Silence suited us best. I lost words, too, on purpose. I played Cary's games; after all, she was playing mine by leaving New York and coming here.

Scratch that – not a game. Everything else had been a game. If you believe you'll find the perfect parking spot, if you see it in your mind's eye, it will come to you. If you believe the clouds will part on your wedding day, if you believe so completely that you don't bother renting a tent, then the sun will shine. But now I wanted to say *so what* to all that, as in: So what if it doesn't work. So what if you don't get that spot; you can try again the next day. So what if a thousand times there's no spot. So what if it rains on your wedding: the best man will hold an umbrella over you as you fit rings onto each other's fingers. So what if your arthritic grandmother has to traverse a muddy field to reach her cocktail: someone will carry her; life will go on, as they say. No, what I'd believed had been faith, hadn't been. *This*, what we were doing, what I'd convinced Cary to do, was faith. No such thing as better luck next time. This wasn't a parking spot; this wasn't a sunny day. This was till death do us part. You can use a rope to lower a piano from a third-floor window, you can believe the knot is secure, but only when that same rope is tied around your waist as you're being lowered will you discover how much faith you have in the knot.

The flies – by late afternoon on our anniversary they seemed to have doubled – didn't seem like a game. We found their point of entry: a sink in our laundry room. We poured bleach into the drain, then plugged it. We went for a hike in the woods, no speaking allowed, only the chirping of birds, the sound of leaves kicked in stride, Ralph navigating through brush in pursuit of a woodchuck. We drove to Lucy Vincent and napped at the base of a rock into which we'd carved the twins' names. The beach was cold and windy; we liked that there were no other people. We saw a fat man sleeping on the sand in the distance, but then we realized it was a seal. We didn't need to move much closer to know it was dead.

When we came home, there were no fewer flies, but no more. This progress, if it could be called that, came with a setback: the toilet was backed up, from what we weren't sure, as we hadn't used it since morning. We flushed, and the water rose; we flushed again, same result, and now the floor was wet.

That night we could hear Ralph's jaw snapping at the flies; we told her to go back to sleep, and for a while she did, but later we heard her biting air.

I felt Cary get out of bed, but she came back and said, 'I need to pee.' I laughed at the word – that she still knew it.

We put on our jackets and took a flashlight outside; Ralph came with us. Our plan had been to pee behind the house, but Cary suggested we walk down the road to the trail. It was after 3:00 a.m. The flashlight was dying. We followed the circle of light I shined at the dirt; we couldn't see Ralph, who had run ahead of us, but could hear her steps, her breathing. We took the trail. In the woods, the flashlight didn't seem like much, but when its batteries died, we missed the little light we'd had. We held hands; we called Ralph to come.

'Let's keep going,' Cary said.

'This is far enough.'

I heard her pull down her pajama bottoms. 'You know what they say,' she said. 'The pack that pees together . . .'

In the dark we could hear Ralph sniffing the puddles between our legs: an honor to be known this way.

When we were finished, we started to walk back, but I stopped. I'd never liked the dark, but there, in the woods, time and space seemed not to exist. We were creatures of smell and sound and touch; blind children kissing.

In the morning, ticks. One red and bloated on Ralph's head, one on my neck, one on Cary's scalp. She checked me, I checked her. All her curly hair, it was impossible to know I'd found everything.

Also, in the morning, more flies.

Also, in the morning, toilet water threatened at the rim of the bowl. A recurring dream I'd been having for years: I walk into a clean bathroom, but the toilet is filthy and over-flowing. I walk into another bathroom, white and sparkling, but the toilet is clogged. Then the light goes out, and soon I can feel the cold water touch my bare feet. We called our plumber, only to discover that it was Memorial Day; we hadn't read a paper in over a month. We peed in the shower – something we were glad, in retrospect, not to have thought of the night before – and waited until dark to return to the woods, where we squatted side by side by side.

Also that day, late in the day, heavy rain that leaked through the roof and into our living room. We sat on the couch, a pot between us catching rain. We slept there, too, alternately soothed, then woken by the change in pitch of water falling into water.

The next day a roofer came out. He was bald – no eyebrows or eyelashes either – and had jaundiced eyes. It was unnerving to look into his eyes, but I did. He had a hacking cough and huffed his way up his ladder. It was difficult to guess his age without hair as an indication; he was just as likely forty as sixty. He evoked in me a desire to do his job for him, to ask him to come down from his ladder so I could climb up; he could tell me what to do while he swung in our hammock. I went inside to make tea, an excuse to get away from him. A few minutes later, just as the kettle started to whistle, I heard a sound I knew immediately was the ladder falling. Cary and I rushed outside, hoping we'd find him still on the roof, the ladder on the ground below, but he was on his back on our lawn, mouth open, eyes squeezed shut.

Cary called 911. I knelt beside him and kept telling him he was all right, even though clearly he was anything but all right. His mouth opened and closed like a fish's. All the air that could come out had come out, and none was getting in. I put my hand on his arm and said, 'You're going to breathe, just the wind got knocked out of you.' I shouldn't have said *just*; the wind had been knocked out of him, yes, but he'd likely broken his back. Maybe worse, depending how he landed.

Cary came out and kneeled on the other side of him; she looked at him, then at me. He was trying to say something, but all he could do was make little puffs of air. 'Breathe,' I said. 'Just breathe.' I put my ear against his mouth and listened: three puffs, a pause, three more puffs.

Then, suddenly, I understood: 'Call my wife.'

'Of course,' I said. 'Of course we will.'

But he didn't have enough air to give us the number; that was all he could say, just those three words.

He passed out briefly, and I said, 'Hey, stay with us – don't go anywhere.'

He opened his eyes, closed them again. 'Hang in there,' I kept saying.

Sirens. Then the lights of an ambulance. In New York there would have been a crowd, but in Chilmark it was just me and Cary.

After the man was gone, we called the number on the side of his truck. His name was Russell, but he went by Sarge. The woman who answered the phone said she'd call Kerry, his wife. Sarge and Kerry, a roofer and his wife. That was all we knew. A few hours later, two men came by to get the truck and ladder.

We were so consumed with what had just happened that we didn't notice, not until hours later, that the flies, every last one of them, were gone. Not dead on the counters and windowsills and couch cushions, just gone, suddenly, as if they'd never been there.

They came back for a few days in July, and a few in August, as if to remind us that they had been real and could return, regardless of our wishes otherwise.

Notes for *The Book of Why*, 2002

PEOPLE MISSING LIMBS *don't grow new ones because they don't believe they can, because they've never seen it done. People don't live to be two hundred because they've never seen someone live to be two hundred. People don't reverse, or at least pause, the aging process because they don't believe that it can be done. People don't understand that the human body is miraculous. The human body isn't meant to break down; we believe it will because it's all we know. But let me tell you: the human body is meant to go on and on. The human body is a self-healing wonder. Just ask anyone who had cancer one day and didn't the next. Believe me — they're out there. I have letters from them. They know the truth: If you can see something done in your mind's eye, it can be done. Anything imaginable is possible.*

Even if you receive a diagnosis of a disease one day, your body can be disease-free the next. If you believe that your body is disease-free, and if you maintain that certainty, that vibration of health, more than you maintain your awareness of the disease, then it will not — it cannot

— remain in your body. It's there only because you believe it's there; it manifested only because you believed it could.

Look around you, no matter where you are, no matter how you may be feeling, and notice something that pleases you. Best not to wait for something pleasing to find you. You aren't creating pleasure, you aren't artificially manufacturing it, you're simply noticing what's already around you. The way sunlight slants through a thin crack in the canopy of trees above you and illuminates your wife's hair as you both pause on your walk through the woods beside your house. The colors of leaves; the rings inside a felled tree; the earthy smell of the dirt trail, a whiff of mint and wet leaves. Focus on the slant of sunlight on your wife's hair and notice how you feel. Focus on keeping, not losing. Focus on what's here, now. Feel good about feeling good. Don't dwell on the tiny bones your dog has dug up; this isn't about finding something upsetting and fixing it. This is about deciding that there's nothing to be upset about — not in your world, not in the one you're perpetually in the process of creating. Best not to dwell on the felled tree; best to imagine the lightning strike that split the trunk; best to imagine that kind of power inside you. The more you practice appreciation, the better you'll feel; the better you feel, the more you'll want to notice pleasing things; the more you notice pleasing things, the more pleasure you'll attract into your life. Every time you appreciate something in the universe, you are saying, 'More of this, please.' But you won't need to speak, you won't need to ask — your thoughts and feelings will be enough. When we say or feel thank you, *the universe says you're welcome*, as in: you're welcome to more of this, to more of anything you want.

PLEASE UNDERSTAND: I'D always believed that I could save things; that it was my responsibility. My father, my mother, strangers, objects, the entire world. Cary, of course.

Foolish, especially when someone doesn't need to be saved, or doesn't want to be, or can't be, but I've never been able to help myself.

Which is ironic, I guess: a self-help author who can't help himself.

I'm tempted to say that this is my first literal self-help book – the first meant to help *me*.

The first time I spoke to an audience, I felt as if I was doing what I'd been put on this earth to do. There was no doubt. It was instantly clear – even clearer when people spoke to me after – that my entire life had been leading to that moment; that everything I'd ever done had been in preparation for this; that this was going to be my life's work.

Here's what it feels like: The right words keep finding my lips; they come from a part of me stronger and more articulate than the me the world normally hears from. I tell the audience that I don't need my notes and toss them onto the floor. I move to the edge of the stage. I walk up and down the aisles. I look directly into their eyes and mean every word I say. I'm not a showman; I'm not loud. If anything, I'm quiet. But the quieter I am, the more hushed the audience becomes, and the louder my quiet is. I have some tics (I'm aware of them; I've seen them on video). I rub my beard too much. I rock my weight back and forth from one leg to the other. I keep my hands in my pockets. I wear a jacket and tie but always sneakers. I take long pauses to allow the audience to think about what I've just said. Sometimes I say, 'I want you to think about what I've just said.' Or 'Take a moment right now and think about that.' Often I'll say, 'Listen to me' or 'Here's the truth' or 'If there's one thing you take away from this seminar, this is it' or 'What I'm about to say – imagine it's written in capital letters.' I'll say things like 'I *know* you can do this, I know every one of you can.' I'll say, 'Be patient – you'll get where you need to go.' I'll say, 'Trust me.' I'll say, 'I've never been more certain about something in my life.'

I can access the feeling even now, nine years since that last talk in Las Vegas. I miss it. The way they lean forward in their seats; the way they write furiously in their notebooks; the way they blink. I've always found something sweetly vulnerable in a blink, something the body must do. During some pauses – long moments of silence during which I'd look from face to face and send my intention for peace and happiness, all their desires fulfilled – I'd see nothing but blinks. I'd become aware of my own. I'd play a game: try not to blink. A minute, two minutes, the eyes water, they hurt, the room blurs, and then, just for a fraction of a second, it's all gone, everywhere darkness, and then the eyes open again and the world is still there, where you'd left it, and you wonder if it's the same world. Games I'd play. Fun, at first. Then something else. During one talk, in Philadelphia, I started to cry. I don't mean that my eyes watered from the blinking game, but that I cried; that I felt something – even now I can't name what it was – that made me terribly sad, and it had something to do, best guess, with the word *must*: all the things a human body must do: blink, eat, shit, sleep, die.

And then I changed my thinking. I thought of all the things the human body does on its own: it grows, it pumps blood, it breathes.

I took a few deep breaths.

I told them that my tears were tears of joy. Something about how miraculous the body is, how limitless.

In the weeks after my father died, I couldn't sleep. I'd wake early and wait downstairs in the dark for the sound of newspapers dropped on the stoop. Then I'd fold and rubber-band them. If it was raining, I'd put each paper in a plastic bag. I couldn't stand the quiet, so I'd put on the TV. A color bar made a long, piercing beep; I kept folding papers while the station flatlined. I changed the channel, changed it again: TV snow, a swirling gray-white blizzard I could get lost in if I moved closer to the TV and stared long enough. An avalanche that could break me until I was nothing but a peaceful thought tumbling through beautiful white. Sometimes, in the snow, I could hear whispers, but never words I recognized.

And then the snow was gone and a man was preaching. His gray hair had been combed over his otherwise bald head; he was sweating, huffing into his microphone. He wore brown polyester pants and a striped tie that hung well below his belt. He stood before a young dark-skinned woman in a wheelchair and laid his hand on her shoulder. *Create a new spinal cord in the name of Jesus Christ our Lord and Savior. Create a new spinal cord right now. All things are possible to he who believeth. We thank you, God, for a new spine in Jesus' name. Hallelujah. Hallelujah.* The woman slumped in her wheelchair, eyes closed. The preacher turned to other people standing in a line. *Well, are you ready?* He went from one person to the next and laid his hand on each head and spoke in tongues, and one by one they fell back into arms waiting to catch them. Then he stopped in front of a child whose legs were in braces. He gestured for everyone to give him space. He hunched over the girl – she was tiny – and touched her head. *I lay my hands upon this little one. By the direction of the Lord, in obedience to the law of contact transmission – oh my, oh my, oh my my, my my my my – the healing power of God Almighty is ministered to this body, to undo that which Satan has wrought, to affect a healing therein from the top of her head to the soles of her feet.* The girl fell back. *In the name of Jesus. Say it again, everybody. In the name of Jesus. Amen. Amen.* Another line had formed; he touched each person, and one by one they fell back. An old woman wearing a red beehive wig. A tall, thin man in a powder blue suit. Twin girls wearing matching red dresses. A woman holding an infant. A teenager with arms crossed in either boredom or defiance. They all fell, and the preacher spoke in tongues, and when he was finished he said, I *felt the electricity of the Holy Spirit go into every one of you. You mustn't lose faith. Keep the switch of faith turned on. A few years back a woman brought me her child, three or four years old. Both of that poor child's feet were deformed. Now, I've seen a child with one club foot, but never did see one with both of them. Well, I took that dear child in my arms and held those little feet in my hands and I could feel the healing power of God go into them. But when I looked down, those feet were just as deformed as they ever were. I told the girl's mother, I felt the electricity of the Holy Spirit go into those feet, your child is healed, that's all I know. You need to keep the switch of faith turned on, don't let Satan bring doubt into your heart. The healing power of God is working on the feet. Well, two weeks later she brought that child back and held her up for the congregation to see, and both feet were perfect.*

Every night that year, the year of healing, I slept with my hand on her head. She fell asleep first, and I would wrap one arm around her, and with my other hand I would touch her head. I would close my eyes, and in the dark beneath my eyelids see whiteness, what looked like TV snow, and I would think, *I send you an intention for complete and long-lasting wellness. I send you complete and long-lasting wellness. I send you complete and everlasting wellness. I send us both complete and everlasting wellness. I intend for you a long and happy life filled with peace, perfect health, and well-being. I am pre-grateful for your long and happy life filled with peace, perfect health, and well-being. I am pre-grateful for our long and happy life together filled with peace, perfect health, and well-being.*

Electricity counts.

Brilliant if you were *it*, infuriating if you weren't.

Tag, the simplest game children play, was my least favorite. A game you don't choose as much as it chooses you: someone tags you, a hand on your back, *You're it*. The other children run away, and the only thing to do is chase. Otherwise you're *it* for the rest of the day. We'd hide in the bushes beside the rectory or behind the statue of Mary. I'd chase, but not to catch, not for the fun of catching, but rather to not be *it*, to relieve myself of that burden. If I was lucky enough to tag someone, that person would tag me back and run away. Sometimes we'd tag each other back and forth a dozen times. One time I had the idea to run around a parked car; the girl who was *it* would never be able to tag me. But after five or six dizzying sprints around the car, she stopped. I was leaning against the hood to catch my breath. She touched the bumper and said, 'You're it – electricity counts!'

I wanted to say, *If electricity counts, then you're it, because your feet are touching the ground and so are mine.*

But then she could have said the same to me.

In which case, the entire world was *it*.

Love connects people at a molecular level; their cells become entangled. If you poke one, the other flinches. Once two particles have interacted intensely, even if you separate them by miles, years, lifetimes, they behave as if they're still connected.

Sounds nice. A story like any other. A fairy tale, some might say. Wishful thinking.

But this one has been tested.

Two people with close ties – in most cases, lovers or spouses – are placed in separate rooms. One of them, the healer, watches a monitor. At random intervals the image of the healer's beloved – sitting in an electromagnetically shielded room – appears on the screen. The healer sends the beloved compassionate intentions upon seeing his or her face. Scientists have found physical evidence – changes in perspiration, temperature, heart rate, and blood flow – that one person's thoughts can affect another person's body.

I didn't need this study to believe – I'd been writing about this, in my own way, for years – but it renewed my hope that I could do this alone, that even if Cary had lost faith in her ability to heal herself, or if she'd never really had it in the first place, then no matter: I would focus my every thought on her wellness. I would meditate on it, envision it, be certain of it. I would take her life in my hands. Literally. Through summer and fall and winter, as long as it took, I would lay my hands on her head and the tumors would shrink, then disappear.

It was winter and we were still in Chilmark, but in my mind it was spring and we were back in Brooklyn: the first bud in our garden, a walk beneath blooming cherry trees, Ralph chasing a tennis ball in Prospect Park. I laid my hand on Cary's head as she slept and visualized the future we wanted. Cary would be writing songs again. I would write *The Book of Why*, and this would be its happy ending: the year of healing, the year of entanglement.

But she lost more and more: words, weight, balance, pockets of memory. Some days, for long minutes, she forgot me; she stared and stared, but couldn't name me. *Husband*, I would say, and she would repeat this word, would stare at me, and I would wait, would push aside my fear that she'd never remember, and eventually she would nod and say, *Husband*, and smile, and I would kneel on the floor at her feet and lay my head on her lap.

The dog she never forgot, even though there were moments when she lost the name. *Puppy* or *Pooch* or *Big Ears* or *Buttercup* all meant *Ralph*. Even on the coldest, shortest winter days, when night came too early, there was always Ralph to lie with on the floor or bed. I'd watch them, or sometimes join them, and visualize a clean brain scan. I'd imagine the tumor shrinking from the size of a cherry to the size of a pea to the size of a mustard seed, to nothing.

I F THIS WERE a fairy tale, I would end with a wedding.

We were married in Flushing Meadows Park; it used to be an ash dump before Robert Moses turned it into the World's Fair. We had the ceremony near the Unisphere, a stainless-steel globe twelve stories high. The fountains surrounding the globe sprayed us, and I wanted us to move, but Cary wanted to stay, so we stayed.

When the officiant, Cary's uncle, pronounced us husband and wife, Cary kicked off her shoes and waded into the reflecting pool; she walked to the base of the globe. If I wanted to kiss the bride, I had to follow.

Our guests cheered when I took off my shoes, louder when I walked across the water, louder when I kissed her, then they took off their shoes and came into the water, too.

Moments earlier, during the ceremony, her uncle had said, 'Life can't be predicted. No life already lived can prepare you for your own. You can't plan your life,' he'd said. 'Because, let me tell you, it's already been planned *for* you.'

Our friends stood around us in the reflecting pool, and we looked up through the world at the sun.

The world had been built to withstand the burden of its own weight. But it was permeable: rain and snow would fall through its latticework; wind would blow from the inside as well as the outside.

When I was eleven, my parents took me to Flushing Meadows to see the monument where a time capsule had been buried the year I was born. The capsule was fifty feet belowground. Credit cards, cigarettes, tranquilizers, a bikini, a Bible, a plastic heart valve – all of it waiting for someone to dig it up five thousand years later.

All I could think that day and night and for the many days and nights that followed was: *Five thousand years from now, five thousand years from now, there will be people five thousand years from now*.

When we walked past the Unisphere that day, there was a man climbing it. His name, I now know, was George, a toymaker from Queens, and he waved to us. There was another man, already at the top of the world, filming the climb. I said to my parents, 'I want to do that. I want to climb the world,' and my mother said, 'Don't be ridiculous – that's a fine way to kill yourself.'

The year my father died, two Voyager spacecraft were launched, each containing a gold-plated record put together by Carl Sagan. People from around the world were asked to record a greeting for beings in the universe who might someday, perhaps billions of years later, find the spacecraft. I kept asking my parents if my voice could be on the record, if someone could hear my voice in a billion years, and they said no, but I could record my own message and bury the tape in the yard. But I never did.

We in this world send you our goodwill. Dear friends, we wish you the best. Good health to you now and forever. We wish all of you well. Are you well? Hope everyone's well. We are thinking about you all. Please come here to visit when you have time. We are happy here and you be happy there. Let there be peace everywhere. God give you peace always. Wishing you happiness, goodness, good health, and many years. May the honors of the morning be upon your heads. Friends of space, how are you all? Have you eaten yet? Come visit us if you have time. Welcome home. It is a pleasure to receive you. Good night, ladies and gentlemen. Goodbye and see you next time.

Also included on Carl Sagan's Golden Record: earth sounds.

Thunder, wind, rain, crickets, frogs, birds, whale song, laughter, a heartbeat, the sound of a kiss, a baby crying.

Also included: data from his wife's brain and heart.

She was hooked up to a computer; all she had to do was think and feel. She thought about war, violence, poverty, the challenges of being human, what it feels like to love.

THIS STORY COULD also end with a walk to Prospect Park. It was her idea to come back to Brooklyn. It was too cold on Martha's Vineyard, too empty off-season. She wanted to be around people again, to see her friends.

A man who looks like me wakes to freezing rain against the bedroom window. His wife has been in bed two days; she hasn't eaten.

The dog cries to go out, but the man who looks like me tells her to lie down. She continues to cry, and he says, 'No more – enough,' and she goes downstairs to cry by the door.

He doesn't want to get up. Doesn't want to leave his wife alone.

But the dog is restless; he hasn't run her for two weeks. She's been regressing. Seven years old, but acting like a puppy: chewing socks, shoes, table legs. She wants attention; she wants to play. Their last run, around the park, he cut short; he panicked and hurried home.

The dog's whine is pitched higher now; she'll do anything not to have an accident. A few more minutes and he'll get up. His wife is facing him, and he's holding her hand, which is warm, and it occurs to him that nothing can go wrong as long as he's holding her hand. He leans his head against hers and thinks how close he is to *it*. Only a few inches. Yet he can't touch *it*. Even the surgeons can't. So close, and he can hear the dog pacing down by the door, and he catches himself trying to befriend *it*, as ridiculous as that might sound, as if *it* has a persona and might be convinced to alter its course. Then, his hand on her head, he grows angry and imagines being able to reach into her, being able to perform the surgery on his own, as preposterous as that might sound years later, as I write about it. As if he can do what the surgeons can't.

He closes his eyes, takes a few deep breaths. He's grateful to be able to hold her hand. The story he tells himself – one that might get him through the morning – is that as long as he's touching her, nothing bad can happen.

He remembers: electricity counts.

He remembers: keep the switch of faith open.

He remembers reading about a couple, married fifty years, that had never been more than ten feet apart. They showered together. When one used the toilet, the other sat on the tub's ledge and read a magazine without the least bit embarrassment. They were both artists and worked in the same room. If one woke inspired in the middle of the night and wanted to paint, the other would come to their studio and paint too, or sleep on a cot near the canvas. If one woke thirsty, the other would come along to the kitchen for a glass of water.

The man who looks like me decides, as he holds his wife's hand and listens to her breathe, that he will one-up that couple. Forget ten feet; he and his wife, from now on, will always be touching.

But there's the problem of the dog.

Not that the dog is a problem. Not that the dog hasn't been a huge help. Not that the dog isn't what his wife still responds most to. Not that she doesn't reach to pet the dog even when she's weak. Not that anything truly bad could happen – another story the man tells himself – as long as the dog is in the room.

He makes a rule: The only time he's allowed to stop touching his wife is to walk the dog.

The dog likes the cold, likes to sniff yellow snow, likes to play invisible dog: she gets low to the ground, on her belly, whenever another dog approaches, as if the other dog won't be able to see her, tail fanning out the snow behind her. She likes to sniff the other dog's mouth and rear. The other dog's owner, an old bearded man who looks like his terrier, likes to talk. Not that there's anything wrong with talking. Not that talking isn't the friendly thing to do when your dogs are sniffing each other and your leashes are tangled. This man wants to know how old Ralph is, is she a pure breed, how do you keep her so lean, how'd she get a girl name. He likes to talk about his previous dogs – names, breeds, how long they lived, how they died. He likes to talk about the weather. Roads are icy, yes. More snow than predicted, yes. Plows were out early this morning, yes. Plowed in his car, now he has to dig it out. Not that there's anything wrong with such conversation. Not that there's anything wrong with saying have a nice day, careful on the ice.

The man who looks like me yanks the leash, but the dog tenses: she won't move until she has thoroughly sniffed a yellow circle in the snow. He pulls harder, and this time she gives in. He says, *Pee*, and she sniffs for a spot, finds one, squats, stands again and circles the spot, sniffs for a better one, squats again, stops, moves a few feet to the right, a few feet to the left, back to her original spot, and the man pulls on the leash, perhaps too hard, and says, *Let's go already – pee, for God's sake!* A woman and her daughter pass, and the man feels like a dope. Not for being angry with his dog, not for pulling too hard on the leash, but for saying the word *pee*. The girl is wearing a school uniform, and she's holding her mother's hand, and the man who looks like me waits for the dog to pee and hurries back to the house.

He'll heat some vegetable broth; he'll break ice into chips to feed her; then he'll get into bed and get up only if she gets up. And to walk the dog, of course. And to use the bathroom. And to eat. And to answer the door if the bell rings. Though he doesn't have to answer the door or the phone; he doesn't have to gather the mail in the foyer. As long as he takes care of his and the dog's bodily functions, he can otherwise keep touching her, and nothing bad can happen.

But when he goes inside after having walked the dog, she's sitting on the edge of the bed, pulling up socks. This after days of her not eating or getting dressed. This after days of having to wash her in bed, her face and arms and legs, and drying her.

When he asks what she's doing she says – she *says* – that

she'd like to go for a walk. This after weeks of her not having said much, of her not knowing the word *walk*, of her having to sign the word, her fingers walking.

This story could end there – with the feeling the man has when he sees his wife pulling up her socks; when he hears the word *walk* come out of her mouth. He has read about such miracles. Spontaneous remissions. His readers have sent him letters. One day not long for this world, the next day dancing. He thinks now that *walk* is the most amazing word in the English language, in *any* language. There need be no other word. The dog knows this word and gets excited. His wife pulls on her boots. Stands. Smiles. Says, 'Let's go for a walk.' I'd like to hook the man who looks like me up to a monitor and record his feelings at that moment – the dog's feelings, too – and send them out into space to be discovered and interpreted billions of years from now, and we could end the story there.

Part Seven

Hello Goodbye

NATURE TRIES TO make amends: storm clouds part for the last minutes of sun. We stand on the lawn and watch a sun pillar rise from the horizon, flicker, then disappear: the umbilical cord connecting heaven and earth has been snipped, and true night, not the false night of the storm, begins to cloak the damage we survey now by flashlight.

Sam's car is still parked by the cemetery gate; a tree limb has shattered the windshield. Beneath the lone working streetlight, water gushes from the hole where a fire hydrant used to be. Boys stand beside the hole, reach out cautiously, pull back their hands before touching the water.

A white cat emerges from the leaves of an uprooted tree with a dead bird, then walks slowly across a street empty of traffic.

The front yard is a mess of roof tiles and glass. Gloria reaches for something shiny in the grass; her grandmother tells her to get back on the porch. She sits in a cloud of smoke from her mother's cigarette. She signs to her mother, pats her hands together twice, right palm over left.

'No school tomorrow,' her mother says. She flicks her cigarette onto the lawn. 'School might not be standing.'

A tree limb impales the house below a second-floor window. Jay brings out a ladder, tells everyone to get out of the way. He climbs up to pull the limb loose, but it's in there good, he says, so he decides to wait until morning, when he can use a chainsaw to cut it into pieces.

Sam sweeps glass too small to pick up by hand. A helicopter hovers above the hospital for a few minutes before landing on the roof. Dinah crosses herself. Gloria mimics her. She looks at me, and I look away. I put on work gloves and gather glass, dumping it in a trash can that doesn't belong to the Fosters but must have blown onto their property as if sent for this very purpose. My ears are ringing. When I straighten after bending, my head becomes light. The world drains of color, and I can see only black and white. I blink, and color returns: the red stripes on my sneakers, the purple sky, the pink ribbons in Gloria's hair.

They offer us a room: water stains on the ceiling, toys piled high in the closet, dozens of empty hooks and hangers. The window has blown in; bunk beds lie side by side. There are no pillows, and the white fitted sheets are covered with glass. We remove the sheets and glass and sleep on bare mattresses.

In the dark Sam says, 'Now what?'

'We go to sleep.'

'You know what I mean,' she says. 'The girl's name.'

'I don't know what we're supposed to do.'

'Do you know her?'

'I've never seen her before.'

'Do you know any of these people?'

'No.'

'Are you sure?'

'I decided years ago that I'm not sure about much, but I'm sure I don't know them.'

Ralph snores on the floor beside me. The buzzing inside my head is interrupted only by the helicopter bringing more wounded to the hospital.

I wake cold in the dark, too tired to move my mattress away from the window. Sam faces away from me, knees to chest, fetal. She's using her jacket as a blanket. Ralph is gone. Probably thirsty, pawing a toilet lid. Probably hungry, too.

I walk through the hallway over the creaking wood floor: a child sneaking out of his room. I'm waiting for a bedroom door to open and my parents to ask what I'm doing up, tell me to go back to bed.

At the top of the stairs I whisper Ralph's name, then listen for her nails on the floor. I say her name again, louder. I hear something downstairs; might be her crying to go out, might be a dog on the street.

When I reach the first floor, I can see that someone left a TV on, the volume low. The portable TV, which sits atop a larger one in the living room, is so tiny that I have to stand directly in front of it and lean in to see the people on screen. A black-and-white movie, a blonde telling a man in a fedora − a poor man's Bogart − that she's sorry, over and over she tells him, while he smokes a cigarette, pours himself a drink. He says goodbye. She says, 'Don't say that – please don't.' He tells her they both knew from the beginning how this would end. The acting is melodramatic, but I don't care. I do the math, as always when I see an old movie, and the numbers tell me the same thing: the actors, all of them, unless they're children, sometimes even then, are gone. Yet here they are – their faces, their voices – in a year they'd never know, in a world they couldn't have imagined.

A voice in the dark, behind me – a whisper, it sounds like, but not words. I turn and wait for my eyes to adjust.

She's lying on the couch, Ralph beside her. White pajamas, pigtails. Her dolls are on her lap, their hair standing up, brides of Frankenstein.

'How did you pick their names?'

She slides the palm of her right hand over the back of her left.

'I don't understand.'

She keeps making the same sign.

'Something about an airplane?'

She tries a different sign; it looks like her hands are galloping.

'Horse?'

Her face laughs, but she makes no sound.

'I'm sorry,' I tell her, and she tries the first sign again – slides the palm of her right hand over the back of her left.

'She never lived near any beach.'

Her mother is at the foot of the stairs, holding a flashlight. She wears white sweatpants pulled up to her knees, a long black shirt that reads: BORN AGAIN? WHAT MAKES YOU THINK YOU'LL GET IT RIGHT THIS TIME?

'She's telling you she used to live near the beach.'

Gloria touches her lips with her index finger, then points.

'If *you* say it's true,' Evelyn says.

'She has an overactive imagination,' Evelyn tells me. 'Probably grow up to be a writer.'

Gloria kisses two fingers, and they fly away from her mouth like birds.

'Oh, that's right,' Evelyn says. 'She's a singer.'

She turns to Gloria. 'What did we say about sleeping?'

Gloria leans her face against her palm.

'Then what are you doing down here?'

Gloria points to the TV.

'That's my own fault,' Evelyn says. 'Shouldn't have taken that out. But I had to watch my shows.'

'I came down looking for Ralph,' I tell her. 'I thought she might be hungry.'

'There's a bologna heel in the fridge,' Evelyn says.

Ralph follows Gloria into the kitchen.

'Smell it first,' Evelyn says.

From behind me comes music, the end of the movie.

'I shouldn't blame her,' Evelyn says. 'I used to do the same when I was little. Never liked to sleep alone. Probably why I married so young.'

She pulls a cigarette from a pack on the coffee table.

'Has Gloria ever spoken?'

'She talks in her sleep,' Evelyn says. 'Some nights we hear her, and we go in to listen. We even recorded her a few times.'.

She finds a book of matches in the pocket of a coat draped over a chair. 'One left,' she says. 'Fingers crossed it works.' She strikes the match and it catches, but it dies as she touches it to her cigarette; she puffs furiously, but only part of the cigarette lights. 'Probably a sign I should quit,' she says. She looks through the coat pockets again, then tries the jackets in the closet. 'Bingo,' she says when she finds a lighter. 'I'll quit when I'm forty,' she says. 'They say every cell in your body's new every seven years.'

Gloria signs to her mother.

'Sorry,' Evelyn says. 'Back to bed.'

Gloria runs upstairs, and Ralph follows her.

Evelyn taps her cigarette over her palm; she holds out her hand as if offering me the ashes. 'Here I am again,' she says. 'Just like when I was a kid – up late with the boob tube. I don't even care what's on.'

The screen goes dark, and with it the room. 'Batteries must be dead,' she says. 'Surprised they worked at all – we haven't used that TV in years.' She stands, groans like an old woman even though she's in her twenties. 'I think we have some batteries in the kitchen drawer,' she says.

I wait to see if she'll find any. 'Shit,' she says. 'I would've sworn we had some in here.'

'I can help look.'

She sighs. 'Soon it'll be morning,' she says.

I leave her in the dark, flicking the lighter.

I find Sam sitting on the windowsill, one leg outside, the moon low above the cemetery. I stand in the doorway, not wanting to frighten her, watching her foot to make sure it doesn't lose contact with the floor.

She moves suddenly, and I take a step toward her.

She pulls her leg back into the room. 'Don't worry,' she says. 'I wasn't going to jump.'

'I wasn't sure what you were doing.'

'There was a couple fighting,' she says. 'The guy said, "You always have to have the last word!" And she said, "No, I don't." And he said, "Right there – you're doing it again." And she said, "No, I'm not." I thought he was going to hit her.'

She closes the window. 'Weird, but it reminded me of my brother.'

'What about him?'

'We had a joke when we were kids,' she says. 'My father would have these mood swings. He'd call us in this voice, and we just knew. He'd put us in chairs, back to back, and he'd circle us for hours, screaming about whatever, pitting us against each other – you know, which one of us was going to get the belt. The joke, if you want to call it that, was that whenever we heard his voice change, whenever we knew it was coming, one of us would say to the other, "Any last words?" and we'd crack up. But, in the end, there weren't any last words – no note, nothing.'

'I'm sorry,' I say. 'Actually, I can do better than that. How's this? Sometimes life really, really sucks, and it isn't fair, and I'm sorry.'

'Thanks,' she says. 'That *is* much better than I'm sorry.'

'I can't take credit for that one,' I say. 'I was jogging one morning, years ago, and I ran past a police officer trying to help this woman. She was in her forties, a big woman. She was wearing a white nightgown and one slipper, and she was having a nervous breakdown right there on the street. She was shaking and crying and she was just – I mean, she was in pain, you could *see* it. She was leaning against a brick building with that one slipper hanging off her foot, and people were watching, and there I was running my five miles, and just as I passed I heard the officer say, "Listen, I know. Sometimes life really, really sucks. But . . ." and I didn't hear what came after *but*.'

'Sometimes,' Sam says, 'I feel like that woman.'

I lie on my mattress, wince when I turn on my side. 'My ribs feel like that woman.'

'Did you check their medicine cabinet?'

'Didn't see one.'

'Are you sure?'

'Nothing above the sink, not even a mirror.'

'My husband was afraid of mirrors.' Sam sits on her mattress, hugs her knees. 'At home, in clothing stores, he'd avoid them. The rearview mirror in our car – he'd turn it so that it faced out. Not the safest way to drive. His own reflection was the only thing in the world he was afraid of.'

'He was probably afraid of many things.'

'He wasn't even afraid of my father,' she says. 'I think my father was afraid of *him*, and I was like, Okay, *this* is the guy – he'll keep me safe.'

She lies back on her mattress and turns away from me. 'He was much worse than my father.'

'Where is he now?'

'Don't know,' she says. 'Don't care.'

A few minutes later she says, 'I'm pretty sure he was gay.'

'Your husband?'

'My brother,' she says. 'I think that's why my father was so hard on him. My father knew, even though my brother never came out. He died when he was sixteen. I don't think he ever had a boyfriend.'

Before I can say anything: 'He used a gun,' she says. 'It was my father's, so maybe that was my brother's last word, his final fuck you. My father found him and made me look. He dragged me into the bathroom and said, "Look what he did to me," as if *he* was the victim. But I didn't want that in my mind for the rest of my life. When my father turned my head, I closed my eyes. He dragged me out of the bathroom, and that's when I realized someone would clean it up, would take my brother away, so I broke free from my father and looked. Just for a second, and I was much calmer then. But I had to look again, to be sure. He was facedown, but it was really him.'

I move my mattress closer to hers and put my hand on her back. 'If I knew what came after *but*,' I tell her, 'I'd say it now.'

I WALK RALPH in the cemetery, letting her off leash even though a sign tells me not to. When she was younger she would have bounded alongside these graves, would have chased squirrels and woodchucks, would have tried in vain to eat bees and butterflies, would have found sticks and played keep-away with me and Cary, but at twelve she stays by my side, sniffs flowers and trees. Cary used to say dogs were made by God so God could slow down and smell the grass. Ralph reminds me time and again that life can be just this – a blade of grass. Then this – a single footprint drying in mud beside a gravestone. But the human asks questions: Whose footprint, why barefoot, why only one? Better to be a dog: the entire universe is one flower, then the entire universe is the next flower – the ever-present present, nothing more. This overturned gravestone, for example, or this one, forced prostrate by the wind, facedown as if to imprint the names of the dead into the earth.

Back at the house, Jay tells Evelyn that he needs to pick up wood from a friend; the storm ripped off the roof of the shed in the backyard. Evelyn tells him to take Gloria for the ride.

I offer to go with him, help load his truck.

'I'll be fine,' he says.

'I'd like to show some gratitude.'

'Unnecessary,' he says.

'It'll make me feel useful,' I tell him, and he says okay.

We drive along roads bordered by farms. The smell of manure wafts in the air and into the open car windows. Cows chew grass and swat flies with their involuntary tails while two horses lie side by side, the water trough only a few feet away. We turn onto another, smaller road, where Amish children bike uphill against the wind, trying to steer while holding on to their hats.

Gloria sits between me and Jay, clicking her seat belt.

Jay says, 'Hey, leave that alone.'

She clicks it once more, then buckles the belt.

Jay swerves the car to avoid a tree limb in the road. My seat belt has too much give, and my side slams into the door. 'Sorry about that,' Jay says. He has a calm demeanor, someone you'd want in charge during a tornado, but he has subtle nervous habits – rubbing his shaved head, straightening his thick eyebrows. I can see now, when I look at him closely, that he really is no more than twenty-three or twenty-four, though already much older – worry lines on his face, dirt beneath his fingernails, in the cracks in his palms. He and Evelyn must have had Gloria when they were teenagers.

We park in a dirt lot filled with dozens of vehicles, mostly pickup trucks. Beyond the lot are tables and booths set up in rows – an outdoor flea market. I feel pulled back into an old self, or perhaps an old self is pulled back into me – the young man who wanted to save everything, who couldn't walk past a stoop sale without bringing home cards, photos, glasses without lenses, any objects that called out to me, and who couldn't help but look for signs in these objects, and who made them into junk sculptures, sold them as art for a few years after college, before I wrote my first book.

I stop to look through old photo albums: the long-ago dead walking along a beach, black-and-white wedding photos, the adult eyes of children at the beginning of the twentieth century. Stacks of postcards, many with notes written on the back. I close my eyes, count to ten, then randomly select a postcard. An old game. A photograph of St Pancras Church in Rome – the same name as my parish in Queens. Coincidence, I tell myself, and even if not, even if it *is* a sign, what to do with the sign, how to know what it means? Perhaps there are signs everywhere, but in the end they add up to nothing – a scavenger hunt with no prize. Thirty years later, I remember the facts we were made to memorize in grade school. Pancras, whose name in Greek means 'the one who holds everything,' was a Christian convert martyred – beheaded at fourteen. An orphan, he's the patron saint of children. The note on the back of the postcard reads, 'Having a nice time but missing you. Nice seeing you recently. Love, GDN.' I can't make out the name of the addressee, but my father's initials are enough to make me buy the postcard.

Years ago, when I told my shrink about the signs I would find in objects, he said, 'Eric, what's the story you're telling yourself?'

'That nothing is random,' I told him. 'That there's an order to the universe, a reason for everything.'

'And if that were true?'

'Then I could make sure—'

'Make sure what?'

'I don't know,' I said.

'What would it mean,' he said, 'if your story weren't true – if there's no reason for the things that happen?'

'I'd probably – I don't know what I'd do,' I said.

'Breathe,' he said, and I tried.

'Eric,' he said, 'I want you to know, it doesn't matter to me what you believe. But here's what I'd like us to figure out – the difference between what you believe and what you really *want* to believe.'

Jay is holding a revolver. On the table behind him are carbines and muskets and rifles with bayonets. They don't look to my amateur eye like the kinds of guns people would use today to shoot deer or ducks or each other; they invoke duels more than anything. Jay points the revolver at his own head. He says, 'Any last words?' Then he puts his other hand on his chin and looks up to the sky as if deep in thought, but just as he opens his mouth to speak, he makes a sound meant to be a gun firing, and this makes Gloria laugh. She signs something, and Jay says, 'Too late. You only get one shot at last words.'

He puts down the gun and picks up Gloria, holds her

upside down by her feet. She's screaming, but I get the sense they've played this game before. The last thing she wants is to be put down. 'Any last words?' he says, and her screams become laughter, and he asks again, 'Any last words?' and now she's gasping, and he lifts her higher and asks again, he pretends to drop her but stops before she hits the ground. He flips her right side up, her hair wild and face red. She signs something, and her father says, 'No more – that's enough.'

We keep walking. I can't not stop to look: rows of lamps in the shape of Greek gods; bins filled with brass doorknobs; baseball mitts flat as pancakes; cast-iron pans people fried eggs in a hundred years ago; old chocolate tins and cigar boxes and castor oil bottles; scalpels and specula, lancets and forceps and curettes; handcuffs and straitjackets and horse bits; stocks and pillories; daggers and swords and military helmets; stacks of Superman comics; dolls dressed in wedding gowns, their eyes rattling in their skulls; mannequin heads in a bathtub; wigs blowing along the ground like skittish animals.

Jay stops to speak with a leather-faced man selling old *Life* magazines and used books. Gloria is looking through boxes of Beatles records. The man brings Jay eight long pieces of wood. They speak in shorthand, the way some men do. Wife is fine, kids are fine, house is fine, business is slow, no need to thank him for the wood, and then we're leaving, four pieces of wood each, and I wonder if I've missed a sign, some clue as to why I'm here, what I'm supposed to say or do next.

In the parking lot, we load wood onto the truck. Gloria is humming your song again. I ask how she knows the song, did she write it. She shrugs. I hear my shrink's voice from twenty years ago: 'The mind can be quite powerful,' he said, 'when we're desperate to believe something.'

During the drive home, alongside horses dreaming their thirsty dreams, cows tail-swatting the same persistent flies, an Amish woman hanging wash, Gloria starts humming your song again.

That night, after dinner, Sam says, 'Good news. We'll have a rental car in the morning.'

Gloria signs something to her mother.

'No,' Evelyn says. 'Ralph can't stay.'

Gloria signs something else.

'She's not your dog,' Evelyn says.

'I told you,' Jay says to Evelyn. 'We need to get her a dog.'

We're sitting on the porch. Through the screen I can hear the evening news. Something about the war – a war I know very little about except whatever my mother can't help sharing when I see her.

Gloria stares at me for a long while. She moves closer. She smiles, points to her own face, then holds out her arms.

'It's a game,' Evelyn says. 'She wants you to laugh big.'

'At what?'

'Doesn't matter,' Jay says.

I give Gloria a fake laugh.

She puts her index fingers on her cheeks, below her eyes, and pulls her fingers down.

'Cry small,' Jay says, and I pout my lips and sniffle and put my hands over my face and make the quiet sounds of crying.

She pulls my hands away from my face.

I stop crying; she looks into my eyes to make sure.

She makes another sign, and Jay says, 'Cry big,' and I cry louder, my shoulders shaking. She pulls my hands away from my face again.

In the morning, as we're about to leave, I tell Sam to wait. 'Forgot my keys,' I say.

I go upstairs to Gloria's room, where she's sleeping on her back, one arm stretched over the side of the bed, the other covering her eyes as if she's trying not to see whatever she's dreaming about.

I want to touch her face, cover her with a blanket. I want to ask, of course, if you're in there – if it's really you. I want to say something, leave a note under her pillow, but I have no idea what the note would say.

This book, I suppose, is that note.

For a few minutes I watch her breathe and imagine her older, a young woman. I see different versions of her life play out in my mind's eye. In some versions an older man who looks like me is telling her a story. We're sitting on a park bench, or in my house in Chilmark, or in the cemetery behind the house in Queens, but always I'm telling her this story. I keep asking her to tell me how it ends.

As we bring her bag up the stairs to her apartment – she lives a few blocks from the Flatiron – Sam says she has a bad feeling.

She'd said that in the car, too. She was afraid to go home, and so was I – to Chilmark, I mean – so I told her she could bring me to New York. No need to drive me all the way to the ferry. I'd see my mother – that would make her happy.

'Sometimes,' she'd said in the car, 'I just know things.'

She hesitates now before walking up the final flight to the fourth floor. Ralph is already up there, waiting for us.

I walk past her. 'What's the apartment number?'

'Four twelve,' she says. 'Second one on the left.'

It's evident right away that she's been robbed: knob broken, doorjamb split.

I walk into the apartment without fear, which is not to say that bravery is involved. There's a difference between bravery, which has to do with courage, and fearlessness, which has to do – at least in my case – with believing you have nothing more to lose.

An efficiency efficiently divided, rooms within a room. A kitchenette just big enough for two to stand back to back – one person can wash while the other dries, chop while the other cooks. There's a messy order to the place: books alphabetized by author on built-in shelves; three paint-splattered wooden chairs around a small table. Atop a large wood desk: piles of papers, coffee mug, laptop. Hanging on the walls are a few paintings and two blown-up photos: a man who could be her father, another who could be her brother. Same red hair, same shape to the lips. An unmade pull-out couch-bed, two armchairs, a small TV. An empty picture frame on top of the TV and another on a small end table. A bare wall with two hooks. Below each hook is the ghosting stain – a dark square – of whatever used to hang there. All of this, door to fire escape, in twelve steps. No other signs of a break-in: nothing on the floor, no drawers open.

'I knew it,' she says from the doorway.

'Your computer's still here.'

'That fucker.'

'Who?'

'Whoever did this.'

'It's safe to come in,' I tell her.

Ralph is exploring by smell: rug, bedsheets, Sam's shoes lined up by the door.

Sam walks in holding three weeks' worth of mail. She stands in the center of the room and turns in place; she drops the mail on the floor. Then she checks the bathroom; I hear her pull open the shower curtain.

She opens her closet door, parts her hanging shirts and

dresses. She looks through drawers – dresser, desk, kitchen – and keeps saying, 'Son of a bitch, son of a bitch,' and then stops at the fridge. A note made of magnets – tiny letters I can't see. I move closer and make out the words YOU'RE STILL MY, but she blocks my view. Then she swipes the magnets onto the floor.

'What did the magnets say?'

'Nothing,' she says.

'You should call the police.'

'Nothing's missing.'

'Not that you know.'

'There's nothing I'd be sorry to lose,' she says. 'Except that.' She points to the framed photo of her brother on the wall behind her desk: long hair, long eyelashes, eyes closed, mouth open as if about to speak.

'Even if nothing's missing, it's still a crime.'

Her cell phone rings in her pocket; she takes it out and silences it without looking to see who's calling.

'You should at least call a locksmith,' I tell her.

She sits on the couch and closes her eyes. Her cell phone rings again; she looks at the number, then removes the battery and lays the two pieces on the coffee table alongside a book called *Conversations with God*, an old *New Yorker*, and an ashtray filled with cigarette butts.

'I didn't know you smoked.'

'I don't,' she says.

Ralph is crying in the doorway; I realize that I've had the leash in my hand the entire time, wrapped around my clenched fist.

'Don't go,' Sam says.

'She's very smart, but she can't walk herself.'

'Okay, but come back.'

'I'm starting to smell,' I say.

'Come back and we'll take a shower.'

Then: 'I don't mean together. I just meant – Listen, I don't feel safe here.'

'I can push your desk in front of the door.'

'Fine,' she says. 'Then you won't be able to leave.'

She lets me have the couch-bed; she uses a sleeping bag on the floor. But when I wake in the night, she's beside me, on the edge of the mattress, one leg hanging off. She's very still when she sleeps; I can hardly see her back rise and fall. A pillow covers her head; she could be almost anyone.

Ralph is a lump in the glow of a clock's light. It's Ralph who makes this strange: she's out of context here. Still, she's happy anywhere and with anyone, a creature of the present; I love that most about her, but I've wished otherwise: that her sense of the past might extend beyond smell. Let me say it: that she might be able to grieve; that we might have shared it.

When I wake, Sam is standing at the stove in a red plaid nightshirt, spatula in hand. The table is set for two: plates, napkins, coffee cups, butter.

She's feeding Ralph pieces of bacon. She lets the dog lick her fingers, then goes back to cracking eggs.

'When's the locksmith coming?'

'Tomorrow,' she says.

'What's today?'

'Friday.'

'Feels like Sunday.'

I hook Ralph's leash onto her collar and open the door; she runs into the hallway and starts down the stairs.

'How do you like your eggs?'

'I'm not hungry.'

'Well, I'm making eggs.'

'I'm really not hungry.'

'If you *were* hungry, how would you want your eggs?'

'Sunny-side up.'

'I should have known,' she says. 'Do you drink coffee?'

'No.'

'Would you like tea?'

'No, thanks.'

'Listen,' she says, 'I was cold in the sleeping bag.'

Ralph is whimpering on the stairs.

'I'll have juice, okay.'

She looks in her fridge. 'No juice,' she says. 'Maybe you can get some while you're out.'

The locksmith doesn't come the next day, or the next, or the next, and I stop asking. I stop pretending that I have somewhere to go. We don't talk about the broken door or the note on the fridge or the fact that nothing was missing. I've stopped bugging her about calling the cops. We eat eggs and toast each morning, and now there's juice. Two walks a day, Madison Square to Union Square, Ralph limping more than she used to; her hips have had enough.

I think about leaving, but go back. No matter where I am

in the room, Sam's brother stares at me. Like the rest of the dead, he must watch over the living with dispassion: dandelion clocks and green streets, a girl's name whispered, clues in our sleep. We don't talk about her brother or you. We don't talk about the cologne I found in the bathroom; we don't talk about the suits in her closet, the men's shoes. We don't talk about the wedding ring still on my finger or the one in a box on her dresser. We don't talk about the electric bill addressed to a man with her last name. She'd be more careful if she didn't want me to know, but still I say nothing.

I look through her medicine cabinet: Prozac, sleeping pills, codeine long expired. An almost-empty shampoo bottle upside down on the lip of the tub; a white towel drying over the shower curtain rod; slippers on the bathmat that have taken on the shape of her feet. A panic rises up my chest and into my throat – I can't swallow – at my not being able to recognize myself in this place. For three days I've used this shower, this towel, this toothpaste. I've dug my nails into her soap to remove her red hair. I've wiped steam from this mirror so that I could see myself. I've dozed on this toilet and dreamed that I was someone else.

On her desk are two obituaries from the week before she found me. From February 7, 2008, Ruth Stafford Peale, 101 years old, wife of Dr Norman Vincent Peale. Her husband wrote a book called *The Power of Positive Thinking*. After it had been rejected by most publishers, he threw the manuscript into their wastebasket. His wife fished it out and encouraged him to try once more. The book was published in 1952 and has sold more than twenty million copies in forty-two languages. Someone – Sam, I assume – has written in the margin, NOT A COINCIDENCE. The other obituary, from February 10, 2008, is for the actor Roy Scheider. Circled in red ink is 'Franklin & Marshall College,' where Scheider had been an undergraduate, and written beside it in the margin is: F&M IN LANCASTER – NOT AN ACCIDENT. Also circled is *Jaws*, Scheider's best-known movie, and written in the margin is: FILMED ON VINEYARD – ANOTHER SIGN. I look through her desk expecting to see my own obituary, but I find other recent ones – Bobby Fischer, Phil Rizzuto, Madeleine L'Engle.

I go out during the day while she writes Charlton Heston's obituary; I don't tell her where, she doesn't ask. She's happy when I leave Ralph with her; that way she knows I'll be back. I don't tell her that I've spent my day hiding books. Moving them, turning in their spines. As many copies as I can find. Easy when there are copies everywhere, when it seems like every person in the world is reading the same book. A hardcover – small, but not as small as a paperback. Dust jacket made to look like parchment, title in white cursive across a red circular seal. *The Secret*. Look closely and you see faded messages, sketches, and codes, the palimpsest's *scriptio inferior*, the ghost of some ancient manuscript. The implied promise that all will be revealed: open the book and discover the answer to every question.

Rhonda Byrne, the author of *The Secret*, gathered quotes about the law of attraction and the power of intention from inspirational authors, my former colleagues in the field, some of whom I sat on panels with at conferences and ate breakfast with at hotels before flying home. According to

Byrne, the greatest people in history – Plato, Shakespeare, Beethoven, Lincoln, Einstein – knew about 'the secret.' It has sold millions of copies, yet I hadn't heard of the book until now.

Now that I do know, it's hard to escape it. Lovers share a copy in the grass at Union Square Park, reading passages to each other like sonnets. A young woman in dreads naps with a copy open across her chest. An old man with the muscular body of a man half his age Rollerblades by with a banana in one hand and *The Secret* in the other. I'm following it, and it's following me. It is, after all, the law the book teaches: If you focus your attention on something, you will attract it into your life.

I go from bookstore to bookstore moving *The Secret* from the 'self-help' or 'self-improvement' section to the fiction section.

There's a display in a bookstore on Broadway called Yellow Book Road, dozens of copies arranged in vertical racks. Beside the rack is a life-sized cardboard version of Rhonda Byrne: a petite middle-aged woman with bright blue eyes and straight platinum-blond hair, black low-cut blouse, blue and white beads around her neck, a tiny red circle – the seal from the book's cover – affixed to her forehead.

'Looks real, doesn't she?'

The store's owner, a plump woman with thinning brown hair, sits behind the counter with a copy of *The Secret*.

'Did you see her on *Oprah*?'

'No.'

She holds up the book. 'My third time, and it's just – my God.'

I smile, unsure how to respond.

'It's changed *every*thing,' she says.

'For the better, I hope.'

'I've lost twenty pounds,' she says. 'I have a ways to go, but.'

'Good luck,' I tell her.

'I'll get there,' she says. 'I have no doubt.'

I take a copy to the reading area in the back with the intention of hiding it in the Fantasy and Science Fiction section. A young woman is sitting there, reading *The Secret*. Her son, a fidgety toddler, burrows his face in the chair's cushion and whines. His mother smiles as she reads, but her fists are clenched, her hands turning white. The boy looks up at me, his hair matted to his head, then buries his face again.

A few minutes later he asks his mother if they can go. She turns a page.

'Mama,' he says. 'Mama. Mama. Mama.'

She puts her index finger to her lips to silently shush him.

He tugs her skirt and asks again if they can go.

She holds up one finger to indicate *hold on, one minute*.

He pulls off one of her sandals. She crosses her legs, but doesn't look up from her book. The boy pulls off her other sandal. She closes her eyes and takes two deep breaths, then opens her eyes, smiles, and continues to read.

'Mama,' the boy says. 'Mama, Mama, Mama, Mama, Mama,' but she turns another page.

He takes the book from his mother and throws it.

She grabs his arm, digs in her nails, pulls him closer. Calmly she says, 'You won't allow me a moment's peace. You won't allow me that, will you.'

The boy blinks up at her, his mouth hanging open.

'Not a moment's peace,' she says.

The woman picks up her book and brings it to the register. I can hear the owner saying, 'I'm doing much better now. It was a challenging year, but everything is better. I'm much stronger because of it.'

Sam is making stir-fry even though I told her I'd be leaving before dinner. Five days, still no locksmith. Ralph is sleeping in a full stretch — her dead-limb position, Cary used to call it — by the open fire escape window.

'I can't stay,' I tell her.

We were supposed to meet, Sam says. Maybe the reason doesn't have as much to do with her brother or Gloria Foster — though she's still open to that possibility — as with each other, she says. We needed to come into each other's life at this exact moment, she says. We can help each other, she says. Maybe we're both lonely, she says. Think about all the signs, she says. There are no accidents, she says. There are signs everywhere, she says. You wrote books about this, she says.

'I burned those books,' I tell her.

'Listen to me,' she says. 'Something strange is happening.'

'I'm done with strange,' I tell her.

'I found us at the Laundromat, then in the park, on the side of a tree.'

She turns off the burner and serves eggplant, peppers, and

baby corn onto two plates of rice; she brings the food to the table. We stand there watching steam rise from the plates. She pulls out a chair, but doesn't sit. She looks at the table, then back at me, then back at the table; I follow her eyes: on top of each napkin is a square of white paper the size of a stamp.

She lays one in each of my palms, then covers my hands with hers. It looks like we're about to play a game of red hands – the slap game.

Eric is on one square, in fading black ink, and *Sam* is on the other square, in red to match her hair.

She found them in separate dryers, she tells me. She thought they were labels that had fallen off her shirts.

That would have been strange enough, she says, but when she stopped to pet a dog in Madison Square Park and looked up, our names were carved into a tree.

'Eric and Sam,' I say. 'Some gay couple.'

'Come *on*,' she says.

'Come on what?'

'I'll show you,' she says. 'I'll take you right now.' She grabs her keys from her desk and walks to the door.

'I believe you,' I tell her.

'I want to show you.'

'Sit down,' I say, but she doesn't move. 'You can put down your keys – you don't need them.'

'I keep calling the locksmith,' she says. 'I swear.'

'I know you're still married,' I say.

She lets her keys drop to the floor. The noise wakes Ralph; she looks at us, then lowers her head and falls immediately back to sleep.

'You were running away,' I tell her.

'It's not *him*,' she says. 'I really did leave my husband years ago, and it was because of you – your first book. But somehow' – she takes a deep breath – 'somehow, despite my best intentions, I married him again. Not *him*, but someone like him.'

'I'm sorry,' I tell her.

She sits on the floor at my feet, but doesn't look up. 'Why do I keep attracting men like that into my life?'

'I don't know.'

'You're supposed to know,' she says.

'I don't have any answers.'

'I asked him to leave,' she says. 'I changed the lock.'

'You should call the police.'

She looks up at me. 'I must be doing something wrong.'

'You're trying your best,' I tell her. I give her my hand and pull her up. I take her other hand too and hold them both and wait for her to say whatever else she needs to say. But she just looks into my eyes, and eventually I let go.

She sits at the table and moves her food around on her plate. 'Don't you believe that all of this is supposed to be happening?'

'Things happen whether we want them to or not.'

'Well, what do you want to happen?'

I want her to be happy and safe. I want her to stop looking for answers. I want her to stop reminding me who I used to be. I want to live entirely in every moment. I want to want only what I have, only what *is*. I want to be more like Ralph. I want to be more like Cary. Like Cary *was*.

'Tell me,' she says. 'What do you want?'

'The truth,' I tell her, 'is that I want to go back in time.'

'Not me,' she says. 'I don't want to relive any of it.'

'No,' I say. 'I'd do things differently.'

'Oh,' she says. 'You and me and everyone.'

Sam sits on the floor again and makes kissy sounds. Ralph gets up and stretches. She walks over, puts her head on Sam's lap, and makes her content noise – low moan, eyes closed – as Sam scratches her ear. 'See,' Sam says. 'I know all her favorite spots.'

'I should go,' I say.

I walk to the door; Ralph jumps up, runs to my side.

'I'm afraid,' Sam says.

'So is everyone.'

'One last question,' she says. 'If you were to write a self-help book now—'

'I wouldn't.'

'Let's pretend,' she says. 'If you were to write another book—'

'I wouldn't.'

'But if you were to write one.'

'Keep trying your best,' I tell her. 'That's what my book would say.'

Part Eight

The End of Every Story

W E COULD END with her sleeping.

We could end with her leaning against a man who looks like me.

They're sitting on a bench in Prospect Park after a short walk after days of not walking or eating or getting out of bed.

The dog's off leash. She's running across a field covered with snow and ice, then running back to the bench where they sit. She shakes snow from her coat, cries for them to throw something, but there's nothing except the pathetic excuse for a snowball he makes. He throws, the dog chases. But the snowball breaks apart midair. The dog makes circles in the field, nose to the snow. She sees it as her duty to fetch whatever's thrown, and it upsets her not to be able to.

The man who looks like me makes another snowball and tosses it high enough for the dog to get under it. But when she catches it, she catches nothing, or so it might seem to her; it disappears in her mouth, it turns to water, and she waits for the man to make it reappear as if by magic, by miracle.

'Here, Ralph,' he says. 'Right here.' And he throws again.

Some books say the past and future are illusions: the past gives you a false identity and the future promises salvation. Some books say the present moment is all there is, there's nothing other than right now.

This would mean that the man who looks like me is an illusion, and so is his wife, and so is his dog running through the snow.

This would mean that the snow isn't real, and the park bench isn't real, and the two boys sledding down a hill aren't real, and the hill isn't real, and the bare trees bordering a running path, and the woman running along the path, and the freezing rain now, and the dog's pain when she walks on rock salt, and her cries, and the man who gets up from the bench to rub her paws.

We could end with the man rubbing the dog's paws.

We could end with the moment he turns away from the dog to walk back to the bench.

We could end with how happy he feels to see her sleeping, her mouth slightly open, her eyes – he can see as he gets closer – tearing from the cold and wind that aren't real as I write this but were real that day.

★

She's sitting up and her mouth is open and the tears could be from the cold and wind, and the boys sledding down the hill might otherwise be forgotten, and the woman running along the path bordered with bare trees might otherwise be forgotten, and the date might otherwise be forgotten, and we might end one second before he – oh my – before he looks and – oh my, oh my – something about the tears and the mouth open and – oh my my – he sits beside her and removes her gloves and holds her hands and tries to rub warmth into her hands and—

It's me.

I shouldn't keep implying it isn't when it is.

I shouldn't keep saying *the man who looks like me* as if he isn't me, as if he doesn't live inside me, as if I wasn't there.

The woman running might otherwise be forgotten had I not called out to her, had she not heard me but continued along the path, her role in this story brief but memorable. The boys sledding down the hill might otherwise be forgotten had I not called them over, too, and had they not come cautiously, and had I not said, 'Never mind – I was going to – never mind,' and pulled her close so they wouldn't see her face. Not that they would have seen anything but a woman sleeping, her eyes tearing from the wind.

And then for a long while, what felt like a long while, what could have been ten minutes or an hour, no one came close enough to call out to, and I didn't yet know what to call out, I didn't want to call out anything at all, I wanted the moment to be, to continue to be, quiet, and yes, hours later and years later I'd have difficult moments when I'd regret not calling out, not doing something, even though nothing could be done, but I decided to wait and bring her closer and keep rubbing her hands, and during all this the dog ran back and forth in the field chasing something I couldn't see. It looked as if she was playing with someone. She lay down and her tail swept the snow behind her, and then she ran as if someone had thrown something, and she kept doing this, and then I heard someone behind me say, 'Beautiful dog,' and I said, 'Thank you,' and then I said, 'I think I need your help,' and hours later and years later I'd think about that word *think* and wonder why I'd used it when I knew very well that I needed his help, and this man, too, might otherwise be forgotten.

Lucy Vincent Beach, Chilmark, 2009

PUT DOWN YOUR *pens. Put down your books. Stop taking notes. Please stop writing in the margins. Please stop writing what I say.*
Close your eyes and take a deep breath.
Let's begin again. Let's start over. Please. Let's have a do-over.

You are here for a reason. Ask yourself why.
Maybe you've lost your job, your home, your spouse, your child, your dog, your health, your peace, your mind, your way.
Ask yourself what you'd like to accomplish today. Ask yourself how you expect me to help you.

Let me be perfectly honest: I can't help you. Not in the way you might like. I can't get you your job back. I can't get you your home back. Or your spouse, your child, your dog, your health, your peace, your mind. I can't help you find your way.
Please hear me when I say this: There are certain things about life, too many things, that we simply can't change.

You see, our lives are stories that have already, at least in part, been written. I'm not sure who the writer is, or the director, or the editor.

Try your best to embrace the mystery of not knowing.

Truth is, we're not in control. We don't always get what we want, what we hope for, what we're expecting. Sometimes, not even close. Sometimes, the opposite.

With practice, we might control how we react to what happens, but even this is difficult.

You're not really giving up control. You can't give up what you never had. But you can give up your false belief in control.

You're afraid that you'll have to feel something painful, that you won't be able to handle what happens.

I understand, believe me.

Here is the only thing you can do: hold your fear in one hand and your commitment to act fearlessly in the other.

That we fall, that we fall apart, are givens. Our goal might be to fall with grace, to sit in the dark.

Don't shake your fist at heaven; it will do you no good. Truth is, anything can happen to anyone at any time. There's virtue in loving one's fate. When you accept the world on its terms, you are living a brave life. Better to greet life with an unconditional yes. Don't ask why, ask now what.

Please, put down your pens. Stop taking notes. Don't write anything that I say. Close your eyes. Take a deep breath.

★

I'm happy to be here today. I'm happy to get to say these things. Even if only in my mind. Even if only on this page, this lecture I never gave. Even if only a whisper to my reflection in the water's edge as I walk slowly with my arthritic dog on a cold fall morning on Martha's Vineyard just after sunrise with not another soul near enough to hear me even if I were to shout.

A T THE END of some songs you'd go off pitch on purpose. Your voice would break, you'd given all you could and the song had failed, but it was as beautiful in its failure as it might have been in its perfection.

You'd get excited when a song fell apart as you were writing it. We'd be eating lunch, and I'd ask how your morning went, and you'd say, 'The one that was stuck broke open and got messy,' and I knew that was a good thing.

A few months later, at one of your shows, I'd hear it: a song that abandoned its chorus, that left home never to return, that lost its way on purpose and didn't care; or a song made up of nothing but choruses, a dozen songs in one.

Mess was the worst thing for me; uncertainty didn't work. Each of my books – before this one – was outlined before it was written. There was a plan, and I stuck to it, no matter what. I had lists, bullet points, goals.

Once, when I was stuck starting *The Book of Why*, you said, 'Just sing it,' and I said, 'But I'm writing bullet points,' and you said, 'So sing your bullet points.'

O N YOUR BIRTHDAY this past September – what would have been your fortieth – I was listening to you sing. A recording, I should say. Which is you. *Was* you, I should say. Evidence that you *had been singing*, that you *had sung*. We may use most verb tenses here except the present continuous *are singing when* ——, and the present perfect continuous *have been singing for* —— *years when* ——, and the future *will sing*, and the future continuous *will be singing when* ——, and the future perfect continuous *will have been singing for* —— *years when* ——.

Let me begin again. It was your birthday, a year and a half after the trip to Lancaster. I was listening to you sing, to a recording of you, when the bell rang. Boxes filled with letters from my readers. I'd told my editor years ago that I didn't want them, but he was leaving my publisher for another one, so he decided to send them to me. I didn't open them for a few weeks, and then one day I said just one, no harm in one, and it began, *I was so sorry to hear*. I decided one a day would be fine. All this time I expected *Told you so*, but so far they've been kind. *I was sorry to read about your. My sincere condolences at the loss of your. After all you've done for me, I wanted to. Keeping you in my. I know how you must be feeling, I lost my. Some might say how could something like this happen to him, but it's not your. I'm so sorry, I was so saddened, I was shocked to hear, I'm keeping you in my thoughts, I'm sending you warm thoughts peaceful thoughts positive thoughts during this difficult what must certainly be a difficult time. I've enclosed a book you might. I hope you don't mind, but I've enclosed my copy of. The enclosed book was very useful to me when I lost my. Please read the enclosed book, I'm sure it will speak to you the way it spoke to me when.*

Healing after Loss. How to Go On Living When Someone You Love Dies. Finding Your Way after Your Spouse Dies. Living with Grief. Traveling Through Grief. Journey Through Grief. Understanding Your Grief. Awakening from Grief. Surviving Grief and Learning to Live Again. Chicken Soup for the Grieving Soul. The Grieving Garden. A Grief Observed. The Courage to Grieve. Getting to the Other Side of Grief. Grieving Mindfully. Grieving God's Way. God Knows You're Grieving. Good Grief. Don't Take My Grief Away. Grieving: A Love Story. Do Not Stand at My Grave and Weep. Sad Isn't Bad. The Mourning Handbook. The Widower's Handbook. For Widowers Only. Widower to Widower. Waking Up Alone. When There Are No Words: Finding Your Way to Cope with Loss and Grief. The Light at the End of the Tunnel: Coming Back to Life after a Spouse Dies. Life after Loss. Life after Death. Death Is Nothing at All. We Don't Die. Love Never Dies. Talking to Heaven.

Hello from Heaven. I Wasn't Ready to Say Goodbye. Help Me Say Goodbye.

Some books say imagine that the worst has happened. Some books say carry on regardless. Some books say write your own obituary. Some books say make tomorrow today. Some books say try yoga. Some books say run a marathon. Some books say don't run before you can walk. Some books say no one sees themselves as others do. Some books say grow a beard. Some books say shaving your beard will take years off your face. Some books say visit your parents, sleep in your childhood bed. Some books say don't wait for a party to blow up balloons. Some books say don't look in the mirror. Some books say look in the mirror, check your pee, take your pulse, smell your own breath. Some books say never skip breakfast. Some books say eat more kale, more blueberries, more prunes. Some books say drink more green tea. Some books say no alcohol. Some books say alcohol in moderation. Some books say celebrate wrinkles. Some books say be modest. Some books say don't be too modest. Some books say volunteer. Some books say take charge, stand straight, smile. Some books say take the stairs, not the elevator. Some books say aim high. Some books say be realistic. Some books say avoid risk. Some books say don't be afraid to take risks. Some books say think big. Some books say be practical. Some books say think before you act. Some books say don't think too much. Some books say agree to disagree. Some books say don't try to make a round peg fit into a square hole. Some books say keep your cool. Some books say don't be afraid to get angry. Some books say turn your enemies into teachers. Some books say don't blame, don't judge. Some books say when you have one finger pointed at someone else, you have three pointing back at yourself. Some books say have a firm handshake. Some books say rigid branches break in the first wind. Some books say don't put rocks in your knapsack. Some books say put the cap back on the toothpaste. Some books say enjoy a traffic jam by listening to music. Some books say take a long bath, take a vacation, go on a cruise. Some books say look up at the stars. Some books say clean your sheets. Some books say focus on the small details. Some books say focus on the big picture. Some books say set your watch five minutes fast. Some books say live in the moment. Some books say plan ahead. Some books say one day at a time. Some books say be here now.

Today is October 1, 2009, the only October 1, 2009, there will ever be, and you are here.

My high-school history teacher used to begin every class this way. Even though he was simply stating the date and the obvious, I think that he was on to something.

Today is October 1, 2009, and you are not here.

Ralph walks stiffly along the water's edge twenty or thirty yards ahead of me; she keeps looking back to make sure I'm still there. She greets each person walking past; even with hip dysplasia and arthritis, she manages to be happy.

The vet tried to make a joke. 'Her caput is kaput,' he said. He explained that *caput* is another word for the head of her femur. 'It's supposed to be round,' he said, 'but hers isn't, so it's causing wear and tear on the joint. Very painful,' he said, and it was way too late to laugh.

'Her stifle joint is showing signs of damage, too,' he said. 'Her stifle is overcompensating because of the caput.'

Tired, we sit on rocks and look out at the harbor. We doze together to the creaking of boats, my hand resting on her back rising with each breath in rhythm with water lapping against the dock.

You used to say, 'I think she'll get old overnight.'

One day a squirrel came too close, but she didn't chase it.

A few days later she dropped her favorite treat on the floor; it stayed there a week. I tried to give her another one, and her eyes and tail were excited to receive it, but she couldn't chew it, or didn't want to, and dropped it beside the other one. Now I give her only wet food and soft treats, which upset her stomach. But I don't mind taking her out a few times during the night; I'm often awake anyway.

When she's not facing me and I call her name, she doesn't turn. Only if I yell, and I don't like to, otherwise she might think she's done something wrong. Her sight's fine, so I sign to her. Days pass without the sound of my voice, without much sound at all except what you hear only when silent – water dripping from a drainpipe, a fly inside a lampshade, the watch I never wear but leave on the bedside table.

Martha's Vineyard is quiet now, the way we like it; the cold is here. In Edgartown and Vineyard Haven window signs say CLOSED FOR THE SEASON SEE YOU NEXT MAY. At the dock in Menemsha boats fill with rainwater; lobster traps lie empty on the sand. NO LIFEGUARD ON DUTY. Sitting on a bed of small rocks is a push-button phone. I pick up the receiver; there's a dial tone. I dial my number and wait for someone to answer. I don't recognize the voice at first: *I'm sorry we're not here right now.* I figured it was all right, given Ralph, to keep the plural *we*.

Later, at Lucy Vincent, a seal surfaces for a few seconds before going back under. Wind, strong waves, the tide is coming in. A man who looks like me walks beside his dog, her breath visible in short puffs. The man pees on a rock; the dog looks away as if to give him privacy. They walk a quarter mile slowly, then turn back; the tide has come all the way in, the sand is gone. Not gone, it just seems gone. But the man's footprints, and the dog's, gone. They should hurry, but don't. The dog tries to catch a few waves as they break; the man removes his sneakers and socks, rolls up his pants, walks ankle deep in cold water that stings.

Eventually the body adjusts: the cold feels warm. By the time we reach where we began, the water is at my knees, waves crashing against the rock wall behind me.

S OME BOOKS SAY a sign is runny eyes. Some books say a sign is twitching or shaking. Some books say a sign is incontinence. Some books say a sign is falling down. Some books say a sign is loss of appetite. Some books say a sign is tail between the legs. Some books say keep her close. Some books say if she cries, the sound of your voice nearby will comfort her. Some books say let her sleep in bed with you. Some books say keep a pad beneath her. Some books say give water through a dropper. Some books say feed her by hand. Some books say gently rub her fur and tell her what a good friend she has been. Some books say every part of a journey is meaningful. Some books say even the saddest times contain beauty and even hidden joy.

A few years back, the water was rough and cold, but she wanted me to throw. She sat at the water's edge, and waves broke and foamed around her, and her eyes and tail said throw. 'Not so far,' you said, but my arm had already started forward, and it felt good to throw as far as I could, and as soon as the tennis ball left my hand, it was too late to say *stay* or *no* or *come here*, she was gone – into the ocean and after what she couldn't possibly see, what even I couldn't see, even though I'd followed its arc, a tiny circle of yellow that rose, fell, then disappeared. That's just a word we sometimes use to mean we can't see something. It was there, somewhere in the ocean, but it had disappeared to us.

Too quickly she was out too far – past where I'd seen the ball drop – and we could hardly hear ourselves call her through the wind and breaking waves. She was biting the water, shadows or slants of light she must have thought were what she was looking for. She was the only small thing out there in all that ocean – the only thing we could see, that is. Not even a boat. Not even, thank God, a fin. She was frantic to find what was lost; we knew she'd never give up.

I had an idea: convince her that she'd found what she had no chance of ever finding. I ran to our car in the parking lot, searched for another ball beneath a seat.

By the time I returned, Ralph had drifted farther out and you were in the ocean up to your neck, trying to coax Ralph to swim to you.

I knew I needed a perfect throw – between her and you, where she could see it. Ralph saw the ball and swam for it. She moved closer, only to be pulled out again. But she was young, and her desire to fetch the ball – the new one, the imposter – was stronger than the tide, and she grabbed the ball with her mouth and swam to you, and together you made it to shore.

Ralph shook off the ocean, dropped the ball for me to

throw again. 'No more,' I said. 'Enough,' and she looked dejected, the way only dogs can. It was late May, the day before our third anniversary.

It was only later, at home, that we noticed Ralph's tail. It wasn't moving, not even at the sound of words that always made it wag. The vet said the waves had probably damaged it. He said the tail might never move, we'd have to wait and see, and it was as if we'd been told our dog would never be happy again when it was just that she might never *look* happy again, like a person who couldn't smile. She'd be fine whether she ever wagged her tail or not; we were worried more for ourselves, that we'd lost some of our own happiness.

For days we watched her tail oddly bent and not moving.

Two weeks later her tail knocked over a wineglass. This otherwise would have upset us. But we were so happy, we left the stain. Some days it was a comforting reminder, other days a frightening one, of how lucky we'd been. We pretended it was all about her tail, not about how quickly the tide could have taken her away.

Some books say it's very quick and peaceful. Some books say within six to twelve seconds after injection she will take a slightly deeper breath. Some books say she will fall into what looks like a deep sleep. Some books say she will take a few more breaths. Some books say look into her eyes. Some books say washing the body can be a last act of loving kindness. Some books say most living creatures are made of mostly water. Some books say you may want someone to drive you home. Some books say you are not alone in your sadness.

Some books say there will be an empty feeling each time you come home. Some books say the loss may bring up memories of other losses. Some books say hold a memorial service if you wish. Some books say buy a stone for your garden in the shape of a paw print. Some books say pet figurines are a popular way to remember. Some books say it's very common to think you've seen her in the home or in the yard long after she's gone. Some books say grief makes people do strange things. Some books say don't make any important decisions in the weeks that follow such a loss.

Stuck, turned around, I can't see where I'm going. Cars keep coming, keep bumping me back. I try to turn, to right myself, but can't move. Hit again – hard – and now I'm facing the right way. A jolt from behind knocks off my sunglasses. I put my glasses back on – I don't want to be recognized – and move forward. Around, around again, and I see you – red shirt, hair longer and in a ponytail. I want to bump you and your father, but can't reach you; someone's always in the way. Hit from behind, I spin around again. A frustration dream that's not a dream.

Sunglasses, hair shorter, clean-shaven; a disguise. An adult alone where no other adults are alone. And if you see me, if your father does, I'll pretend not to know you at first – it's been two years, after all – then act happy when I remember, ask how you've been. I'll tell your father that I'm here with a friend and his kids.

The red shirt passes me, a flash of your face, your hands gripping the wheel, then gone where I can't see.

I'm after you again – red shirt, red car. Closer, closer,

but the cars stop – mine beside yours. Ride's over. I drop my keys on purpose, hide my face bending to pick them up.

I don't go on every ride with you and your father; too suspicious without a child. A frog-themed ride that free-falls fifty feet, then 'hops' back up; smiling pandas circling a beehive; a space shuttle that swings like a pendulum; a small Ferris wheel. Close, but not too close. I pretend to study the park's map, look at my watch as if waiting for someone, tighten my shoelaces for the nth time.

I keep following.

Cotton candy turns your lips blue. You walk beside your father, waving the paper cone like a maestro.

I sit behind you on a roller coaster with two drops, not too steep. You raise your arms, but don't make a sound. If I reach out I could touch your hair blown back by the wind.

Later, I sip lemonade on a beach chair and watch you slide down a water tube, your father waiting to catch you. All around me children lick grease from their fingers, then run back to scream under waterfalls. I'm the only person not wearing a bathing suit or shorts. Sunny and seventy, the weekend before Memorial Day. I reach to pull on my beard, a nervous habit, but it's gone. My hands don't recognize me.

The waterfalls go dry; it startles the children. Spouting water is sucked back into holes in the ground. No one is allowed down the slides; no one is allowed to leave. I'm convinced this has something to do with me: they know what I'm doing here; they know I've followed you from your house to Dutch Wonderland.

A girl is missing: seven years old, brown hair, green bathing suit. The name comes garbled through the speakers. I wait to hear it again, rather to hear it for the first time. I want to shush the girl behind me who keeps asking her mother if they'll play the rest of the song that had been playing.

I've done nothing wrong.

Not ever, I mean, but now, in this moment, as far as I know. But it's possible to do something wrong without knowing you are, while intending, in fact, to do what's right, or what you believe is right. It's possible, I know, to intend to do one thing but to do something else entirely, to do the exact opposite; or to do exactly what you intended to do, but to see that action or decision result in exactly what you didn't want, or what someone else didn't want, or what no one wanted.

The girl is found in a bathroom stall; everyone applauds at this announcement. The music resumes – a different song, yet always the same. Waterfall water falls; the slides come back to life; water shoots up from the ground, sends children running. They run back to run away again.

I run and watch, fear being watched: a lap around the cemetery, rest, another lap, rest. I lean against a tree and stretch my legs, then sit in the tree's shade and wait.

An old man walks through the cemetery with his dog. He

waits patiently while the mutt – barrel-chested, black and tan – sniffs roses left in front of a nameless stone. I wonder how someone dead that long can still be remembered by someone living. Maybe a great-great-great-great-great-grandchild left the flowers. Maybe the person's life story has been passed down through generations; it must be fiction by now, a game of Chinese whispers.

After three days, I know your routine. Swimming at the Y in the morning. I've seen you return home, hair wet, jean shorts over a bathing suit. A walk to the library with your grandmother after school. Your mother works half days; she leaves in the morning with a cigarette between her lips and returns home after three, smoking a different cigarette. Late afternoon, usually around four, she sits on the porch – there's an old couch and three white plastic chairs – and drinks a beer while waiting for your father to get home. She drops her cigarette butts in an empty bottle.

You sit on the lawn, a small square of grass and flowers, and draw. You show your mother. She sips her beer, tells you how pretty you've drawn her, gives the pad back to you.

I have my routine, too. Run, rest, watch. A drive downtown for lunch. Later, while you and your family eat dinner – your father grills, and you eat on the porch – I sit across the street on a bench outside the hospital and pretend to read the paper.

At dusk the air grows chilly and TV light flickers in your darkening house. I walk past the house a few times;

I hear gunfire from a cop show or an old movie. Your mother comes out for a smoke. You follow her out in your pajamas to catch fireflies. Then you go back inside, and I hear the lock turn.

I drive back to the hotel, where I order room service. I don't have a plan. I'm not sure how long I'll stay. I've considered ringing your bell and telling your parents the truth – the names of your dolls, the song you were humming, the crying-laughing game, the fact that you don't speak, that you want to be a singer, that you believe you used to live near a beach. But when I practice what I might say, when I imagine what this might sound like from their perspective, what I'm saying – I practice aloud – begins to sound crazy. I can't imagine what your parents would say. I can only imagine what I might say if I were them. I'd be open-minded, to a point. I might even believe. But after that, I'd probably say, 'I'm very sorry for your loss. Best of luck with the rest of your life.' And so I can't bring myself to ring the bell, can't summon the nerve, or the stupidity, to say something to your parents. What I really want, I suppose, is to speak with you. I want to tell you this entire story from beginning to end. But you're seven years old, and I'm not sure what you could possibly say, or sign, in response. So I'm left with this book, which I hope you'll find when you're older, in a used bookstore, and then – but, you see, there's only one ending to this story, to every story.

The next morning, a Saturday, one last look at you.

I'm sitting across the street in the cemetery, leaning against a gravestone, when you come out of the house, a puppy in your arms. You sit on the lawn and bait the puppy, a German shepherd, with a stick.

And then I hear your voice. 'Hello,' you say, and now you're standing, looking at me. 'Hello,' you say again, and wave.

I wave back and walk across the street to your lawn. My legs are shaking, my mouth has gone dry. The words I've practiced saying – to your parents, to you – are lost. 'Cute dog,' I say. 'May I pet him?'

'Yes, but he might pee on you.'

I crouch beside you in the grass and pet the puppy. He tries to bite my fingers with his needle teeth. He wants anything in his mouth. I let him chew on my shirt sleeve, and then we play tug-of-war with it.

'How old?'

'Ten weeks,' you say.

'What's his name?'

'Harry.'

'How'd you come up with that name?'

'I don't know,' you say. 'He just looks like a Harry.'

I'm afraid to look at you – to really look at you. But I'm leaving soon, and, unless something unexpected happens in the next few minutes, I may never see you again. Seven years old now, one of the most expressive faces I've seen. Big brown eyes, big lips, dimples.

I'm about to ask if you remember me, but your mother comes outside to smoke a cigarette. She sees me and says, 'Can I help you with something?'

I stand, brush off my cords. 'I saw the puppy and couldn't resist.'

She comes closer. 'You,' she says. 'I know you from—'

'Two years ago,' I say. 'The tornado.'

She snaps her fingers. 'That's it,' she says. 'I *knew* I knew you.'

'Eric,' I say.

'Do you live here now?'

'Just visiting.'

'You know, your friend came back – what's her name.'

'Sam.'

'She was here about a year ago, asking questions.'

'What kinds of questions?'

'Something about her brother,' she says. 'She kept asking if his name meant anything to us.'

'Did it?'

'No, but I'm not sure she believed us.' She takes out a new pack of cigarettes and slaps it against her palm. 'She asked about you, too.'

'What did she ask?'

'I don't remember. Whatever it was didn't make much sense to me.' She takes a cigarette from her pack, puts it in her mouth, but doesn't light it. 'She was a strange bird. No offense.'

'I didn't know her well, but I know she's been through a lot.'

'Everyone's been through a lot,' she says.

I pick up the puppy and let him lick my face. 'Sorry, I'm going through dog withdrawal.'

'You didn't bring Ralph?'

'You remember her name.'

'You don't forget a girl Ralph.'

'I lost her,' I say. 'About six months ago.'

'Oh, I'm sorry,' she says, but I'm watching *you*. You give no reaction, as if you didn't hear. I give the puppy my finger to nip.

'She's speaking,' I say.

'Funny, it was the day you left,' she says. 'She came down for breakfast and said *Mom*, and I nearly fell over.'

'It's nice to hear her voice.'

'I always knew,' she says. 'If she could speak in her sleep, then she could speak when she's awake.'

I lay the puppy in the grass beside you. 'Do you remember Ralph?'

'No.'

'Do you remember me?'

You look at your mother. 'Do I know him?'

'You've met before,' your mother says.

'I don't remember,' you say.

'I remember you,' I say. 'You want to be a singer.'

'Not anymore,' your mother says. 'Now she wants to be a vet.'

'What's that song she used to hum?'

'She's forgotten all that — whatever it was.'

Despite my terrible voice, I want to start singing the song, want to see if you sing along or react in any way, but your attention is focused entirely on your puppy, and I don't blame you. I might as well not be here.

'I'm sure she'll be a great vet,' I say.

The puppy runs across the lawn, and you chase him behind the house, where I can no longer see you.

There are so many things I'd like to say, but none of them is willing, despite all my practice, to come out of my mouth.

'Well, I should be going.'

'Nice to see you again,' your mother says.

'Take care,' I say.

'You, too,' she says. 'Be well.'

'Goodbye,' I tell her, and then I call out to you, wherever you've gone, 'Goodbye, Gloria. Goodbye.'

SOME BOOKS SAY start a garden, sing to your plants. Some books say join a book club, take music lessons, start a stamp collection, get a pet. Some books say brew your own beer. Some books say try paintball, enter a local trivia competition, take dance lessons, learn to rumba. Some books say listen to James Brown. Some books say give yourself a hug. Some books say when someone hugs you, let them be the first to let go. Some books say let a dog lick your face. Some books say swim naked. Some books say kiss a stranger. Some books say climb a mountain. Some books say overcome a phobia. Some books say change begins with pain. Some books say get busy living or get busy dying. Some books say never say the word *try*. Some books say there's nothing you can't do. Some books say accept your limitations. Some books say don't take no for an answer. Some books say buy a karaoke machine and invite friends over. Some books say learn a new language. Some books say leave no regrets. Some books say beware a person who has nothing to lose. Some books say do no harm. Some books say never cut what can be untied. Some books say admit your mistakes. Some books say you are not your mistakes. Some books say forgive everyone everything. Some books say never criticize what can't be changed. Some books say don't be afraid to say I don't know. Some books say don't bore people with your problems. Some books say when someone asks how you feel, say terrific, never better. Some books say ask questions. Some books say don't ask too many questions. Some books say carry someone. Some books say let yourself be carried. Some books say there's nothing to fear. Some books say it's okay to be afraid. Some books say whistle in the dark. Some books say give more than you take. Some books say God never gives you more than you can take. Some books say God never blinks. Some books say God grant me the serenity to accept the things I cannot change, the courage to change the things I can, and the wisdom to know the difference. Some books say read the Psalms. Some books say if something seems too good to be true, it probably is. Some books say choose your life partner carefully. Some books say tape-record your spouse's laughter. Some books say that if you live with a partner, one usually dies first. Some books say surrender. Some books say do not go gently. Some books say recognize that you are lost. Some books say put yourself back together piece by piece. Some books say it's never too late. Some books say it's not unusual to live to ninety. Some books say you will probably be old for a long time. Some books say you can't kiss your own ear. Some books say it's nice to meet someone after a long absence. Some books say reunion is a type of heaven. Some books say there's no good in goodbye. Some books say never say goodbye, better to say see you later, see you soon, see you someday, until we meet again.

Acknowledgments

Saying *thank you* is one of the great joys of life. So it truly *is* my pleasure to express gratitude to the following:

Jill Grinberg, my agent, who has believed in my writing since day one.

John Parsley, my editor, and everyone at Little, Brown who helped give life to this book.

The writers whose work raised important questions for me as I wrote this novel: Wayne Dyer, Deepak Chopra, David Richo, Esther and Jerry Hicks, Louise Hay, and Rhonda Byrne.

Martha Collins, whose villanelle 'The Story We Know,' one of my favorite poems, was an important trigger for this novel.

Tara Potterveld, for her help with sign language.

Nicole Michels, who waits for me when I fall behind, and our son, Dangiso, the most joyful human being I've ever met.

Finally, of course, Ralph — best dog in the universe.